Matt Thorne was born in 1974. He is the author of *Tourist* (1998), *Eight Minutes Idle* (Winner of an Encore Prize, 1999) and *Dreaming of Strangers* (2000). He also co-edited the anthology *All Hail the New Puritans* (2000).

By Matt Thorne

Tourist
Eight Minutes Idle
Dreaming of Strangers
All Hail the New Puritans (as co-editor)
Pictures of You

Pictures of You

~~Matt Thorne~~

Dear Chris,

my fellow prisoner... in memory of our times with that "nasty, brutish race."

All the best

Matt

PHOENIX

A PHOENIX PAPERBACK

First published in Great Britain in 2001
by Weidenfeld & Nicolson
This paperback edition published in 2002
by Phoenix,
an imprint of Orion Books Ltd,
Orion House, 5 Upper St Martin's Lane,
London WC2H 9EA

A CIP catalogue record for this book
is available from the British Library.

ISBN 0 75381 344 0

Printed and bound in Great Britain by
Clays Ltd, St Ives plc

For Lesley

Monday

the sting

Martin sat up in the back of the cab, taking a moment to adjust to no longer being in motion. He felt less drunk than he had at the party and wondered whether to go back to one of his clubs. It was always safer to get home after Claudia had gone to bed, and his hangovers never seemed as bad if he ended the evening with a cocktail. An extra drink smoothed over the nasty bump of drunkenness between getting home and going to bed, and as long as he followed it with a few glasses of water and a smoked ham sandwich, he usually awoke feeling fine.

'She your girlfriend?' asked the cabbie.

'Naomi?' He smiled. 'No.'

'Would you like her to be?'

'Oh no, she's far too high-maintenance for me.'

Naomi reappeared in the illuminated doorway of her building, holding the disk. Carefully padding across to the taxi, she slipped it into his inside pocket as she lifted Martin by his lapels and kissed him on the lips.

'Mmm,' he murmured as she broke away, 'what was that for?'

'Keeping my secrets.'

She pushed a finger against his lips, then slammed the door shut. He could taste the mint of her chewing-gum and reached into his pocket to check how much cash he had left.

'Where next?' asked the driver.

'Change of plan. Take me back to Soho.'

The taxi deposited Martin outside his favourite club. He took out his membership card and walked over to where a large man in a camel-hair coat guarded a nondescript doorway. The man stood back and ostentatiously unhooked the velvet rope, allowing Martin inside.

Martin only went to clubs alone during the first part of the week, when he could guarantee that he could get somewhere to sit undisturbed by the afterhours activities of C-list celebrities. He'd implemented this personal rule after being forced to share a wrap with a disheartened soap star who'd recognised him from the photo above his editorial one desperate Thursday the previous autumn.

When this club had opened, all the staff had been impeccably well-groomed. Over the last year, however, these fash-mag automatons had been phased out in favour of talkative ex-travellers, who having earned their way round the world with their cocktail-shaking skills, were much better equipped to titillate the club's clientele with cocky tricks like making an orange-peel noose to hold the cherry in an Old Fashioned.

Martin took his drink and went through to the empty back room. Pleased to see a copy of *Force* alongside some other magazines next to a pile of food menus, he picked it up from the table and thumbed through it. Even though the issue was only a couple of months old, it already seemed a world away from him.

Usually Martin could safely sit alone until he'd finished his cocktail. Tonight, however, a toothy woman with dark blonde hair tapped his arm and said, 'Psychiatrist.'

'What?'

She swirled her drink. 'I'm guessing your job. Go on, now you do me.'

'But I'm not a psychiatrist.'

'I know. I only said that because I didn't want to freak you out by getting it right straight away. So come on, what d'you think I do?'

Martin put down the magazine and looked at the woman again. Although he was pretending it was only for the purpose of the game, he knew he was really trying to decide if she was attractive. He knew she knew this too, and that she'd only started the game to speed up the seduction process. She was sexy, but her prominent teeth and slightly bulging eyes gave her a predatory look that unnerved him. Still, it was a pretty ballsy pick-up technique, and no matter how often this happened, he always felt flattered.

'PR?'

'Fuck you,' she replied, immediately standing up and striding out of the room.

Martin was about to get up and follow when he realised she'd left her drink on the table. So this was part of the game too. He felt too tired to play along, but wanted to thank her for making the effort, so he stood up and checked the other room. She wasn't there either so he went through to the toilets. She was standing outside the ladies, smoking a cigarette.

'You,' she said.

'Yeah. Look, I'm sorry, you're very nice and everything, but I was drunk enough even before I came to this club and I'm really wasted now. How about I give you my number . . . ?'

'Oh, Martin, you were so close.'

'What?'

She extended her hand. 'You don't remember me, do you? Claudia said you wouldn't. We met at your wedding. My name is Jane.'

Tuesday

sushi

Every morning for the last five years Alison Hendry had awoken to a song called *Lize* by the band Smog. It was one of the most depressing songs she'd ever heard and having it on her stereo-alarm always ensured that she had a terrible day. But no matter how many times she implored her boyfriend to change it, he always refused.

She'd even pulled the tape out and thrown it away twice, but on both occasions he'd simply bought another C-90, rerecorded the song and replaced it. The current cassette was even more annoying as two years of constant play had stretched the tape so badly that it sounded like one long strangulated whine. She'd got so used to the song that now she awoke the second it started, pressing pause before the singer had chance to launch into fully-fledged misery.

The reason why Alison's boyfriend Adrian forced her to listen to this was to remind her of a minor infidelity she'd committed in their second year of university. At first Adrian had been deadly serious about this punishment, but since then she'd caught him in similar circumstances and he now seemed to view playing the song as some kind of monotonous joke he was going to keep up for as long as they stayed together.

For the last year, Alison and Adrian had been living with Alison's sister Suzanne, who was a slut. There was no nice way of putting it, and slut sounded better than promiscuous, which carried the spectre of disease. But she was monstrously proud of her success-rate with men, at one time even keeping a condom-collection on her window-ledge. When Alison had found out about this, she'd forced her sister to get rid of them. Unfortunately, Suzanne had simply peeled them off and thrown them into next-door's garden, and ten minutes later Alison had been confronted by a furious neighbour with one condom slapped across his forehead and a second swimming in his cup of tea.

When Alison first started working, she was terrified her sister might seduce Adrian. So far the only restriction she seemed to accept was not to go after either family members or Alison's boyfriends. But Alison worried that the boredom of being home all day together was just the sort of excuse Suzanne needed to justify shagging Adrian. Every evening she looked for changes in their behaviour, searching for the subtle clues that would reveal they'd been up each other while she'd been at work. But unless the two of them were exceptionally discreet, it seemed they were genuinely un-interested in upsetting her.

Or maybe Suzanne was simply too scared about what would become of her if she incurred Alison's wrath. Although in her personal and professional lives she seemed blithely uncon-cerned about alienating people, especially at the night-club where she gave new meaning to the job title *door bitch*, Suzanne genuinely seemed to value her home-life, and understood that Alison would spare no compassion should she catch her tampering with Adrian's trousers.

Before Alison had landed her job working as Martin Powell's personal assistant at *Force* magazine, the three of them had been enjoying an extended adolescence, living on a combination of parental hand-outs, jobseeker's allowance

10

and the odd flirtation with Reed. Adrian and Suzanne now continued this life alone, indulging in the kind of days that could only be enjoyed by people with too much time on their hands. Over the last few weeks, they'd been going through Adrian's extensive collection of old music magazines, attempting to recreate seminal moments from recent pop history. Yesterday she'd come home to find them dancing round the living-room with four purloined window-mannequins, claiming they were converting them into robots to re-enact Kraftwerk's appearance at Tribal Gathering in 1997.

Alison's journey into work was long and irritating, forty-five minutes on a heaving double-decker bus. But it was a relief when she arrived at the *Force* offices in Euston. Most of her friends who worked on magazines were stuck in con-verted factories in East London. All those buildings had fantastically stylish insides, but it didn't feel like proper work when you were slouching about on foam off-cuts with a bunch of arty kids whose clothes folded up into bags. She much preferred working in a proper high-rise. She loved the dated glass and chrome, she loved the open-plan space, she even loved the mere idea of working on a men's magazine. And of course everything that went with that. She loved the illicit feeling that seemed to be shared by every woman in this masculine space. She loved the way every male employee knew he was on show. She loved the effect that constantly writing about after-shave and suits and the best way to remove bristles had on them, giving her a floor full of well-groomed specimens to admire every morning.

Most of all, however, she loved her boss. It was a secret crush, and even though she knew he was frequently unfaith-ful to his impossibly posh girlfriend, she never did anything to reveal her feelings. This wasn't because she feared rejec-tion, but because she worried she'd stop fancying him if he returned her affections. This was the sort of thing Suzanne would never understand. For her, a scalp was always better than sustaining the pleasures of possibility. Alison had been going out with Adrian for almost five years now, and before him there had been two other long-term relationships. Apart from her one genuine act of infidelity, Alison's secret love-life consisted of unrevealed crushes and low-level flirting, days and nights of unfulfilled promise. And when someone did see through her hidden desires and make a pass at her, there was always a brief moment of satisfaction before she told the interested party that she didn't want to betray her boyfriend.

Martin was an easy person to look after. He never expected her to read his mind, and didn't trouble her with the small stuff he could sort out himself. He wasn't lazy, didn't really gossip, and avoided office politics. But Alison did think there was something scummy about his adulterous love-life, and preferred to indulge in fantasies where he left his wife and changed his life for her rather than actually committing herself to an affair.

'I had a dream about you last night.'

Alison looked at Gareth's reflection in the mirrored door as the lift took them up to the seventh floor. He was one of the few men employed by *Force* she didn't like, although she tried to hide this aversion. Other people on the magazine thought Gareth was a great laugh, mainly cause he could get away with saying the most obscene stuff without anyone taking offence. His main task was editing the dirty joke page, and although he was supposed to use readers' submissions, everyone in the office knew he faked the letters and pocketed the prize money.

'We were having this big orgy,' he continued, 'you and me and all the people from floor seven.'

'I see.'

'And you and I were separated by about three bodies and someone was sucking my dick and someone else was fucking them and you were rimming that other person.'

'Lovely.'

'No, no, it's OK, right, cause my hands were stretched out underneath all these bodies and I had my fingers in two girls' vaginas. I wasn't really fingering them, I was just like holding on to them through their vaginas, and one of the girls said, "Who's finger is that in my cunt?" and then Nicole said, "Are you kidding, it's Gareth's finger, Gareth's got his finger in everyone's cunt."'

Alison stared at Gareth, wondering what had happened in his life to make him so confident. It seemed incredible that she had to listen to him, that he could come up to her muttering about dicks and cunts, and if she told him to fuck off she'd be the one being impolite.

'Sounds fairly fanciful.'

'Well, maybe, but that wasn't what you said in the dream.'

The lift stopped.

'What did I say?'

'You said, "You know, I don't think I've ever had Gareth's finger in my cunt."'

'True enough.'

They walked out into the office.

'So I looked at you.'

'Over the bodies.'

'Exactly,' said Gareth. 'And our eyes met and I asked you if you'd like to have my finger in your cunt.'

'Is this a come-on?'

'No, of course not. I'm just telling you about my dream.'

'OK. Go on.'

'Well, of course you said yes . . .'

'Of course.'

'So we went off to this private room and I laid you out on this big bed and opened your legs and instead of a cunt you had like this weird piece of sushi or something.'

'That's so disgusting.'

'I know,' he replied. 'What do you think it means?'

As much as Alison hated Gareth's cheerful vulgarity, she felt determined not to be embarrassed and to respond in kind. Turning towards him, she looked him in the eye and said speedily, 'It's fish, isn't it. Your joke is that I've got a fishy fanny. Was that just a trick? Did you make the whole thing up?'

'No, no, of course not. It was my dream.'

'Right.'

She knew she was supposed to laugh now. Slap him on the back and praise his ingenuity. But she was too irritated, and started walking away. He reached out and touched her shoulder.

'Sorry, Al, didn't mean any offence. Look, I'll tell you what, I'll make up for my rudeness with some shit-hot gossip.'

'I'm not interested.'

'Even if it's about your beloved boss.'

She looked back. 'What about him?'

Gareth ran his finger across his neck. 'End of the month. They're bringing someone new in to revamp it.'

'Who?'

'No one knows, a woman probably. They've been talking to someone who used to be at *Nova*.'

'And this is true?'

'Absolutely. They're telling him on Thursday.'

Alison spent the hour before Martin arrived agonising over whether she should tell him what she had heard. Gareth's reliability as a gossip was second only to his smutmeister skills, and almost every story he passed on turned out to be true. There was always the possibility that someone had deliberately leaked a false story (maybe trying to get him to resign so they wouldn't have to sack him) but even then, the fact that these sorts of rumours were doing the rounds was almost certainly something he should know about.

But would Martin thank her for being the one who told him? Alison hated bearing bad news, and while she believed her boss to be an essentially decent man, she didn't really know him well enough to second-guess how he would handle losing his job. Martin was always closed-mouthed about career stuff, and avoided seeking the sort of publicity craved by most of his rivals. Whenever he ended up in the newspapers, he invariably looked embarrassed and was usually sitting with friends rather than drunkenly clutching Denise Van Outen or Nick Moran. And although Alison had no illusions about Martin, knowing how much he enjoyed his decadent nights with Naomi, she also knew he was a much more innocent soul than most of the people he hung around with.

Alison could also understand why they wanted to get rid of him. Martin seemed to have little enthusiasm for *Force*, and few real friends among his staff. People who'd worked with Martin before told Alison that he'd always been a rather isolated figure, having spent years cultivating a persona designed to prevent people coming up to him with irrelevant questions. She didn't mind protecting him, but she always felt scared whenever she sensed his fragility, and felt terrified that he might not be able to cope with getting the sack.

Nevertheless, she decided she would share what she had heard. It would be much worse if she didn't say anything and then he discovered that she'd known before him. She had until Thursday, and there was always the hope that someone would get in before her. Quite a few of the staff writers admired Martin, and most were career-minded enough to want to cover their bases in case he moved somewhere else and could offer them a better job. Pleased to have reached a decision, Alison turned back to her computer and checked to see if she'd received any e-mails in the last five minutes.

Martin

Martin Powell knew he didn't make a very convincing editor. He didn't photograph as well as Dylan Jones (*GQ*), lacked the cast-iron connections of Peter Howarth (*Esquire*), and had never been able to muster the successful authority of Mark Ellen (*Arena*). He saw those guys around (usually separately, especially since the big argument last September about who had the most ABs among their readership, a confrontation he'd kept out of as he doubted his magazine had any at all) and although they were usually friendly towards him and always interested in the fortunes of *Force*, he couldn't help feeling a fraud. Their respective magazines, while not having the largest circulation of the Big Seven, were definitely the ones that still seemed stylish, and in spite of the continuing tail-off after a decade and a half of rapid growth, retained their dignity, occasionally achieved the odd flash of original-ity, and were bolstered by their counterparts in Europe and America. The American connection was the thing Martin envied most, especially as when reading the US edition of *Esquire*, he was frequently struck by the sense that they had got it absolutely right. As far as Martin was concerned, a good men's magazine should make you feel part of an exclusive club, colluding in a confident fantasy of masculinity that was impossible to find in real life.

Force, on the other hand, was an artificial creation with a constantly changing target-audience, and no real sense of itself as a magazine. It had managed to avoid the tat of the handful of post-*Loaded* titles, but the only people who seemed to be buying it were the magazine junkies who already had everything else on the shelf.

One of their most recent failed experiments was to try to come up with the *Force* man. Not the average reader, but the idealised embodiment of the magazine. The *Force* man is . . . in his early thirties, probably a bit of a lone wolf, but not without male friends. Someone who'd take you to Alaska for a stag-week instead of getting you drunk, stealing your clothes and abandoning you on a train. A lover, not a fighter. Beginning to look at his CD collection as a whole and buying those Beatles albums that twelve years ago in a field seemed irrelevant. Comfortable in a dinner-jacket and these days only wearing trainers to go running. Disdainful of last year's Cole Haan *Michael's*, and all of this year's knock-offs. And round about there they got stuck, aware that *Force* man was beginning to sound a bit of a bore.

At first, Martin didn't foresee a problem with becoming an editor. He'd spent most of the nineties as a freelance writer, and felt he was adept enough at writing about music, film, style and TV to handle taking on a whole magazine. He didn't know that much about cars or sport, but knew he could entrust those sections to someone else. But since taking on the position, he'd discovered that being good at his job wasn't as important as having the right personality.

Martin wasn't a natural leader. He disliked being in a position of authority and had never been the type to take pleasure in doling out favours. And although he knew he had some support from the staff-writers, he found it hard to motivate them and knew it was only a matter of time before someone decided a new editor was needed to steer the magazine to success.

Right from the start, Martin had decided he wasn't going to fall into the usual pitfalls that went along with a day-job. Too many of his friends had driven themselves frantic by turning their office lives into an unpleasant soap-opera. He was unfaithful to Claudia on a regular basis, but wouldn't dream of having an affair with anyone at the magazine. He even avoided flirting with the women in the office, which no doubt contributed to his unpopularity. Appointing an assistant, he had chosen Alison because she seemed serious and professional, the kind of person who would protect him from the rest of the office. She was undeniably attractive, but he prided himself on not having any lustful thoughts about her, even in idle, unguarded moments. He knew this made things easier for her too, although he sensed she would be pleased if he took greater interest in her life outside the office. Today, as always, she was in before him. He smiled at her as she looked up, striding purposefully towards her desk before anyone had chance to interrupt him with a stupid question.

She looked worried. 'You know you've got lunch.'

'Who with?'

'Gina. She's only in London for three days and this is the last one so you can't cancel.'

'OK,' Martin said, walking through to his office.

Alison followed him. 'Do you know where you're meeting her?'

'Of course.'

'Really?'

'Remind me.'

He should've remembered. Gina only ever ate in Joe Allen's when she was in London. For someone so fêted for her supposed coolness, Gina had surprisingly conventional tastes. Martin liked that about her, and it was true of all the major taste-makers he knew. Let everyone else go to the clubs and restaurants she recommended but rarely visited. She already had her life.

Martin had first met Gina five years earlier. The two of them had been booked together to appear on a short-lived discussion show on Channel Four. He'd heard about her beforehand (in those days they'd both been more generous about giving up their time to newspapers, magazines and television), and seen her across the room at several parties, but this was the first time they'd been properly introduced. The show had gone well, and they'd gone out to dinner afterwards. Taxi back to her place and everything was progressing so smoothly they both couldn't stop grinning. Convinced he was in for a memorable evening, Martin felt more relaxed than he had on any previous one-night stand. But when they got back, things started to get a little bit strange. First she startled him by immediately stripping out of her *Kiki Bridges* T-shirt and black bra as soon as they got through the door. Then she led him into a room that had not only a mirrored ceiling, but also mirrored walls and a mirrored floor. Somehow she'd had this reinforced so it was perfectly safe to walk on, and although he started off feeling like he was trapped in a kaleidoscope, as soon as the two of them were making love the sensation of the cold glass on his skin was incredible.

The next time he saw her was in New York. In a Krispy Kreme in Chelsea. Martin was supposed to be getting breakfast for the people putting him up. Instead he disappeared with her for two days. She was going through a vampire phase

19

and although he was prepared to wear the cape and fangs, he drew the line at actual bloodletting. But he had so much fun that the next time she was in London they had a proper two month affair. Gina was staying in a hotel so he dropped in whenever he could get away from Claudia, which worked out fine, as one of Gina's best qualities was that she was just as happy if he showed up for breakfast or a midnight fuck.

After that, they had limited themselves to the odd secret screw whenever she was in London or he was in New York. They had got attached to each other during those two months, and each time they went to bed now it was an emotional experience. But Martin still enjoyed having sex with Gina, and hoped that was how lunch would end today.

He entered the restaurant. Gina had arrived early, and already looked at home. She was sitting at a table next to the piano, drinking her usual vodka and cranberry.

'Gina.'

'Martin. Do you like my T-shirt?'

Girls are Evil. Red gothic script on a black background.

'Nice.'

'What about my hair?'

He checked it out. Black with a red fringe.

'It's great.'

'My new therapist. Any time I get any destructive impulses I'm supposed to take it out on my hair.'

'God. I don't think I could ever do anything to my hair.'

She chuckled. 'It's always been like that then?'

'Pretty much. Except for an unfortunate crew-cut incident when I was thirteen.'

He pulled back his chair and sat down opposite her. He could tell she wasn't done with this topic, but the thing about Gina was that she could talk you to the wall, and if he didn't try to move things on, he knew it'd be three o'clock before he'd even ordered a starter. He smiled indulgently.

'You should dye it, Martin.'

'Are you kidding? Most people would kill for this colour.'

'You've never wanted to go blond?'

'For about five minutes, when Kurt Cobain was still with us. But even then I couldn't quite cope with the idea. It felt like taking a wax crayon to an Old Master.'

'You're so vain.'

He picked up the menu, gave it a cursory once-over then ostentatiously tossed it into the centre of the table and focused on Gina.

'What's good here? I can never remember.'

She leaned onto her arms, a pose he recognised from her press photographs. 'The hamburger,' she told him, 'it's so incredible they don't even put it on the menu.'

'I didn't know you ate meat.'

'I go through stages. But it's purely faddism . . . I could never give it up for good. Hey, wait up, I want to show you something.'

She lifted her bag onto the table. A copy of *Force* jutted out from the two zippered lips. He felt touched that she'd been reading his magazine, but didn't say anything, knowing she'd snap at him if he brought it to her attention. She rifled through her bag and pulled out a black plastic camera.

'It's a bit out of date now, but I thought you might get a kick out of it.'

'What is it? A digital thing?'

'No, no, just a toy polaroid. But the size is nice, don't you think? *Smile.*'

He smiled. She clicked, waited, then tore out a strip of film. She shook it a couple of times and handed the strip to Martin.

He looked at the small picture of himself, took the camera from Gina and returned the favour.

Since its opening six months earlier, The Tenderloin Hotel had quickly established itself as the only place to go for an afternoon assignation. Management freely acknowledged their rapidly required reputation with a full-size cut-out of CC Baxter in reception. Martin liked the idea of the place, but wasn't comfortable with certain gimmicks, like the small S&M bag they handed out with room-cards to favoured guests. This was the first time he'd been to the hotel with Gina, and he was surprised it was to her taste. She usually preferred eccentricity and showbiz history to gimmicky design, and in spite of her willingness to sleep with Martin whenever the opportunity arose, he knew she didn't treat sex lightly and assumed she would hate the sniggery rock-star feel to the hotel.

They walked across the lobby to the lift. Their room was on the fourth floor. The doors opened and they stepped inside.

'So who are you seeing now?' Martin asked Gina.

'My guy.'

'Which guy?'

'My WASP guy.'

He tried to remember details. 'The one who cheated on you?'

'I didn't tell you that, did I?' She looked up at him, embarrassed. 'God, I can't believe I told you that.'

'I haven't told anyone.'

'Liar. But it's OK. You don't know anyone.'

'So how are you handling it?'

'What do you mean?'

'Well, the last time I spoke to you you'd set fire to his wardrobe.'

The lift stopped at their floor. They walked out. 'You don't really want to know this, do you?'

'Yes.'

'Which way is it? This way?'

'I think so. The room numbers are so confusing in this place.'

She started walking. 'OK. Basically, he was away when I found out, so I burnt his wardrobe and flew to LA.'

'The Chateau?'

'Where else? And when he didn't try to track me down I called him and he didn't mention the wardrobe or anything, so, to cut a long story short, I went back to him.'

'And things are OK with you?'

'They're alright. He makes me feel too much like a man, but that's something I can cope with.'

They'd reached the right room. 'This is it.' He looked back at her as he slid the card into the slot. 'I don't understand what you mean.'

'He's just so beautiful. And so dumb. His favourite book's *Bartleby* for God's sake. And that's not even a book. He's just so inferior to me. And I know I'm only still with him because he's so good looking.'

The door opened and they walked inside. Gina looked through her bag again as they found their room.

'They have CD players here, don't they?'

Martin nodded. 'Of course.'

She handed him a copy of *Station to Station*. 'Put track six on repeat. It's the only thing that does it for me these days.'

Martin walked across the room, opened the black wooden cabinet beneath the TV set and loaded the CD into the player. He looked back at Gina, surprised by the ecstatic look on her face as the song's cinematic sweep filled the room. She stepped out of her red kitten-heels and smiled at Martin with her head tilted on one side. Then she took off her T-shirt.

'Why do you always do that?'

She looked over at him, her face anxious. 'What?'

'Strip like a streetwalker. Don't you like to be undressed?'

Gina's expression was hard to read. Martin never felt entirely confident when playing these sorts of games with her. He always had the sense that one day he would say something that would result in him losing contact with her forever. But, in the meantime, an aggressive approach seemed more likely to keep her interest than over-caution.

Her face relaxed. 'Yeah, I like to be undressed. When I'm having sex with my boyfriend. It's different with you.'

He crossed the room towards her and looped his arms around her back. 'So you won't let me undress you?'

She looked up at him, her eyes quizzical. 'Would you like to undress me?'

He smiled. 'Very much.'

'OK, but do it roughly.'

'Why?'

'I don't want you to be sensitive with me, Martin, OK? Things'll go wrong if you start being sensitive.'

He released her. 'Give me your camera.'

'Oh, no,' said Gina, 'I'm not letting you have pictures of me.'

'We'll burn them afterwards. Come on, that'll stop you thinking of me as sensitive.'

Gina opened her bag, located her camera and threw it to him. It bounced beside him on the mattress.

'OK,' he said, 'give me your best Liz Taylor.'

She smiled and leaned backwards, pushing her breasts up from below. Martin took a picture and she quickly came across, wanting to see it. He shook the strip and showed it to her.

'What d'you reckon?'

'You've made my chin look funny. Let me take one of you.'

Martin took off his jacket and lay back on the bed.

'Pull up your shirt,' Gina told him.

He did so.

'You look like a skate-kid in a snuff movie. Can't you make yourself more manly?'

Martin laughed and changed his pose. She put her hand on his shoulder and bore down on him. After a moment it started to hurt and he tried to shake her away. But she held firm, snapping again. He wrapped his legs around hers, then twisted her body over so he could get back on top. Remembering her instructions, he forcefully pulled down the cups of her bra, kissing her breasts as they sprung free. He sucked hard on her nipples, before reaching to unclasp her. Then he laughed, took the camera and snapped another picture.

'There's one for the internet,' he laughed, just before her foot came hard up into his face, knocking him off the mattress and onto the floor.

the 5.30 phone call

Alison had known since four that Martin wouldn't be coming back in. Until this point she'd found it hard to concentrate on her work, but hadn't at least felt actively miserable. She didn't know for certain that Martin was spending the afternoon screwing Gina – often after a long lunch he went straight home – but a strange, sad, psychic feeling told her this was probably the case.

She waited ninety minutes before calling her boyfriend,

wanting to get a handle on her mood first. Adrian's emotional state was fairly consistent – the only thing she could imagine sending him into a depression was a worldwide shortage of bacon sandwiches – and she knew he always got ultra-observant if he detected anything was wrong with her.

'Alright?' she said cheerfully.

He was laughing at something. 'Yeah.'

'So what are you recreating today?'

'Nirvana's appearance at Reading. The second one, when they were really big and there'd been all those drug stories and they went on after Nick Cave. Suzanne's stolen a wheelchair from the hospital.'

'What?'

'It's OK, it's an old one, no one will miss it. We needed it because that was how he got on stage.'

'Right.'

'Don't be cross,' she heard Suzanne shout from elsewhere in the room.

'I'm not cross.'

'I haven't managed to do the shopping yet, but don't worry. Suzanne's going to help me.'

'Actually, Ade, that's what I was calling about. I wondered whether we could go to a restaurant instead. We can take Suzanne, if you want.'

He went quiet. 'Where?'

'I don't mind.'

'Not somewhere posh. Let's go somewhere round here.'

'Henry's,' shouted Suzanne.

'Oh God, no,' Alison told Adrian, 'tell her we're not going there. Say she can come, I'll pay, just as long as we go anywhere else.'

'I like Henry's.'

'Please, Adrian, we go there all the time. We might as well go to a fucking Harvester.'

'She wants to go somewhere posh,' she heard her sister tell Adrian.

Feeling defeated, Alison said, 'OK, Henry's it is. Can you book the table?'

the sting II

Martin knew better than to buy flowers. And although he knew he was following scumbag logic, in some ways he thought it would prove useful that he'd spent the afternoon with Gina, allowing him to feel suitably guilty. The trick was not to be defensive, but also not to be overly apologetic, lest Claudia sensed he'd done anything worse than getting caught out in a club.

He was home two hours before her. He'd showered at the hotel, but that had been with Gina, so he took a bath, wanting to make sure there was nothing of her left on him. After that he checked the plug-hole in case he'd carried home any of her hairs and went over his suit with a brush. He cleaned his teeth, gargled, and cleaned his teeth again. Then he checked his body for scratches, and, finding two red nail-crescents in his left buttock, slapped and squeezed the offending area until they were gone.

Then he got himself a beer from the fridge and sat down to watch some cable television. He was ready for Claudia's return.

'Have you spoken to Jane today?' he asked the moment she got in.

'Yes.'

'So you know your little sting worked?'

27

Claudia put her bag down in the hallway and strode into the lounge. He looked at her legs, trying to work out how aggressively she'd attack.

'Well, it wasn't completely successful. Especially as I was hoping you'd go home with her and give me grounds for divorcing you.'

'Is that what this is about? You want to break up? Cause there's a lot easier ways of doing it than trying to get me to fuck one of your friends.'

She advanced towards him. 'Why did you give her your number, Martin? Were you going to sleep with her?'

'No, of course not. I was just being polite. I knew she wouldn't call.'

'Jane really likes you, you know. That's why she gave the game away. I'm fucking furious with her for doing that.'

Martin put down his beer and stood up. Claudia backed away slightly, reaching up to let her hair down. He'd stopped finding her work clothes sexy, especially as she no longer looked that different at weekends, sliding happily into a comfortable, but smart, conservative appearance at all times.

'Is this how bad things have got? Cause if they are I'm not so sure I want to stay in this relationship either.'

'Martin . . .' she said, her voice softer. 'Why won't you just tell me what you get up to? Maybe if you were open with me we could sort this out.'

'Open about what?'

'The other women.'

'There aren't any other women. Not any more. And I told you about every single one. And it's not as if you don't have Clive.'

'I don't fuck Clive.'

'Not any more, but you did before. And it was while we were going out.'

'And you were being unfaithful to me. I sensed it then, and I sense it now.'

'I promise you, Claudia, that's not true. I haven't slept with anyone other than you since we stopped going to those sessions together.'

'Maybe we should start again.'

'Why? We're over all that. Listen, it's silly for you to get upset about last night. You know everything about me. You know where I am during the day, you know who I go out drinking with at night, you even know which clubs I go to when I . . .'

'Want to pick up women,' she spat.

'Want to be alone. Look, Claudia, please, it doesn't make sense for us to always be at each other's throats.'

She sat down opposite him. He tried a smile, not wanting her to see how wretched he felt. Martin knew she was as close to throwing it all in as he was, and sometimes he wondered what drove her to expending so much energy on keeping their marriage going.

Martin had first met Claudia when she was twenty-five. At that time neither of them had been especially interested in settling down. Although Martin believed that he hadn't changed that much over the last ten years, Claudia had undergone several radical personality shifts, each one accompanying a major change in her life. The first big alteration happened when they decided to stop mucking around with other people and make their relationship monogamous. Previously, Claudia had been quite a heavy partier, and unlike most of the big drug-takers he'd known at that time, she took a good few years to give in to the broadsheet scaremongers and upgrade from Ecstasy to Coke. Martin had never been a big drugs man, happy to try everything once and then stick to the odd line on special occasions, so he was pleased when

Claudia cut back to just booze and prescription pills. Then, when they moved in together, she ditched the pills and moderated her drinking. This was followed a few months later by her decision to stop switching careers and stick to her job at Christie's. After their engagement she became virtually tee-total, and when they got married she cut back on all but the most important parties. It had occurred to Martin that she was preparing to become a parent, but he was so scared that she might be serious about wanting a baby that he made sure he changed the subject every time it looked like the question might come up.

All of these changes had taken Claudia so far away from the person he'd fallen in love with that sometimes he found it hard to remember just how fun-loving she'd been when they first met. The magazine world was an aggressively hedonistic one, with a history of fatalities on both sides of the Atlantic, but even so, Claudia had seemed more serious about her after-hours pursuits than anyone else he'd ever met. Her friends had all seemed the same, and in those days he'd been the one with the quiet life. He'd always had Lenny and Naomi, and their gang of weirdoes, but it was interesting how carefully that particular social-circle was self-regulated. Anyone too seriously intent on destroying themselves was slowly, almost imperceptibly ostracised, allowing the others to live danger-ously for a while without having to face the nasty aftermath of another friend's funeral. And sometimes these outcasts did die, although by that time their digits had long since disappeared from Naomi's speed-dial.

The phone rang. Martin walked across to answer it. It was Naomi. She was in a panic because she'd arranged to meet her friend Laetitia before going to the gallery party they were all attending that evening, but now her brother Lenny had called with a problem he needed her help to sort out and she wouldn't be able to keep her earlier appointment. Martin didn't understand her worry, wondering why she couldn't just call Laetitia and tell her to meet them at the gallery. Naomi explained that Laetitia was a space-cadet and the chances of her getting to the gallery unaided were slim. At this point Martin realised what was being asked of him and agreed to pick up Laetitia and take her to the gallery, even though he knew this would infuriate Claudia, who was glaring at him throughout the phone-call.

'Naomi?' she asked, as he replaced the receiver.

He nodded.

'I knew it. That fucking slut. Where are you going with her?'

'Some opening that Lenny's mates are involved in. Silk scarves and razor blades, or something similarly sixth-form. An S and M art evening.'

'Sounds right up your street,' she said acidly.

'Thank you, darling.'

'And when should I expect you back?'

'I don't know. Three or something. Does it matter?'

'No, I suppose not. I guess I'll just have to give Clive a ring.'

He stared at her. 'Fine.'

Henry's

Alison was two years older than Suzanne. Alison's parents put her problems down to an unfortunate combination of the age-gap and sibling rivalry. Alison had enjoyed a straightforward, conservative childhood. Suzanne had spent the whole of her adolescence getting in trouble for wanting to do the same things as her sister two years too early. So while their parents were perfectly happy when Alison lost her virginity at a sensible seventeen to a boy she'd been dating for a year, they were much less impressed when Suzanne lost hers in a sewer outlet two weeks later to a man named Dirty Wheeler who lived in the woods.

'Hi, sis,' said Suzanne, 'you OK?'

'Yeah,' she told them, 'just recovering from an annoying journey.'

'We didn't order yet. I wanted to, but Adrian told me to wait.'

'Thanks, Ade, that was kind of you.'

'See,' said Adrian, nudging her.

Suzanne laughed. A waiter came across and offered to take her coat. Alison handed it to him and sat down.

french boys and german girls

Lenny and Naomi Bentata were Martin's oldest friends. Although Naomi had started off trying to be nice to Claudia, and Lenny had even been best man at their wedding, for some reason they'd never managed to make a connection with her. This was something Martin didn't really mind, and in fact was privately pleased about, as he wanted to keep his social life relatively secret from his wife.

Unusually close for brother and sister, Lenny and Naomi came from a Jewish family that had long since stopped celebrating their faith. Naomi was small, blonde and funny, while Lenny had been shown the Dustin Hoffman movie about his namesake at far too early an age and had spent several years trying to ditch his method mannerisms. Both siblings worked in television, Lenny producing, Naomi as a presenter, although it seemed increasingly unlikely that she'd achieve the Sara Cox/Zoe Ball level of success she desired.

They were also his last link with serious decadence, two people who would (he hoped) never get married, never have kids, never stop going out somewhere stupid every single night of the week. Most of their friends were maniacs, but his nights spent with them were the most memorable of his entire life.

He had never met Laetitia, although he'd heard Naomi talking about her. She was younger than Naomi, someone she'd adopted on one of her most recent jobs. Lenny had said she was very sexy, but then again, he said that about almost every woman he ever met.

Martin hailed a cab. He climbed into the back and told the driver his destination. Then he reached into his suit pocket and pulled out his photograph of Gina. She'd saved the picture when they burnt the others, and handed it to him as they were leaving the hotel, a sentimental touch that was typical of her, and a nice gesture after an awkward afternoon. The sex had been great (although Martin had worried that Gina's choice of background music was a secret clue to a new upsurge of self-loathing), but afterwards they had both cried, clutching each other with a ferocity that surprised him. This had prompted Martin to talk too much about his current fears, letting her know how worried he was about losing his position at *Force*. He knew Gina found self-pity a total turn-off (unless it was her own) but he couldn't stop himself babbling, telling her his worries because Claudia wouldn't want to hear them. After his disclosure, Gina dressed in double-quick time and asked Martin if he didn't have to get home.

The taxi reached Farringdon Station. Martin paid the driver and got out, wanting to walk the final stretch to the bar. He needed a short burst of air to clear his head, to set him up for his next social interaction. It was raining, and he turned his face upwards for a few seconds, feeling the tiredness in the corners of his eyes.

He wondered whether he was upset by Claudia's threat to call Clive. He supposed it was a source of social embarrassment that his wife's relationship with her confidant was a matter of public knowledge, but then again, as far as he was aware these days they no longer slept together, and at least it meant she wasn't running around with anyone else.

He reached the bar. For some reason he had assumed that he'd instantly recognise Laetitia and now, confronted by a room full of strangers, he didn't know where to start. He approached the only woman sitting alone.

'Hi,' he said, 'are you Laetitia?'

She shook her head.

'I'm Laetitia,' said a voice behind him. 'Who are you?'

He turned round and was confronted by a dark-haired woman in her early twenties. Her long hair was parted in the middle and came down in a straight sweep over her left cheek. She had thin, plucked eyebrows and a full, self-confident smile. Like most of Naomi's friends she was tall, expensively dressed and unafraid of her own elegance. Which made it all the more surprising that she seemed to be accompanied by a man who was immediately identifiable as a foreign-exchange student. He had the look down pat: wire-brush hair; a smattering of acne obscuring an otherwise OK face; cheap *Raybans* hooked round the wrong way so it looked like he had eyes in the back of his head; a *Phoenix* badge on a denim jacket over a white T-shirt; trousers with too many pockets; New Balance trainers. From his moustache, Martin identified him as French.

'I'm Martin,' he told Laetitia, offering her his hand. 'Naomi sent me.'

'Hi, Martin, this is Benoît.'

'Hello,' said Benoît.

'Naomi's going to meet us at the gallery.'

'Is she? OK. I guess there's no hurry then. Would you like a drink?'

'Thanks,' said Martin.

'I will get his drink,' Benoît announced in an over-formal voice, 'what would you like?'

'Just a lager, please.'

Benoît nodded and walked up to the bar. Martin sat down opposite Laetitia. She leaned across and whispered, 'He just came up to me.'

'Benoît?'

'Yeah. I was surprised they let him in here.'

'Maybe they think he's in a band and being ironic.'

'He's not, though, you know. He's a genuine exchange student.'

'Let's go through his rucksack. I've always wanted to know what these guys have got that's so fantastic they have to carry it around with them all the time.'

Laetitia shot Martin a mischievous glance and passed him Benoît's rucksack. He opened it under the table. An A-Z, a pencil-case disguised as a can of 7-Up, and a large hunting knife. He was about to show the latter to Laetitia when she hissed, 'Put it down. Quick. He's coming back.'

Benoît returned with Martin's drink. He placed it on the table in front of him and patted Martin on the shoulder. There was something about this gesture that deeply irritated Martin, and he had to force himself to be gracious and thank Benoît for the drink.

All the staff at the art evening, which was really called

'Bloodlove: 21st Century BDSM' were tall women with long, clean black hair tied back with red ribbons. They were also all wearing blindfolds, which was fine for the women at the signing-in point, but less sensible for the ones wobbling around with canapés. Martin quickly separated from Laetitia and Benoît, and started a circuit round the gallery. The crowd were surprisingly well-dressed for this sort of event, and he spied a few wealthy-looking artists' parents. This confirmed his suspicion that the artwork wasn't exactly cutting edge.

As he walked into the main room he recognised two of Naomi's stockbroker friends. Both of them were dressed in dark pinstripe suits, although they were quite different in appearance. One of them, Aubrey, was tall, blonde and physically intimidating. The other, whose name Martin had forgotten, was squat, with round glasses, floppy hair and a frogish face. Just by looking at the way the two of them were standing together, Martin could tell the squat man was in awe of Aubrey, and he wondered about their business relationship.

'Hi Martin,' the taller one said, turning to his friend, 'you know Blake, don't you?'

'Yes,' said Martin, shaking Blake's hand.

'Aubrey reckons the girls have been instructed not to wear underwear,' Blake said.

'Really?' said Martin.

Aubrey nodded. 'You can tell by the shadow.'

The three of them looked at the nearest girl. The fact that she was blindfolded only made Martin feel more guilty.

Blake adjusted his glasses. 'You know, I think he's right.'

Naomi arrived an hour later, just as they were about to give up on her. Watching her move through the crowd, Martin considered how different she was to Gina. Although both women were on the small side, they always managed to be the centre of attention. Naomi projected outwards, rarely going anywhere without an intimidating coterie, of which Martin was proud to be a member. Although she was the one who took charge of an evening's organisation, talking to taxi drivers and gallery owners and greeting girls, she refused to tolerate anyone coming up to talk to her unless they had been introduced by another member of the circle. With Gina, however, everyone was encouraged to become part of her entertainment. Strangers were invited along to private parties; no one was allowed to feel unwelcome. Being out with her quickly became tiring, while Naomi made sure that no one in her circle was allowed to overexert themselves.

'Can we go now?' moaned Blake.

'Relax, guys, I shan't stay long. But I do have to check who's here.'

'Where's Lenny?'

'The spot of bother turned out to be bigger than we imagined. But he sends his love. Did you pick up Laetitia?'

She held Martin's gaze, her small, angular jaw set stern. Her doubt surprised him, as he couldn't remember ever having let her down.

'Of course.'

'Where is she?'

'Outside. With Benoît.'

'Who's Benoît?'

'A French exchange student.'

Naomi raised her eyebrows. 'Where are they?'

Martin walked with her to the doorway and pointed them out. They were sitting at a white metal table, talking intimately. Although it was too dark outside to tell for sure, it

37

looked like they were holding hands. Martin fought the urge to intervene. As Naomi went to join them, he walked back to Blake and Aubrey. The two men smiled warmly at him, stepping back to let him rejoin their small group.

'God, she's gorgeous,' said Aubrey.

'Who?' said Martin. 'Naomi?'

'No,' he replied, 'that lady over there. The one in the baggy white shirt.'

'It looks like she's wearing school uniform,' said Martin.

'Exactly.'

'But not in an attractive way. She looks like a surly sixth former.'

'Mmmm. Just my type. Is she German? I bet you she's German.'

'Aubrey's got a thing about German girls,' Blake told Martin, then turned to Aubrey. 'I bet you twenty English pounds you can't persuade her to come to dinner with us.'

'You're on,' said Aubrey, immediately striding towards the girl, who was standing in on the edge of someone else's conversation.

'You'll lose,' Martin told Blake.

'I know, but I'll get it back off him tomorrow. It's a little game we play, to build up each other's confidence. Aubrey will do anything for money.'

They stood there watching Aubrey. Naomi came back to Martin's side.

'Where's Aubrey?'

Blake pointed him out.

'Oh God,' said Naomi, 'what is this, fuck a foreigner night?'

'How can you tell she's foreign?' demanded Martin.

'Haircut. Blake, give me your mobile, I'll have to call Christophé and tell him there will be two more for dinner.'

'In Germany my father is very famous,' the girl said, hanging onto the strap as the taxi swung round a corner. 'Since I was a little girl, my father ... he's a barrister ... well, he would introduce me to his clients. Actually, he would take me out for dinner with them on the night before they went to trial. Often when we got home he would ask me what I thought. Whether I felt they were innocent or guilty. Anyway, there was a very, very famous case in our town where my father was defending this very vicious sex-criminal who did terrible things to women. Things I can't even begin to tell you about. And, of course, my father let me come to dinner with him just like he did with all the other people he represented. Anyway, this man went to prison for only three years and when he came out he kidnapped me ... it was in all the papers.'

'We're here,' said Naomi, tapping the glass partition.

The taxi driver stopped and they all climbed out. Naomi paid the driver and they waited for the second taxi carrying Benoît and Laetitia to arrive, before walking into the restaurant. They were greeted at the door by the maitre d'. Naomi told him that she'd spoken to Christophé about the addition to their party, but he said they'd still have to wait. They went to the bar.

Aubrey looked at the German girl. 'That's terrible.'

She shrugged. 'It wasn't so bad. He didn't want to hurt me. Only to photograph. He'd been taught to act out his desires in that way by the prison psychiatrist. I still have the pictures ... some of them are quite nice.'

Aubrey and Blake exchanged looks.

After dinner, they all went to Aubrey's club. It wasn't their favourite hangout, but it was a good place to hide, especially as it had only been open four weeks and few of their friends had got round to joining yet. The club operated a rather stupid policy, where the tables were given out to the oldest members who'd called that evening. Aubrey was member number fifteen which, as there were fourteen tables, meant he was almost certainly guaranteed a place to sit, unless all fourteen previous members were in the house. Also, if you had been given a table and an earlier member arrived and there were no tables left, you had to surrender your space to them, an arrangement which led to no small resentment.

They all sat at their table and ordered three bottles of champagne. Martin was always careful to keep an eye on how much he was spending when he was out with Naomi's friends. Going out with Naomi was a once or twice-a-week extravagance for him. Blake and Aubrey went out with her four or five nights on the trot, and even though they were single stockbrokers and not short of spending money, they tended to take advantage of Naomi's more fair-weather friends, and he had frequently been stung with extravagant bills. He had happily paid for Naomi's dinner as a thank-you for the evening, but was keen not to settle the drinks tab as well.

Martin knew Aubrey would get edgy if he started talking to the German girl. There was a strange kind of code among the men in their group that until someone had gone to bed with a girl, it was still acceptable for one of the others to cut in. Martin had witnessed this happening on several occasions among Lenny and Naomi's male friends, although he'd never executed the manoeuvre himself. He wasn't planning to tonight, either, although he did want to talk to the girl. Her story in the cab had intrigued him, and he was eager to hear more. Swapping seats with Naomi, he asked her, 'Did you think he was guilty?'

'Who?'

'The man who kidnapped you. Before it happened, when you went to dinner with him. Could you tell he was guilty then?'

'Of course. I always knew when a man was guilty.'

'Really? How could you tell?'

'A child's senses are more aware. I cannot tell now any more. I have met too many guilty people.'

'Do I seem guilty?'

'You?' she said, smiling. 'What would you be guilty of?'

They finished the champagne quite quickly, and were about to order another bottle when the German girl started to look anxious.

'Is anything wrong?' Aubrey asked her.

'You guys, are you, y'know, anti . . .'

'Anti-what?'

'Pick me ups.'

'Oh,' Naomi laughed, 'of course not. Why?'

The girl laughed, relieved. 'I have to go for a while.'

'To the bathroom?' Aubrey asked.

'No . . . an aftershow.'

'Fine,' said Naomi, 'would you like one of us to come with you?'

'No,' she said, 'that's OK.'

The German girl took her mobile from her bag, and moved into the corner. Naomi raised her eyebrows at Martin and smiled.

'Cool.'

Martin looked at his watch. 'Actually, Naomi, I think I'm going to have to duck out.'

'Why? You aren't on some new regime, are you?'

'No, nothing like that. I've just got something I need to sort out with Claudia.'

'OK. Call me, OK?'

work

It was just after midnight when they got back from the restaurant. Suzanne had left them to go off to work at ten-thirty, but they'd stayed for a few drinks after she'd gone, trying to be nice to each other and make friends again. Although Alison had initially felt reluctant to come to this restaurant, she had to admit that she'd had a much better time than she'd anticipated. The management seemed fond of Adrian and Suzanne, and every time the waiter came across, he indulged in a quick spot of banter before reluctantly leaving, waiting until Suzanne had come up with a suitably witty end-line.

She even began to feel less alienated by her boyfriend's awful appearance, knowing that when he made an effort he looked better than most of the diners here ever would. She understood that dressing down was a game for Adrian and Suzanne, just as the restaurant was a new setting for the sit-com they continued day-in, day-out.

'Thanks for tonight,' Alison told Adrian as they walked through to the lounge, 'it was really enjoyable.'

They sat together on the settee. Adrian wrapped his arm around Alison's shoulders. 'I'm sorry I didn't want to go somewhere posh.'

'It's OK,' she said, 'we can't really afford it anyway. I was just feeling down and wanted to cheer myself up.'

'What were you feeling down about?'

Alison thought quickly, knowing her boyfriend was much

more observant than he made out and not wanting to give herself away.

'I dunno. Work.'

'But I thought you loved your job.'

'Yeah, I do, it's just, I don't know, I guess if I'm honest what's hard is seeing you and Suzanne.'

'Is this about you supporting us again? Cause if it is, my dad did say he'd send us more money . . .'

'No, it's nothing to do with the money, it's more . . .' she took his arm from around her shoulders and looked into his eyes, 'knowing that even if I don't think of what I'm doing as a real job, that's how everybody else is going to see it.'

Adrian nodded, and she could see the self-satisfaction tilting his lips as he settled back in the settee. She decided to work on this a little longer before letting him lecture her.

'I just wish I either had the confidence to do nothing, like you, or was laid-back enough to stick to casual work, like Suzanne. It wouldn't be as bad if I'd had a gap year or something, but I feel like we just had that little time together after university and now I'm in a career that I'm probably going to end up sticking in for at least the next five years.'

'You don't want to work in magazines any more?'

She sighed. 'I don't know. What do you think?'

'Well,' he said, 'I can see what you're saying about how easy it is to get sucked into a job, and if you remember, I did say all this to you before you started at *Force*. But, to be honest, Al, I think a lot of this is down to your personality.'

'What d'you mean?'

'Well, you were never really happy being at home all day. You don't remember it now, but at the time you got all tense and depressed.'

'No, I do remember. But I might've felt different if I'd

thought of that time as a holiday rather than being so worried about money and scared that I'd never get a proper job.'

'And that's the other thing. The reason why you can't do what Suzanne does is because you're so ambitious. Which is why you're freaking out now.'

'I don't feel ambitious.'

'Come on, Al, don't be ridiculous. You can't do anything without working out the quickest, most efficient way of doing it. And I expect the reason you're getting frustrated is because that sort of stuff doesn't get noticed when you're a secretary.' He leaned forward. 'I mean, it does get noticed, but the absolute best that can happen is that someone thinks you're a good secretary, and while that in itself is great, it doesn't inspire them to promote you. Especially if you're doing too good a job of cleaning up behind them.'

Alison nodded, bored listening to him. 'No, you're right. I expect too much too soon.'

'What you really want is something to happen to your boss.'

She looked at him, surprised. 'He's getting sacked on Thursday.'

Adrian grinned enthusiastically. 'That's great.'

'Is it?'

'Yeah. Of course.'

'But what if they decide to sack me too?'

'That's not going to happen. You said he wasn't much good at his job. Everyone's obviously realised you're the power behind the throne. You wait, I bet you get promoted. They might even give you his job.'

'Don't be stupid.'

'Why not? It could happen.'

'Adrian, I'm his assistant. They're not going to make me editor of the magazine.'

'Well, I think you should at least put yourself forward.'

Alison looked at her boyfriend. He was perched right on the edge of the settee, clearly ready to launch into a full scale explanation of how he thought she could further her career, even though he himself had never worked a day in his life. But she wasn't in the mood for further argument.

'Come on,' she said, 'let's go to bed. See if we can't enjoy ourselves a bit before Suzanne gets back.'

Adrian grinned. 'Good idea.'

Wednesday

the eighties

Alison knew it was silly that her appearance had been defined for the rest of her life by an argument she'd had with Suzanne when she was seventeen. Hennaing her hair was such a teenage thing to do, and although the look fitted in fine at the time, it took incredible presence of mind to keep it up when for everyone else her age it was as embarrassing as still wearing Dr Martens after the second year of university or overhearing a friend in a pub ordering a pint of Cider and black.

Her argument with Suzanne had been mainly to do with music, although it was such a serious conflict that the implications also extended to boys, friends, and the two girls' relationship with each other. Up until Alison's thirteenth birthday, neither sister had been that interested in music. Their parents had the normal parents' record collection (Cat Stevens, Van Morrison, Santana, the red Beatles album) and they both occasionally sat with a tape-recorder and a microphone in front of *Top of the Pops*, but as far as their own purchases went, their music tastes didn't extend much beyond *The Kids From Fame* album, the *Dirty Dancing* soundtrack and, for a couple of weeks, the first Five Star album. Then, in an incident Alison still didn't understand to this day, Suzanne accidentally sat on the Five Star record and snapped it in half, and was so upset that she temporarily gave up on the whole music thing.

It was their Uncle Eric who stirred up the trouble. Nine

years younger than Alison's mother, he prided himself on still buying the NME and keeping up an interest in modern music into his thirties. For Alison's birthday, he gave her a copy of *Kiss Me Kiss Me Kiss Me*, and to Suzanne as a sibling-pacifying unbirthday present *Strangeways, Here We Come*. The idea, he told Alison's parents (who were slightly freaked out by the potential dangers of these exciting presents) was that the two sisters could listen to each others' records and swap them if they wanted, or just think of them as a joint present.

Uncle Eric had only given Alison *Kiss Me* rather than *Strangeways* because *Kiss Me* was a double, and therefore more expensive. He himself preferred the Smiths album, as did both sisters. Alison tried her best to get into her present, but aside from *Catch* and *Just Like Heaven*, the record sounded too samey, and had little of the swagger of the best tracks of *Strangeways*, like *Girlfriend in a Coma, Last Night I Dreamt Somebody Loved Me* or *I Won't Share You*. Also, although Robert Smith's interviews in *Smash Hits* were very entertaining, she got the impression that he was a more comical figure than Morrissey, and on the few occasions that she saw teenagers in her area wearing T-shirts for either band, the ones sporting Smiths shirts looked grown up and intelligent, while the Cure fans just seemed odd.

Looking back, Alison was aware that she could have rectified the situation in countless ways, but even though she was the elder sister, her reaction was to pretend she wasn't really interested in music, so that as they both grew a few years older, even Alison's closest friends started to think of her sister as the cool one. For a long time this didn't really upset her, but then as Suzanne started hanging out with a crowd who were much older than either of them, she realised the only way to avoid turning into the most unfashionable teenager in town was to persuade Suzanne to start taking her out with her. At first, Suzanne was fine with this arrangement. Alison would convince her parents to let Suzanne do things they never would've condoned had Alison not accompanied her, and, in return, Suzanne would allow her sister to hang around with her exciting older friends. This deal worked out well for several months, until the two sisters had the most serious argument they'd ever had in their lives.

Among their new group of friends was a cheerful, mop-haired, vaguely druggy man named Paul who both sisters had fallen for after he'd lured them (separately, but on the same night) to the back of a dank indie club to do blowbacks. In the taxi back from the club, Alison had told Suzanne how much she liked Paul and how she planned to ask him on a date. Suzanne had been outraged, telling Alison there was no way Paul would ever find her attractive, and that the only reason he even talked to her was because she was her sister. Then she laid into Alison for spending all her time copying her, stealing her friends and compilation tapes, and being so boring that everyone felt sorry for Suzanne for getting lumbered with her.

Alison's response was immediate. Going out to the nearest supermarket, she bought herself some henna dye and, ignoring the warnings on the packet about using it on blonde hair, turned her head a defiant orange. Although later she would use coffee to get the colour back to a more socially acceptable shade, at the time she was delighted with the change. She gained a whole new credibility, and even managed a few weeks of going out with Paul before he realised she wasn't prepared to sleep with him and moved onto Suzanne. But by then she didn't care, and the initial intoxication of this acceptance was so overpowering that she'd never been able to go back.

Jennings

One of Martin's greatest regrets was sleeping with Nick Jennings' wife. It wasn't cuckolding his friend which bothered him – if you were going to have any sort of fun in London it was important to get over that sort of squeamishness early on – but the fact that Jennings had behaved so sportingly about the whole thing that Martin had felt honour-bound to make him a contributing editor and give him plum assignments every other month, even though he was the magazine's weakest writer by far.

If Jennings was merely a terrible journalist, his company would've been bearable. But the fact that he was also a second-rate novelist made Martin feel ashamed to be seen out with him. Once a year, a proof copy of Jennings' latest travesty appeared in Martin's post, and he would have to avoid him until he'd received enough compliments and it was safe to assume he'd stopped bringing up the book in conversation.

Jennings' journalism was so bad that Martin forced him to file each piece an issue in advance to give him time to knock it into shape. He couldn't imagine how his publisher managed to edit his novels, and the mere fact that they remained in print convinced Martin that Jennings' wife had also done the rounds at her husband's publishing house.

Jennings pulled back a swivel-chair and sat down. He was looking unusually confident today, and Martin wondered if he'd benefited from one of those inexplicable successes that occurred only to his most mediocre friends.

'You look good,' he told him, 'have you been on holiday?'

'Not yet. Kazakhstan at the end of the month.'

'So why are you here again?'

Jennings looked hurt. 'I've come to take you to lunch. You pick the place and I'll pay.'

Martin considered his offer. Part of him wanted to sting Jennings with somewhere expensive: payback for all those terrible articles he'd forced him to publish. But then there was the danger that they might run into someone he knew.

'There's a quiet place just down the road from here. It is a restaurant but they do mainly sandwiches and stuff.'

Jennings shrugged. 'Fine.'

As they walked down to the restaurant, Martin wondered if he was fooling himself to think that the only reason he kept in contact with Jennings was because of his unexciting evening with his wife. It was definitely true that if it hadn't happened he wouldn't have taken such good care of him, but he doubted he would've completely cut him out of his circle. Martin had always had a soft spot for losers, if only because he'd come so close to becoming one himself. Before *Force*, Martin had been just another hustling freelancer, the kind of person editors hated talking to on the phone. And he'd been bad at it, always accepting immediately when someone said no. He'd hoped that by not pushing he'd get a reputation for integrity, and that next time he'd get a warmer response, whereas now he was an editor himself he knew if you weren't regularly commissioning someone you rarely thought about them, and it was insane to imagine anyone marking each rejection in a log-book in the interest of fairness.

They reached the restaurant and found a table. A waiter came across and took their order. Martin leaned back in his chair and asked Jennings, 'How's Jemima?'

'Good,' he replied, 'I told her I was meeting you today.'

Martin nodded, trying to seem unconcerned. 'You don't have any work outstanding for me, do you?'

'No.'

'Any pieces you want to pitch?'

'A few. But I'm going to put them all on a fax and let you choose.'

Martin smiled. 'So this is just a social call then?'

'Yeah. You know what it's like, working from home. Sometimes you get desperate for company.'

'What made you so sure I'd be free?'

'We had an appointment,' said Jennings, sounding confused.

'Did we? Oh God, I'm sorry, I've been so distracted.'

Jennings looked away. 'It's OK.'

They were halfway through lunch when Naomi's stockbroker friend Aubrey came into the restaurant. An odd-looking teenage girl accompanied him, and Martin remembered Blake and Aubrey having an unsavoury conversation about schoolgirls. Her hair was fixed in unflattering plaits and she was wearing a green dress and small round-framed glasses not dissimilar to Aubrey's. Jennings noticed Martin was distracted and stopped eating his sandwich.

'Someone from the magazine?'

'No. A friend of a friend. Aubrey somebody.'

'Not Aubrey Webster.'

'Maybe. I don't know his surname. That's him over there.'

Jennings twisted round, trying to get a better look.

'Yes, that's Aubrey. And his sister, Anita.'

'How d'you know them?'

'I was in Morocco with Aubrey's parents.'

Martin looked at Jennings, waiting for further elucidation.

Jennings had said Morocco in the same way that someone might say Oxford or Cambridge, but surely Jennings hadn't gone to university in Africa? And although he was a little older than Aubrey, Jennings couldn't possibly be the same age as his parents. Martin wondered whether it was some sort of societal or political thing he should know about. When he realised Jennings wasn't going to explain, he asked, 'Was that for the magazine?' 'Good God, no. Let's go say hello.'

'You go. I need the toilet.'

Jennings nodded, and got up from the table. Martin walked slowly to the gents, trying to keep out of Aubrey's line of vision while at the same time checking how he reacted when he saw Jennings. If he seemed pleased to see him, Martin was prepared to go over to the table after he'd finished in the toilet. But if Aubrey looked distressed, Martin planned to walk straight out of the restaurant. Then, when he got back to the office, he'd phone Jennings' mobile and claim there was something urgent that'd slipped his mind and needed instant attention.

Unusually for a stockbroker (at least, the ones Martin had met), Aubrey was scrupulously polite. Apart from the odd laddish remark every now and again, he was a consummate gentleman, but even from across the restaurant, his pleasure at running into Jennings seemed genuine. Martin wanted to check for a funny handshake, but he was already at the gents and there was someone behind him. So he pushed open the door and walked to the nearest urinal.

When he came out of the toilet, Jennings had his hand on Aubrey's shoulder and the two of them were sharing a joke. Feeling it was now safe to approach, Martin went across to the table.

Aubrey seemed surprised. 'Martin! Are you having lunch here as well? Oh, I see, you're here with Nick.'

Amazed Jennings had managed to initiate a conversation without mentioning him, Martin tried to hide his irritation with a brief nod.

'You know, it's stupid, but I'd completely forgotten that you two knew each other. Even though he writes for your mag and everything.'

'That is stupid,' said Martin, in no mood to be polite.

'I know, I know, but anyway, listen, I've just been telling Nick that he must come to dinner at my place tomorrow night. You know about this, right? Naomi's told you?'

'No, I hadn't got that message.'

'Oh. Maybe your secretary has yet to pass it on.'

Aubrey took Martin's e-mail address and promised to send him details of the dinner. Martin and Jennings returned to their table to find their food had been cleared away, and the bill waiting in a black leather wallet. Jennings picked it up, checked the amount, and put his credit card inside, before handing it to a passing waitress.

'Have you got to get back to the office?' Jennings asked.

'Yeah,' said Martin, 'I've got a busy afternoon.'

'So I'll see you tomorrow night?'

'Seems that way,' he replied. 'Thanks for lunch.'

subterfuge

Alison finished her sandwich and looked at her watch. She knew Martin would soon be back from lunch with Jennings and had already decided that this afternoon would be when she'd tell him what she'd heard from Gareth. The rumour was now common office knowledge, and it was obvious no one else was going to tell him first. She didn't like the idea of being associated with bad news, but saw no other option available to her. At least until the phone rang.

'Hello?'

'Hi, Alison, it's Mandy.'

Mandy. 'Hello, Mandy. Martin's at lunch, I'm afraid.'

'That's what I was hoping. When do you expect him back?'

'Imminently.'

She laughed. 'Imminently, eh? I like that. Can you come to my office?'

'Now?'

'Yes, now. And hurry.'

Alison hung up, slid her feet back into her shoes and stood up. This was the first time she'd ever been summoned to Mandy's office. As she walked down the corridor, she allowed herself the brief fantasy that maybe Adrian had been right last night and she was about to be offered editorship of *Force*. It was a job she knew she could do, and she'd often considered how she'd get the magazine back on track. She believed the best thing would be to soften it, to turn *Force* into a men's magazine that not only could be read by women, but, crucially, would be a magazine that women would want their boyfriends to read. And she would also target the huge disenfranchised male readership out there: boys like her boyfriend, who wouldn't dream of buying any of the existing men's magazines but would probably go for something less style-orientated and more laid-back.

The door to Mandy's office was open. Alison decided to walk straight in, show her she wasn't lacking in confidence.

'Alison, hi. Shut the door please.'

Alison did so.

'Sit down,' Mandy told her. 'I have something I want to discuss with you.'

'You're getting rid of Martin.'

Mandy looked at her, left eyebrow raised in surprise. 'It's already common knowledge?'

'Office gossip.'

'Does Martin know?'

'I don't think so.'

'Good. Now, I realise you're close to Martin, and that I'm taking a risk in telling you all this. But if you respect the trust I'm placing in you, I can guarantee you'll be amply rewarded. I want you to help me make things as painless as possible for Martin. Obviously he's not going to be leaving the office immediately, and I expect he's going to feel a bit alienated from his colleagues. So, for the next few weeks I'd like you to become . . . even more than you are already . . . his right-hand woman. And then, when he does leave, I'll make sure you're given a much more exciting position.' She smiled at Alison, all red lipstick and smoker's teeth. 'How does that sound?'

'Good.'

'Great. There's more one condition.'

'Which is?'

'If Martin doesn't know I don't want you to tell him. You've been doing a very good job of keeping it to yourself so far. You can manage one more day, can't you?'

Alison considered this. 'OK.'

'Good. Thanks, Alison.'

Morocco

'How was lunch?'

Martin turned back and looked at Alison. She was sitting at her computer, wearing a thick white cardigan over a maroon top. She looked slightly worried, and he wondered what she knew that he didn't. Moving closer towards her, he replied,

'Horrendous. Have I had any messages?'

'While you were at lunch?' she asked. 'No.'

'No, I mean over the last few days. Are there any messages that have come in that you haven't given me?'

She considered this. 'I don't think so. Anyone in particular?'

'Not really. Naomi hasn't called, has she?'

'No.'

He shook his head and continued through to his office. Sitting down at his desk, he told himself he would not let this get the better of him. He held out for about twenty seconds before calling Naomi on her mobile.

'Martin . . .' she said eagerly. 'What's up?'

'Do we have any plans?'

'What? You and me?'

'No, everybody, you know, this week?'

'Well, there's Aubrey's dinner tomorrow, but apart from that . . .'

He tried to keep his voice even. 'Aubrey's dinner?'

'Yeah. I sent you an e-mail.'

'I didn't get it.'

'Really? Hang on, I'm in front of my computer, I'll just check.'

He listened on the phone as he heard her tap some keys. He

switched across to his own e-mail account, looking through his old mail even though he already knew it wasn't there.

'Yeah,' she said, 'I sent it Friday. Don't worry, I'll send it again. Why do you ask? Are you double-booked?'

'No, it's not that. I just ran into him.'

'Who? Aubrey? Where?'

'Oh, just this little sandwichy-bar restaurant place.'

'Doesn't sound like you.'

'No, I know, I was with Nick Jennings and I didn't want to go anywhere I might be spotted.'

'But Aubrey was there?'

'Yeah. With his sister. I didn't know Aubrey knew Nick.'

'Oh yeah.'

'He's invited him to dinner tomorrow.'

'And you thought we'd forgotten you. I'm sorry, Martin, I did send the mail.'

He pushed his backside down into his chair, attempting to wheel himself across the office, before using his foot to kick his office door closed.

'No, it's OK. What do Aubrey's parents do?'

'His Dad's a painter and his Mum's a poet. Why?'

'No reason. So do they live in Morocco?'

'Not any more. They used to have a writers' and artists' commune there. You know, all very Bowles and Burroughs.'

'Ah,' said Martin, 'so that's the connection.'

'With Jennings? He's, like, their disciple. He loves them so much he even let Aubrey's dad bugger him.'

'You're not serious.'

'Well, it's just a rumour, but I believe it. And he's written rave reviews of all of Aubrey's mother's collections.'

'So how come Aubrey doesn't have any artistic ambitions?'

'He's published two books of poetry.'

'Really?' Martin asked, surprised.

'Yeah, the year after he finished university. He said it was the only way to resolve his relationship with his parents. Then once he'd got that out of the way he decided what he really wanted to do was work with money.'

'I see. How come I know so little about my friends?'

'You go home too early. Guys like Aubrey don't start opening up until at least five a.m.'

'Well, I'll stay late tomorrow.'

'OK. See you.'

She hung up. Martin still felt edgy, annoyed with himself for getting so worked up about Aubrey's dinner, especially in front of Jennings. He knew he'd lost face when he allowed himself to get so anxious about not having an invite, and wished he'd managed to be more blasé. He had to stop thinking that everything was a trick designed to humiliate him. He knew it was the magazine that made him like this, and wondered why he didn't have the presence of mind to rise above it. A certain amount of social paranoia was inevitable for someone in his position, but lately it'd really started to get the better of him. It was clear the answer was to walk away from this whole world, but that would be career suicide, and he wasn't ready to face that yet.

He picked up the phone again and called Claudia. She wasn't in, so he left her a message to expect him home early tonight.

the reward

Alison stood in the centre of the lounge, looking down at the sprawled bodies of Adrian and Suzanne. Although they'd both smoked so much this afternoon they were unable to sit up straight, she could tell they were both excited.

'But that's brilliant, Al. What do you think she meant?'

'I don't know. That's why she kept it vague. Mandy's got a reputation for being a really Machiavellian bitch. She knew I wouldn't press her on what my reward might be, and then when I've sold out Martin I'll find all I've got is a longer job-title.'

'So she didn't say you'd be paid more?' Adrian pressed, looking as if he was about to attempt sitting up.

'No, well, you know, she was all vague. The first thing she said was that I'd be amply rewarded, then she changed tack and seemed to imply that the reward would be a better job.'

'But if it's a better job you're bound to get more money.'

'Maybe.'

'You are going to do it, though, aren't you, Al?' Suzanne asked. 'You're not going to chicken out and tell your boss.'

'I don't know. It doesn't feel like chickening out, it feels like being dishonourable. And what happens if Martin gets a really exciting new job and I want to move with him?'

'Right,' said Adrian, finally getting vertical, 'let's think this through logically.'

'OK.'

'Do you trust your boss?'

Alison considered this. She'd never really thought about Martin in this clear-headed, appraising way. She knew he was genuinely reliable in the office and unreliable elsewhere, but on a personal level she wasn't sure. Especially as the question was really could she trust Martin to take the fact that she'd been told he was going to get sacked in an adult manner? After all, there was nothing to be gained from telling him if he was just going to get cross. Also, she had to be sure that he would respect her working in her own self-interest. Because what she'd really be trying to do would be to have it both ways, something Martin might not respect if he reacted the wrong way to losing his own job.

'Yes,' she said, having thought about it, 'I think so.'

'Good. Now, do you think he's going to be offered a better job by someone else when he leaves the magazine?'

'Maybe.'

'OK. And do you think that if you told him about your meeting with Mandy he'd be able not to give it away?'

'I'm not sure what you mean.'

'Would he reveal to Mandy that you'd told him you knew he was going to lose his job?'

'I don't think so.'

'Then it's obvious. Tell him. And if he gets a good new job you can go with him and if not you can stay at *Force* and enjoy your more exciting position.'

Alison nodded. Adrian was right. She'd tell Martin tomorrow.

Thursday

shoot the messenger

Martin walked past Alison and sat down at his desk. The phone rang. Working at *Force*, Martin got so many calls that most of the time he didn't pick up, suspecting it would be a current affairs show or one of the more upmarket broadsheets, wanting his opinion on something stupid. But there were a few people he enjoyed talking to, and in order to weed out the unnecessary callers, he let certain key individuals know in advance at what hour he would be picking up the phone. This week he was only taking calls between ten and eleven. It was ten past ten, so he picked up the phone.

'Martin Powell. Hello,' he said.

'Hi, Martin, it's Nick Jennings.'

Shit.

'Hi, Nick, I enjoyed lunch yesterday.'

'Me too. Look, I really don't want to be the one to tell you this, but there is something you should know.'

'OK.'

'I was going to tell you yesterday, but the right moment didn't come up, and then we ran into Aubrey . . .'

'Yeah?'

'And I thought I might tell you at dinner tonight, but by then it'll probably be too late.'

'What is it, Nick?'

'Well, I heard this rumour, maybe you know about this already, but, well, the word on the street, and I don't want to be too specific about my sources, but like I say, the word is that you're about to get canned.'

'What?'

'I'm sorry, Martin, and please don't shoot the messenger here, but . . . well, I thought you should know.'

Martin didn't say anything.

'You're upset. But don't worry, I'm sure you'll sort something out. And I'll see you tonight, right?'

mere pseud mag ed

Alison walked into Martin's office. He was holding his phone receiver but didn't appear to be either making or taking a call. She waited for him to notice her, then smiled.

'Yeah?' he asked.

'I have something to tell you.'

'I know. Jennings just told me.'

'Oh, Martin, I'm sorry, it must've been horrible to have to hear it from him.'

'It's OK.'

He replaced the receiver but remained at his desk, not moving. Alison knew she should leave him alone, but instead she sat down opposite him. Most of the time she tried to avoid thinking of her boss as a father-figure, but the way Martin was behaving now reminded her exactly of what her dad was like when he got bad news. He had the same silent bewilderment, a mood that fell slightly short of indignation, but nevertheless conveyed that he felt it was wrong that he should be punished for making an effort. He looked back at her.

'Alison, would you like to go to lunch later?'

'I'd love to,' she said honestly, gratified to see him smile.

She was expecting him to take her somewhere cheap and local, maybe even the same place he went to with Jennings yesterday. So she was amazed when he told her to make a reservation at the Firebird, a Russian restaurant she knew was one of his more extravagant lunch-haunts.

'I got the call,' he said, as they got into a cab together.

'They did it over the phone?'

'Oh no, I've got a meeting with Mandy and Giles this afternoon.'

'What time do you have to be back?'

'Oh, don't worry, I'm not going.'

She looked at him. 'How come?'

'I'll think of an excuse and get you to e-mail them. I can't be bothered facing those two today. I'll let 'em get angry and then show up for the meeting tomorrow.'

Alison nodded. 'Sounds like a good plan.'

Alison waited behind Martin as a smartly dressed woman greeted him. After a brief exchange, a suited man came through from the restaurant and showed them to their table. The decor reminded her of hotels she'd stayed in with her parents as a child, and she felt strangely pleased that this was one of Martin's favourite restaurants. All her family holidays had always been organised by her mother, and her family always divided into two camps during their weeks away. For Alison and her mother, going to an expensive hotel was a chance to live out a fantasy. Suzanne, however, would team up with their dad, mocking Alison's affectation and embarrassing her by starting food-fights and blowing raspberries at each other. That, she realised, was one of the reasons why she'd been irritated the other night when Suzanne made them go to Henry's. She didn't always want to go to expensive restaurants, and would rather die than swap Adrian for some Hackett-wearing Hooray. But she did occasionally crave a little bit of glamour, especially if someone else was treating her.

'You OK?' asked Martin.

She smiled. 'Yeah. It's nice here.'

He looked touched. 'You like it? The food is incredible. Order whatever you want. Let's make this a celebration.'

his own man

Four hours later, Martin kissed Alison goodbye and climbed into a taxi. He felt so full he doubted he would eat anything at Aubrey's later that evening. Alison had proved good company throughout the afternoon and Martin wondered why he hadn't taken her out more often. He supposed it was because, having decided he definitely wasn't going to have an affair with her, he didn't want to give anyone in the office a false impression. But now he was leaving, his previous worries seemed foolish, and he felt sad he couldn't really count on her as a friend.

He wondered how Mandy and Giles would react when they found out he'd skipped their meeting. He felt guilty sending Alison in with his excuses, but it'd been worth it for the childish pleasure his evasion had brought him. Now that he was looking at his career in retrospect, the one thing of which he felt proud was that he'd always been his own man. He may have failed as an editor, but it seemed likely that *Force* would soon fold anyway, and in a few months he could probably spin the story to suggest he left of his own accord when the magazine lost its *raison d'etre*.

Now that he'd had time to adjust, he realised there could be a certain glamour in losing his job. He was upset because it seemed to suggest that people didn't like him, but after all, it was probably only Mandy behind this. It would be more enjoyable if he was single. Then he could wallow, go out and buy a bottle of whisky and drink it while stumbling around his apartment and cursing the world. The fact that he had to explain what had happened to Claudia took the edge off his enjoyment, and not for the first time, he wished he didn't have this commitment.

The taxi pulled up outside Martin's house and he got out. Overtipping the driver as he always did when he'd had too much to drink, he got a receipt and stumbled up to his front door.

As he fiddled in his pocket trying to find his key, Claudia pulled the door open. Martin stared at her. He couldn't understand why she wasn't at work, and in his befuddled state, wondered whether *Force* had already called his wife and told her what had happened. He was about to throw himself on her mercy when he decided it would be prudent to try a question first.

'How come you're at home?'

'I've got a cold. They sent me home early.'

'Oh.' No need to tell her then. 'Well, it's nice to see you.' He entered the house. Claudia turned on him.

'Did you show Kelly your cock?'

'What?' he slurred.

She pushed his shoulder, forcing him to face her. 'Did you?'

'Yes.'

'Oh, Martin, why?'

'Truth or dare,' he said with a sigh.

'When was this?'

'Three fucking months ago. You were in Brazil.'

'That's no excuse.'

'I know. It's not supposed to be. You just asked me when it happened.'

Claudia turned away from him and walked through to the lounge. He went into the kitchen, made two martinis and followed her. She was stretched out on the sofa, holding her hair out of her face. He offered her the drink and she accepted it, before asking in a calmer voice, 'So where was the game taking place?'

'Lenny's.'

'So Lenny was there too?'

'No.'

'No?' she repeated, surprised.

'Well, he was there, but he wasn't playing. He'd drunk too much and passed out in the bathroom.'

'So who else was playing?'

'No one.'

'Just the two of you then?'

'Yes.'

She rubbed her eyes. 'What is wrong with you, Martin? I know you're not a stupid man. Didn't the two of you consider having a nice cup of coffee and a sensible conversation?'

'It wasn't my idea.'

'No, of course not. Did you kiss her?'

'No.'

'Did she show you her cunt?'

'Yes.'

'Open or closed?'

'What?'

'Flaps. Open or closed?'

'Oh, closed, of course. It wasn't that gynaecological.'

Claudia straightened her legs and brought them down onto the floor. She looked wretched. Martin could understand why, although he didn't know whether it was better to make light of it or apologise profusely.

'It was just something stupid,' he told her. 'Not even fun. It definitely didn't mean anything.'

'I know it didn't mean anything,' Claudia said quickly, 'that's the whole point. I'm fed up with everyone I know acting like oversexed students. It's bad enough when it's just you and your bunch of freaks, but when my friends start acting like that too . . .'

'I really wouldn't worry, Claud. It's not the sort of thing I'm going to make a habit out of.'

'But that's not true, Martin. You do make a habit out of it. You wake up every morning and check you're wearing underwear in case you end up playing spin-the-bottle. It's pathetic and childish and I don't want to live like this any more.'

'OK,' he said, 'it'll all stop, I promise. You'll never hear an embarrassing story about me again.'

She looked at him, suspicious. 'You mean it?'

'I mean it. And if I break my word you can leave me. Now, come on, give me a kiss.'

soft-headed cuckold

Alison got back into the office to find six messages from Mandy on her voice-mail. She felt irritated that Mandy was using her as a point of contact, and after Martin had taken her for such a pleasant lunch she didn't feel like siding against him. Still, as it didn't seem that Martin had any immediate career-plans, she realised she still had to be careful and picked up the phone to call her back.

Mandy was angry, not even giving Alison chance to explain

where Martin had gone and calling her into her office immediately. Alison did as she was instructed. The office door was open and she went straight in.

'Did you tell him?' Mandy demanded.

'No, of course not.'

'But he knows?'

'Yes.'

'How?'

'Nick Jennings.'

'Fuck,' she said, and Alison was shocked by the genuine venom in her voice, 'I thought you said no one in the office would tell him.'

'Nick Jennings is freelance. And Martin's friend.'

She snorted. 'Nick Jennings is a soft-headed cuckold who'd fuck his granny for fifty pee and a bag of boiled sweets. Does Martin have a new job?'

'Not that I know of. Jennings only told him this morning.'

'So where is Martin now? Has he resigned?'

'Oh, no, he's only gone home early. He told me to apologise to you for him missing the meeting but he's not feeling that hot and he'll come see you tomorrow.'

Mandy came round from behind her desk. 'Are you fucking him?'

'No.'

'You turned him down?'

'He's never tried anything.'

'OK. I'm sorry it's turned out like this, but I'm afraid I'm going to have to withdraw my offer of finding you a better job.'

'I'm sacked?'

'No. Did I say that? No, don't be silly. But you're going to stay in the same position. And you can assist the new editor when they're appointed.'

'When's that going to happen?'

'I don't know yet. It depends on Martin.'

Alison nodded. Mandy squashed out a cigarette in an ashtray and returned behind her desk. 'Thank you Alison, that'll be all.'

'But that's not fair,' said Suzanne, 'you didn't say anything to him.'

'It's OK,' Alison sighed, 'I didn't feel right about it anyway.'

Adrian suddenly became animated. 'Do you remember what her exact words were to you when she first said you'd get a better position?'

'Not really. Well, yes I do, but it doesn't really matter, does it?'

'Well, if she promised you something you can probably hold her to it.'

'How? There's no record of what she said, and she's hardly the sort of person I can bully.'

'You'd be surprised. A lot of people respect strong-arm tactics. You may have missed your moment now, but I still think if you go back in hard you might be able to get something out of her.'

Alison sighed, and slumped down on the sofa. She knew Adrian would get angry if she challenged him in front of Suzanne, but she did wonder how he could pretend he knew everything about work when as far as she knew he'd never even been inside an office. She supposed it was probably because of his parents – both management gurus – but it still surprised her that he'd take on this role given how much he actively disliked their business talk.

Suzanne moved up on the settee to give her more space. She had a bowl of Monster Munch balanced on the roll of her tummy just above the waistband of her skirt. Alison stole the remote from beside her and turned on the TV.

sexy and provocative also

Aubrey opened the door to his apartment. He took Martin's coat and showed him through to the sitting-room, where Naomi, Blake, Helena and Anita were already waiting. Everyone held a tall, thin-stemmed wine glass and Aubrey quickly returned with one for Martin. He took it and sat alongside Naomi on a large, overstuffed sofa. She smiled and curled her legs up, bringing her spiked heels so close to Martin that they almost punctured his leg. Martin leaned in and whispered to her, 'No sign of Jennings yet?'

Naomi shook her head, then said, 'He's not so bad, you know. It's not his fault his wife's a slut.'

The door-buzzer sounded. Aubrey extracted himself from the conversation and went out to answer it. Martin took a box of cigarettes from his pocket and lit one.

'So how are you, Blake?' he asked.

'OK, I guess, I've had a bit of a hairy day.'

'Anything you can talk about?'

He smiled. 'Oh, you know, nothing serious. Money matters.'

Aubrey walked back in with Jennings.

'OK, everybody, help yourself to more wine and chocolates. Dinner should be ready in about fifteen minutes.'

He left Jennings in the centre of the room and went back out to the kitchen. Jennings looked awkward, his eyes darting round the assembled guests to see if anyone was going to help him out. Feeling charitable, Martin asked, 'Is that a new jacket?'

76

Jennings pulled his sleeves down over his hands. 'Do you like it? An ex-girlfriend bought it for me two years ago, but I've never worn it. I didn't think it really suited me.'

'No, it's great. It looks very American.'

Naomi looked at him suspiciously, as if she thought he was building up to some terrible put-down. But Jennings was flattered.

'Thank you,' he said. 'I suppose it's like that with clothes that are different from what you normally wear. They become like a costume or something.'

Martin looked at Helena. 'Do you think of your clothes as a costume?'

'My clothes?' she replied. 'Why are they a costume?'

'No, I don't mean they are a costume. It's just that every time I've seen you, you've been wearing the same sort of thing. I wondered whether that was deliberate.'

Helena seemed more bemused than offended, as if pleased that Martin had noticed her appearance. She ran a finger around the space between her neck and her shirt collar and glanced back at him.

'I've always dressed like this. Lots of people in Germany, like in many countries, I think, although less so in London, they go to extremes with their appearance because they find it hard to achieve being an individual. I had many, many friends who were punks, even from age nine or something. And I wanted to be with them in their gang, but my father, he is a very clever man, and he played many successful mind-games with me ... so I was aware already that for me to become punk would be a very obvious kind of conformity. But I wanted to have these punk people as my friends, because, although it is not the same here, they were very much the coolest, and also the most intelligent of the young people. So what I did was to pick an outfit that could seem both conservative and punk at the same time . . . the idea that I should be able to move freely between both sides was very important to me . . . and the obvious choice seemed to be the schoolgirl, especially as it is sexy and provocative also.'

Jennings looked even more lost now that everyone was so intently focused on Helena, and he took this moment to sit down. The clothing conversation had clearly come to an end, and everyone fell into separate exchanges until Aubrey came back in to announce the start of supper.

It was during the after-dinner coffees that Jennings started arguing with Aubrey. Martin hadn't been paying attention to their conversation, and only noticed something was wrong when he heard Aubrey exclaim, 'That's bullshit.'

Jennings shook his head. 'It's true.'

Aubrey stood up on the table and used the spring of the wood to launch himself at Jennings, breaking his chair and bringing the two of them down onto the floor together. Punching Aubrey in the face, Jennings shouted,

'You're a vicious, lying cunt.'

Jennings put up little resistance, and Aubrey was soon on top of him, fingers tightening around his throat. It was clear someone needed to intervene, so Blake stood up and put his hand on Aubrey's shoulder.

'For fuck's sake, old chap, don't do this here. Not in front of your guests.'

Aubrey thought for a moment and loosened his grip. He looked up at Blake and his other guests.

'I'm sorry,' he said, 'you're absolutely right. Can someone kick this wanker out?'

Blake nodded and escorted Jennings out of the apartment. When he came back, Martin couldn't stop himself breaking into applause.

Naomi and Martin caught a cab home together. Naomi sat with her feet up on the partition while Martin looked out of the window.

'Strange night,' he murmured.

'Yeah.'

'What d'you reckon it was about?'

'Oh, the obvious, I expect. Jennings probably told Aubrey something he didn't want to hear about his parents.'

'Does he know about the buggery?'

'Probably. Although, you're right, maybe that's what tonight was about.'

'How's Greg?'

'Fuck Greg.'

Martin looked at Naomi, surprised. 'That sounds serious.'

'It is serious. He's going off the deep end.'

'What does that mean?'

'Exactly what I said. He tried to strangle Jamiroquai.'

'What?'

'It's true. He was at some party Greg was at and Greg ran across the room and started throttling him.'

'Why?'

'Who knows? It was Damon the week before.'

'He tried to strangle Damon?'

She nodded. 'He took him by surprise, otherwise I imagine Damon would've bloody slaughtered him.'

'How come he hasn't been arrested if he keeps attacking celebrities?'

'God knows. It's probably only a matter of time. I just hope they send him away before he kills someone.'

'You don't mean that.'

'I do. I've had enough of him, Martin, I really have.'

Naomi was crying. Martin took her head in his hands and gently kissed along her eyebrows.

'Trust me, Naomi, I know things are bad now, but he'll get better. It's probably just an odd phase or something. Would you like me to talk to him?'

'No, you can't. He hates you.'

'Right,' he said, laughing. 'I forgot.'

'But you're right,' she said, stifling her sobs, 'it probably is only a phase. I just wish I knew what to do to bring him out of it.'

Later that night, Martin lay in bed, unable to sleep and thinking over the events of the evening. Claudia was out cold and the two Nytols he'd taken weren't working. He knew he should go back to prescription sleepers, but the last time he'd taken those sort of tablets regularly he'd found himself permanently stuck in an unpleasant chemical fog.

He knew why he couldn't sleep. He felt ashamed of himself. For applauding when Blake had walked Jennings out of Aubrey's apartment. Martin didn't often regret things he had done. When he did it was almost always something that'd happened right at the end of the evening. He had once calculated that he could eliminate ninety percent of his social embarrassment by leaving any given gathering ninety minutes earlier.

It wasn't that Martin liked Jennings (especially since he'd been the first to tell him that he was about to be sacked), but he felt cross with himself for so quickly accepting the violent end to the evening. Nights out with Naomi and her friends almost always ended in unpleasant arguments, but this was the first time dessert had been followed by a fist-fight. And, who knew, maybe Aubrey even had a good reason for punching Jennings. At least he wasn't a coward, like Martin, sitting there childishly endorsing the violent acts of others.

Martin was also troubled by Naomi's story about her boyfriend. He kept hearing her saying *I just hope they send him away before he kills someone* and every time the phrase repeated on him it sounded more unsettling. He was used to his female friends having unsuitable boyfriends, but he worried that what with tonight's fight, the German girl's peculiar background and this new celebrity-strangling development, their group had let something scary into their circle that would prove impossible to exorcise.

He closed his eyes and held onto Claudia, telling himself that he would take his wife's advice and become more cautious from now on.

Friday

people will talk

'So what happened between you and Martin?'

Alison couldn't believe her bad luck. Twice in one week she'd got stuck in the lift with Gareth. She worried that he'd started waiting for her to come in, hiding behind the blue wooden barriers outside the office before running after her when she went through the rotating doors.

'What are you talking about?'

'It's gone all round the office. He missed his big meeting cause he didn't come back from lunch. And you were also conspicuously absent.'

'OK, Gareth, I know I can confide in you. We've been having this big affair.'

'Really?'

'No, of course not. He took me out for lunch and I was a little late getting back. That's all.'

'And is he coming in today?'

'Why wouldn't he be?'

'I don't know. There was a rumour going round that he couldn't cope with the idea of being sacked and has completely flipped out.'

'Take it from me, that's not what's happened. I'm sure he'll be here later, and I shouldn't think being sacked will trouble him at all.'

The lift stopped and the two of them got out. They separated without further comment, and walked to their opposite sides of the office.

porno chic

Martin hated upsetting people. He knew Claudia would be crushed if she found out about his most recent affairs, and while he had previously regarded the strip-clubs and drinking-games as an essential part of the laddish hedonism necessary to create the right atmosphere for a successful men's magazine, he made a decision that morning to start being more discreet about his lifestyle. After all, he rationalised, it wasn't the fact that he did this sort of stuff that upset Claudia, it was that she got to hear about it. He had fairly moderate appetites, and was always open about most of the things he did. Such a relaxed attitude meant that people spoke more openly about him than they ought. If he started letting his friends know that he intended to clean up his act, it might take them a while before they believed he was serious, but eventually he'd find himself afforded a newfound respect that would stop people spreading gossip about him.

He was musing on this when the telephone rang. As it was still during his answering hour, he picked up.

'Hello,' said the American voice, 'I'd like to speak to Martin Powell.'

'Speaking.'

'Hi, I got your name from Caroline Grieder. My name's Brad Russell and I have a proposition I believe might interest you.'

Martin looked round. 'OK.'

'It's not really something that'll make sense over the phone. Would you be free for a meeting this evening?'

'I think so.'

'Great. Seven thirty?'

Martin considered this. He and Claudia always went down

to her parents at the weekend and if he took this meeting it would mean calling her and checking out whether she minded setting off later. He knew she wouldn't take this well, especially as he didn't yet want to tell her about losing his job and would have to keep the reason for his delay secret, but he was curious enough to risk upsetting his wife.

'Fine,' he told his caller, 'but just so I've got a clear idea what you're talking about, is this . . .'

'It's a job offer. If you're up for it.'

'And you got my number from Caroline?'

'Yeah. But she doesn't know what I'm going to offer you. I'll make everything clear this afternoon.'

'Right, OK, um, where are you?'

'Essex. I've sent you an e-mail with the exact address.'

shoot the messenger II

Alison found it very hard to control her temper when Mandy and Giles both phoned her within five minutes of each other, wanting to make sure Martin would be available for a noon meeting. She felt like asking them why they'd gone through her instead of contacting him directly, but didn't want to further antagonise her superiors. So she told them both she would check with Martin and then call back.

She felt nervous as she went through to his office, worried that he would continue avoiding the meeting and make her come up with more excuses for him. But he seemed in a much better mood than the day before, thanking her for passing on the message and telling her to inform Mandy and Giles that he would be happy to see them at noon. Surprised, Alison went back to her desk and did as she'd been instructed.

getting sacked

Although this was the first time Martin had experienced being fired, he'd been through enough negative business meetings to know it was suicide to go in without a strategy. And he'd decided that the best option was to play hard. They knew his contacts, and even if they could stop stories being printed in most magazines, a feature about Martin would be incredibly attractive to the *Observer* or the *Guardian* media-section. And as he lacked a drug-habit or reckless nature, it would be hard to present him as a villain. So it would definitely be in their interest to ensure he was given a generous sum of redundancy money, especially if he presented himself as having nowhere else to go.

He had already decided that he would stay at the magazine as long as possible. There would be no craziness, no best-dressed Nazi fashion spreads, no coked-up final blowouts. Just a careful conclusion to a quiet reign. He needed time to check out other opportunities, put out feelers, see if there was anyone else out there who still liked him. The people he considered successful were always experiencing set-backs, but their good humour meant you didn't lose faith in them.

And then there was always this Brad Russell. He had no idea what this mysterious job offer might be (he'd tried calling Caroline Grieder several times to no avail) but even if it did turn out to be something he didn't want to do, the fact that other people were aware of his new predicament and were recommending him for other positions had to be a good thing.

Alison appeared in his office doorway. 'Alright?'

'It's time for my meeting, isn't it?'

'Fraid so. Want to hide in The Firebird again?'

'Definitely.' He smiled. 'Nah, I've dragged this out long enough.'

He pushed back his chair and stood up.

'OK,' she said, 'good luck.'

options

Alison stepped back and let Martin past. Returning to her desk, she immediately checked her new e-mails. Alison loved Fridays. She especially enjoyed the way that as the work slowed, social interaction intensified. If she was intending to socialise at the weekend (and she usually was), she'd send out four or five e-mails early on, finding out if anyone else had plans, and then see whether it was possible to shape everyone's intentions into a group activity, or whether she'd have to choose whose night looked the most interesting. Often this appraisal would be tempered by her sense of social obligation, and she might take a less exciting option if she hadn't seen a particular person for a while. As Adrian had lost contact with most of his university friends, and the people he had met since then were such inveterate stoners that getting them to a club was about as likely as flying to the moon, he tended to tag along on her evenings, letting her pay his way as he attempted to chat up the most attractive woman in their group.

Today the planning had become fevered unusually early. E-mails had gone back and forth all morning after her friend Emma had announced that she had twenty tickets for a party in a film studio somewhere in the Elephant & Castle. Although the party wasn't until Saturday night, sixteen of the tickets were already spoken for, and Emma needed to know immediately whether Alison and Adrian were interested in coming along.

She picked up the phone and called home.

getting sacked II

Martin came out of Mandy's office, feeling deflated but also aroused. He thought Mandy and Giles would sack him in tandem, but she'd clearly decided to relish the pleasure alone. He had always felt nervous around Mandy, but today was the first time her sexually predatory older woman routine had worked on him. He supposed it was because this was the first time he'd actually wanted to fuck her. He knew she was getting off on the sexual tension and thought if he returned into her office now he'd probably catch her masturbating. When he was first given his job, Mandy had taken him out for lunch on several occasions, but although he tried to fall in with her flirting, he'd never been able to convince her that he found her as sexy as everyone else pretended they did, and had been suffering for this failure ever since. He didn't think this was the only factor that had led to his dismissal, but knew that was what gave Mandy the most satisfaction about getting rid of him.

He started walking back towards the office. Mark – the features editor – came up to him holding a piece of paper and a pen. He had a smear of blue ink on his nose and was looking extremely agitated.

'Top ten sex soundtracks.'

'Haven't heard any.'

'No, you know, records to have sex to.'

'*Station to Station*.'

'What? Bowie? No way.'

Martin took the page from him. 'Who have you got so far?' He looked down the list. *Sex Style – Kool Keith. Soundphiles – Kinobe. Deep Throat OST. Isn't Anything – MBV. Avant Hard – Add N to (X). The Smurfs' All-Star Show.*

'That last one is Gareth's,' Mark told him.

'Is that all you've got? This list is pathetic.'

'We chucked out all the rest because they were too dated. Cocteau Twins. Portishead. All the sad old shit.'

'What about Prince? R Kelly? Barry White? The usual suspects.'

'Which albums?'

'I don't know. Go ask the guys.'

'OK, Martin, thanks.'

Mark walked away. Martin wondered whether Mark knew he'd just been sacked. He supposed he must do, and felt grateful to his features editor for not avoiding him in the way the rest of the office had done over the last twenty-four hours. He imagined the sort of nasty conversations which were probably already doing the rounds, and wondered if Gareth already had a Martin Powell joke. Not feeling up to going back to the office just yet, he went to the office kitchen and poured himself a cup of coffee.

He took the coffee and went down to the meeting room that was situated at the far end of the floor and always empty on Friday afternoons. Sitting alone at the large table, he sipped his coffee and pondered his future.

a sign of mental strength

Alison checked her watch, wondering if Martin had done another runner. Even a long meeting ought to be over by now, and if he didn't come back soon she'd have to leave without checking everything was alright. She knew he was planning to go from the office to a meeting somewhere in Essex so she doubted he had gone home, but maybe Mandy had made him so mad he'd forgotten all about his appointment and stormed out of the building.

Getting up from her desk, she walked slowly down towards Mandy's office. Just as she reached it, Mandy opened her door and walked straight into her.

'Alison,' she said sharply, 'what are you doing?'

'Nothing,' she replied.

Mandy squinted at her suspiciously, but let her pass by. Alison noticed Mark standing by someone's desk showing them a piece of paper. She walked over and tapped him on the shoulder.

'Seen Martin?' she asked.

'Yeah. I think he's in the meeting room.'

She nodded. Walking down to the end of the office, she stopped outside the glass wall and looked at Martin sitting with his back to her and finishing a cup of a coffee. She pushed open the door.

'You know that's a sign of mental strength.'

'What?'

'Sitting with your back to the door. It shows that you're not intimidated by whoever comes in.'

'It's OK,' he said, 'I'll only be a minute.'

'I know,' she told him, feeling the time was wrong to say anything more supportive, 'I just came to tell you that Caroline Grieder called back. She said she wanted to talk to you before you go to your meeting this afternoon.'

He nodded. 'Thanks, Alison.'

a sense of entitlement

'Oh, come on, Caroline, surely you can tell me whether this job offer is worth going all the way to Essex.'

'Jump in a cab and you'll be there in no time. I don't want to tell you anything. It'll be much more fun if the whole thing is a surprise.'

Martin rubbed the corner of his left eye, finding the sensation so satisfying that he worried he'd got some kind of infection. 'Will it make me happy?'

'At the very least it'll make you laugh. Please don't make me tell you any more, Martin. All you need to know is that when the call came through asking me if I knew anyone suitable for this job, yours was the only name that came to mind.'

'So it's something weird then?'

'A bit, maybe. But that's it, that's all you're getting out of me. Have you had your big showdown with Mandy?'

'Just.'

'Did I tell you our daughters are at school together?'

'No, I didn't know that.'

'Her girl is a frightful mare, of course, as you would expect. Anya positively quakes with fear every time she phones. And the worst thing about her is her hideous sense of entitlement. As you can probably tell, she's very much her mother's girl.'

'She sounds awful.'

Caroline laughed. 'Exactly. Let me know what you make of Brad.'

'Oh, Car, one more thing. I'll understand if you don't want to tell me and it's not that I think there's a big conspiracy or anything, but can I ask you who told you I was getting sacked?'

Her reply was immediate. 'Nick Jennings.'
'Thanks, Caroline. See you soon, I hope.'

end of the day

Alison booked Martin's cab, said goodbye and walked across to the lifts. Quickly making sure Gareth was still at his desk, she stepped inside and went down to the ground floor. She'd agreed with Adrian to make Saturday their big night out, and to spend Friday getting stoned and watching TV. The romantic potential in this arrangement was diminished slightly by having Suzanne staying in with them, but at least she had to get to the club by ten on Fridays and wouldn't have time to make too much of a nuisance of herself. Alison, for some reason she'd now forgotten, had even agreed to cook. She was planning to stop in Safeway on her way home and had spent the last fifteen minutes making a shopping list.

Alison had had so many showdowns with her boyfriend and sister over domestic duties that these days she didn't even bother trying to persuade them to share the workload. Even making sarcastic comments about their laziness only encouraged them to bond together against her, and although she realised that her lack of complaint meant they'd won, Alison found their joking and wheedling so infuriating that she preferred not to even give them the opportunity to feel hard done by. It was depressing to go home every night knowing that no one would have ever done anything nice for her, but she didn't want to feel sorry for herself and no matter how annoying they were, just having them in the house was preferable to living alone.

She caught her usual bus from the stop just down from the *Force* offices. Showing the driver her travel-card, she immediately headed for the upper deck. Alison knew if she sat anywhere in the lower saloon, she'd soon feel guilty and have to give up her seat. She hated the expectant look in the eyes of senior citizens when they boarded the bus, aware that if there was anything interesting upstairs – a bingo game, perhaps, or a fresh cup of tea – they'd forget all their infirmities and be up their in a flash.

Alison found a seat near the back and squashed in close to the window. Unzipping her small leather bag, she took out a copy of next month's edition of *Force* and thumbed through looking for any articles that might feature observations staff writers had stolen from her.

getting fucked in the garden shed

The taxi pulled up outside a development area of ten adjoined offices. Martin paid the driver and walked across to the small, prefabricated hut that housed an elderly man in a black uniform.

'Hendon Publications please.'

'Third building along. Doorcode is 0743.'

Martin thanked the man and followed his directions. As soon as he got inside he was confronted by a confident man with a firm handshake and a thinning head of hair.

'Martin, hi, come through.'

He led him down a dimly lit corridor into an office where two other men were already waiting. Brad nodded in their direction and introduced them as Howard and Jerry. Martin sat in an empty chair, watching Brad lower himself behind a desk. He closed his eyes for a moment and tried to flip back into interview mode, which was especially difficult as he didn't know what sort of job he was up for. Maybe the first question would give him a clue.

'Do you masturbate?'

Martin looked up at his potential new boss, wondering if he'd misheard. 'What?'

'Masturbation. Do you indulge?'

'Of course,' he said, recovering himself and deciding that he was being interviewed for the position of editor at one of the new very laddish magazines that weren't doing so well.

'Good,' said Brad, as if he was a comedian getting into the swing of his routine, 'and when you masturbate, what do you think of?'

An easy one. 'Girls.'

Brad laughed. 'I know that. But what kind of girls do you think of? Do you think of your girlfriend? Your ex? Belinda Carlisle?'

'I don't know. I suppose I think of women I've either not done it with, or women I've done it with recently.'

Brad looked him in the eye. 'And who have you done it with recently?'

Martin squirmed. 'I can't tell you that.'

'Oh, come on, we're all men here,' said Brad in an exasperated voice, swinging round in his chair so he could make eye contact with his two minions, Howard and Jerry. 'And I give you my word that nothing you say here will be repeated outside these four walls.'

'OK,' he said, looking at Howard and Jerry, 'I did it with a New York friend called Gina.'

'But you have a girlfriend as well, right?'

'Yeah.'

'Excellent. You know, guys, I really think we've got the right man for the job here. OK, so when was the last time you wanked?'

'This morning.'

'At home?'

'Of course,'

'OK, OK, I'm not saying you sneaked off to the executive washroom to shoot your load. Not, I hasten to add, that there would be anything wrong with that.'

Howard and Jerry giggled.

'The boys know what I mean. Working here, well, sometimes you can feel like you need to tie a knot in it.'

Martin smiled. So it was a lad's mag then. Brad came round from behind his desk and sat on the edge of it, clasping his hands together.

'So, come on, Martin, what do you use?'

'Excuse me?'

'Props, Martin, props. Letters? Dirty knickers? A magazine?'

'Oh,' he said, 'nothing like that. Just my hand, my imagination, and some Vaseline.'

'But you do use it?'

'What? My cock?' he said, trying to sound matey, but feeling a crushing embarrassment as he realised he'd failed to get the tone right.

'No,' said Brad, grinning at his minions, 'porn.'

It was at this point that Martin noticed the magazines on Brad's desk. He hadn't properly clocked them before, mainly because they were turned at an odd angle away from him and the desk lamp shining directly onto their glossy surfaces made the covers indistinguishable. But now he was looking at them closely he realised they were pornographic magazines. Not well-known titles either, although thankfully they all seemed softcore. He felt nervous. Surely Caroline hadn't put him forward for editing a porn mag?

'Ah, well . . . ' he began.

'You don't use it?'

'Well, no, I do, but not magazines. I have some videos a work-colleague duped for me, and I'm a regular visitor to

Adult Tonite on the web, but magazines, well, I'm just too embarrassed to buy them.'

'Embarrassed,' Brad repeated, 'yes, that's another reason why you're perfect for this job. Take a look at these . . .'

He picked up three of the magazines that were fanned across his desk and dropped them into Martin's lap. Martin waited a second and then began to thumb through one. There was less text than he expected, just a short side-bar at the start of each pictorial. The first girl was dressed in a pale blue cardigan and matching knickers. He flicked through the subsequent pictures of her at various angles, the final shot showing her with legs spread aside a chair. The only thing he found shocking about the magazine was that so many photo-sets featured women smoking. There was something deeply unsettling about the number of pictures of women holding cigarettes next to their labia, and a photograph of a sexy, smiling blonde balancing a blue lighter on her pubic hair worried him so much that he immediately put the magazine back down.

'What do you think?' Brad asked.

'They're . . . um . . . very sexy.'

'Could you wank to them?'

'Yes, of course.'

'And how would you do it?'

'What?'

'The wanking. Would you read the magazine first and then go to your bathroom or bedroom afterwards, or would you wank with the magazine in one hand, or would you come onto the photographs. What would you do?'

'I'm not sure. I think I'd lie on the bed and start wanking using the photographs and then when I started to get close, I'd push the magazines away and start using my imagination.'

'And why would you do it like that? Guilt?'

'What?'

'Would you push the magazine away because you felt guilty about looking at the girls?'

'No, it's not that.'

'Or because you think it's better to come thinking of someone you know rather than someone you'll never meet?'

'Something like that. I always have my best orgasms when I'm using my imagination.'

'Good. Now we're getting somewhere. What about you, Howard?'

Although Howard was sitting behind Brad, he froze as if he was still being watched. Jerry continued smiling, as if pleased to see his friend caught out.

'What was that?'

'Wanking, Howard. When you're using a magazine, what's the routine?'

He still looked shocked, saying cautiously, 'It's different for me.'

'Why?'

'Well, I know most of these girls. My girlfriend's the one who fucked her neighbour in the garden shed.'

'Show me,' he said.

Jerry took another of the magazines and opened it on the desk. Brad leaned over and took a long look at the pictorial.

'Mmm . . .' he said approvingly, 'not bad. So what are you saying, that it's too close to home?'

'No, it's just that I don't think I'm the average porn consumer. I mean, that's what you're trying to get at, aren't you?'

'Top marks, Jerry, top marks. OK, so who do we think is the average porn consumer?'

'Well,' said Howard, 'it's pretty safe to say that we've covered the schoolboy market. But there's a surprising number of schoolgirls too. They tend to go for the older, more traditional titles, probably because they start off with what they find under their father's bed.'

'That's another big market,' Jerry interrupted, 'the fathers.'

'True, and then there's the single men. But it's a certain type of single man. That's not a value judgement. It's just that there's something in some men, men like you, Martin, that stops them buying a magazine. Now, tell me a bit more about your experiences working at *Force*. There's a bit of nudity in your mag, isn't there?'

'Yes. Not as much as some of the others.'

'Could you imagine someone wanking to your magazine?'

'Yes, I guess so. In the same way you could imagine someone wanking to *Cosmopolitan*. Although to be honest, it's more likely they'd be going for the articles than the pictures. Unless they were really desperate.'

'OK, Martin, let me tell you what this is all about. As you don't buy porn you probably won't have noticed this development, but a lot of the major publishers have spent the last year trying to broach the barrier between the lad-mags and the softer end of the porn market. They've done this by introducing new titles with less smutty covers and making their strap-lines a bit more sophisticated. But so far the major reason for their lack of success is all to do with advertising. At the moment the only people who'll advertise in porn-mags are video-companies and sex-line operators. And because their adverts are designed for a porn-reading audience, they've got tawdry pictures which immediately identify the magazine as pornography the moment the customer takes it off the shelf. Hendon Publications, however, have had a very good last three years, and because of that we're prepared to take a risk. Bear with me, Martin, because this is going to sound absolutely crazy, but what we want to do is say fuck the advertisers . . . I mean, we'll try to sell space, we always try to sell space, it would be suicide not to at least try to sell space . . . for an issue or two and see if we can't create the world's first mainstream porn magazine. The style magazines have been pushing back the barriers for months now . . . I take it you've seen this?'

He held up a copy of *The Face* from the previous October. Martin had seen the magazine, and knew exactly which article he was referring to – a Sean Ellis photo-set of a fashion spread entitled *nothing left to the imagination . . . but i think her name's deborah* that featured a dead-looking model naked apart from John Galliano boots, a Sylvia Fletcher straw hat and various thin ribbons. The *Force* team had spent several meetings looking through these photos and wondering whether this meant the start of open season before deciding that *The Face* had only got away with it because the model's pubic hair was so thick she might as well have been wearing a pair of black knickers.

Martin was surprised he didn't also have a copy of the following month's *l'edition sexe*, sold in a pink plastic bag to hide the cover shot of a topless model. Most magazines tended to have at least one sex issue every couple of years when circulation was flagging, but *The Face's* attempt had been one of the more extreme, and, he thought, a possible example to follow.

'Yeah,' said Martin, 'we've been following that debate pretty closely.'

'Kylie's bum, *Nerve*, Taschen, *Richardson*, all that?'

He nodded. 'So, just to get this straight, you're offering me a job editing a mainstream porn mag?'

'Creating, Martin, creating. You have complete *carte blanche*. So long as there's enough cocks and cunts in there for it to count as genuine porn. We don't want anything half-hearted.'

'But how can it be mainstream if it's full of cocks and cunts?'

'You let us worry about that. How long do you need to make a decision?'

'How long have I got?'

'Is a week long enough?'

Martin considered this. 'I guess so.'

'Good. Don't hesitate to give us a call if you have any questions.'

flying the flag

Alison put her bag down in the hallway and went through to the lounge.

'Alright?' asked Suzanne, looking up from beneath her frizzy blonde fringe.

'Yeah.' Alison sat down and surveyed the lounge, taking in the Union Jack flag and puzzling at the small change scattered across the carpet. 'The death of Britpop?' she guessed.

'Close. Morrissey supporting Madness. At Finsbury Park.'

'Right. Where's Adrian?'

'In the bath. What are we having for dinner?'

'Wait and see.'

'Did you confront that woman?'

'What woman?'

'Your boss?' She thought for a minute. 'Madge.'

'Mandy. No. She's not the sort of person you can just walk up to . . . I have to wait until she talks to me again.'

'Won't it be too late by then?'

'Probably.'

Adrian came into the room, wearing only a towel. Alison reminded herself of her pledge not to get annoyed with them, but couldn't stop herself asking sarcastically, 'So, can we tidy away your installation or does it have to stay up for a couple of weeks first?'

Adrian turned and looked at her, confused. 'What installation?'

Alison didn't bother replying. He sat down in a chair opposite them and lifted a hairy foot up onto his right knee, about to start cutting his toenails with a large metal clipper. This gave both sisters a prime view of his penis and testicles, and although Suzanne wasn't looking, Alison couldn't help feeling irritated. She knew if she told him to cover up, Suzanne would look and defeat the point of her comment, but she couldn't bring herself to stay there, instead telling them, 'I'm going to make a start on dinner.'

'Great,' said Suzanne.

She went back into the hallway for her bag and carried it through to the kitchen.

the latest in-thing

'Do you think you'll ever learn to drive?'

'Oh, I don't know, Claud. Is it important?'

She looked across at him, briefly, before returning her eyes to the road. 'Yes,' she said, 'it's important. Do you think I like doing this journey every weekend?'

'You're right. Let's cut down to once a fortnight.'

'No, Martin, that's not the point. You know, you don't have to always be this selfish.'

He stared ahead, wondering if it was going to start raining.

'How am I selfish?' he asked. 'Just because I don't want to drive? It's bad for the environment.'

'Oh, don't be ridiculous. And you're selfish because you spend all week running about with your weirdos, and then every weekend make a big deal just because I want you to come down and spend a few hours detoxing with my parents. God knows what would happen to you if I left you alone in the city.'

'I am a big boy now. I can take care of myself. And besides, it's not as if I'm having fun being out all week. I'm working when I go out with those weirdos.'

She snorted. 'Sure, work. Thinking up a story to use as an excuse for your latest bacchanalian display. Sometimes I have no idea why I'm married to you.'

'Because you find me irresistible?' he tried, smiling sweetly.

'No.'

'Because your parents love me.'

'My parents do not love you, Martin. In fact, they don't even like you. They tolerate your company.'

'So why inflict me on them?'

'We've already discussed this. Shut up and find a decent CD to put on.'

He opened the car CD box and started flipping through.

'Naomi's boyfriend tried to strangle Jamiroquai.'

'And that's cool is it? That's the latest in-thing for you and your bunch of freaks to run round doing. Strangling celebrities.'

'Hey, I barely know the guy. I just thought it was odd. He did it to Damon too.'

'That's sick.'

'I know. Naomi's really worried about him. She thinks he's going to get arrested.'

'Good job too. I'm surprised they haven't done it already. Why didn't his minders kick his bloody head in?'

'I don't know. He's quite posh. And rich. And a very smooth talker.'

'And a psychopath, clearly. Don't tell me any more, I don't want to know.'

Claudia stared at the road, ignoring him. Knowing it was unwise to antagonise her further when she had the whole weekend to make him suffer, he put on a classical CD and turned the volume down until it was just audible over the engine.

Claudia's mother called the mobile five minutes before they reached her house. She talked to Martin as Claudia completed the journey, coming out onto the driveway just as she pulled onto it.

'Hello, Martin,' she said as he climbed out of the car, 'good journey?'

'Not bad.'

She pulled her coat around her shoulders. 'I'm afraid Stephen's going to be late tonight, but he said to go ahead and eat without him.'

'Nothing serious, I hope.'

'It's always serious.'

Martin nodded and looked at his feet. Claudia released the car-lock and he took their bags from the back seat.

'Is Abigail coming?'

'She's already here. And your brother's brought his girl-friend.'

'What girlfriend? I always thought he was gay.'

'Don't be ridiculous, dear, your brother's not gay. He just doesn't fall into bed with the first woman who asks, that's all.'

'But he's twenty-eight.'

'And he's had plenty of girlfriends before.'

'None that I've met.'

'That's because he takes his family commitments very seriously. He doesn't want to introduce us to any old Tom, Dick or Harry.'

'Mum, Tom, Dick and Harry are men.'

'Don't be facetious, dear. You know what I mean.'

Claudia's mother led them through the open door into the large hallway. Martin took their bags up to the guest bedroom and went through to the main dining-room, where Claudia's brother was sitting with his new girlfriend. Martin recognised her immediately.

'Tilly.'

'Yes,' she said, before standing up and gasping, 'oh my God, Martin.'

'Tilly,' he repeated, swiftly moving across the room, 'you look fantastic.'

'So do you. Oh, that's amazing. I had no idea you were Julian's brother.'

'I'm not.'

'Oh, right, I see, yes of course . . .'

'I'm Claudia's husband.'

'Right, right.'

'Claudia's my sister,' Julian said sulkily.

'Well, isn't this wonderful,' said Tilly, ignoring him, 'you must sit next to me at dinner. We've got so much to catch up on.'

'I'd really like that.'

'How are you, Abby?' Claudia asked her sister. 'Everything OK at the hospital?'

'Of course not. That's why it's there.'

'Oh, you know what I mean. Don't be so bloody difficult.'

'Darling,' said Claudia's mother, raising her eyebrows.

'Well, she is. Just because she works on an AIDS ward doesn't mean she has to be so bloody sanctimonious all the time.'

'Why don't you have a sherry, dear? Something to relax you after the long drive.'

dopeheads

Adrian and Suzanne were sitting in the corner smoking when Alison brought their dinner through. Looking at them together, Alison was reminded of Paul, the first man they had fought over. In a way, she still held him responsible for the way their lives had turned out. Almost all the men she'd been with since him had been the same: feckless, but somehow exciting, even though she knew deep down Adrian was more conservative than most men she knew. Maybe, she considered, that was even why she liked him. He was quietly rebellious, but still safe, and given this about him, she supposed she ought to feel proud that her sister liked him so much.

She wondered what her parents would think if they were witnessing this evening. Although her mum and dad were not exactly impressed with Adrian's lethargy, they did seem to have realised he was a warm-hearted soul, and had always been proud that they'd raised two sisters who got on well enough to share a home. But what she didn't know was whether they'd be unsettled by their constant smoking and laziness, or whether they'd side with Suzanne and think Alison was being uptight.

They came to the table. The strain of cooking had made Alison feel she didn't even want to eat the meal she'd prepared, and when Adrian came to the table she lifted the spliff from his lip and took two deep drags, telling herself that no matter what happened she would manage to control her temper.

secret societies

Martin and Tilly chatted away all through supper, much to the irritation of their respective partners. They talked about what had happened to them in the years since they'd left Cambridge, and then moved on to the exploits of various high-fliers from their year. Very early in the evening, they agreed – mainly through eye-contact – to avoid any sensitive areas of conversation, including the circumstances under which they had met. Claudia quickly picked up on this, and although she refrained from raising the subject at dinner, it was the first thing she asked once she and Martin had retired to their room.

'Are you sure you want to know?' Martin asked, playing for time.

'You know me well enough to know that's a stupid question.'

'OK. We both belonged to a secret society.'

She sat on the bed and took off her beige top. 'What sort of secret society. Spying, you mean?'

'Not exactly.'

'A drinking society?'

'Well, yes, it started like that. It started, as a matter of fact, as a girls' drinking society.'

'Which one?' she asked, getting back up and going across to the dressing table for a pot of Vitamin E moisturiser.

'The Thélèmites.'

'Oh yes, I remember. You used to go out with one of them. Was Tilly a Thélèmite?'

'Not at first. She sort of became one. Around the time that the society changed.'

Claudia unscrewed the pot, dipped her fingers into it, and began rubbing the cream into her face. 'What d'you mean? It stopped being a drinking society?'

'It was the year that girl died at an initiation ceremony when they tied her to a tree and made her drink seven pints and eat a bowl of cat food and then covered her mouth with sticking-plaster when she tried to vomit.'

'Right, yes,' she said, briskly, 'I remember that too. That was when they had the big clamp-down.'

'Yes. And some of the drinking-societies disbanded in honour of the dead girl, and others went underground, and some just stopped for a bit and waited for the fuss to die down.'

'What happened with the Thélèmites?'

'Well, the Thélèmites went weird.'

'What d'you mean, weird?'

'Well . . . gosh, this is embarrassing. You know how most of the drinking societies weren't really about drinking. They were more about . . .'

'Sex,' she said, putting the cream back down and unclasping her bra.

'Yes, sex, that's exactly it. Of course, there were girls who were genuinely interested in seeing how many pints they could sink without falling over, but most of them, well, most of them just wanted to get drunk and lose all their inhibitions and go to bed with the rugby team.'

'So, you're saying that the Thélèmites was a secret sex society?'

'Yes.'

'What sort of sex society? I mean, what did you do? There must've been some sort of rules?'

'Well, the rules were that everyone drew lots and the winner got to have their fantasy acted out.'

'And what was Tilly's fantasy?'

'I'm embarrassed to tell you.'

'Tell me.'

'I can't. It's against the Thélèmites' code. If I told you that, I'd be betraying not just Tilly, but all my fellow Thélèmites.'

'You will tell me this minute, Martin Powell, or you can find somewhere else to sleep tonight.'

He exhaled. 'Pearl necklaces.'

'What?'

'And baths. With lots of men . . .'

'What? Lots of men what?'

'You know.'

'What?'

'Ejaculating.'

'On her?' she asked, her tone shrill with disbelief.

'Exactly.'

'Oh my God.'

'I know,' he said quickly, 'but it was years ago, and everyone's a bit weird at university.'

She stood up. 'You have to tell him.'

'Who?'

'Julian. You have to tell him.'

'Claud, I took an oath.'

'Martin, you cannot sit back and let my brother go out with some kind . . .'

'Some kind of what?'

'Some kind of . . .'

'What?'

'Some kind of fucking cum-queen. There, I said it.'

'I'm sure she doesn't do it any more.'

'I mean, God alone knows what kind of diseases she's got. And Julian hates condoms . . . he's going to end up at Abby's bloody clinic.'

'How do you know that?'

'What?'

'That your brother hates condoms.'

'He told me.'

'You talk to your brother about sex?'

'Of course. Don't you?'

Martin thought about his brother. He hadn't spoken to him in over three years. 'No, I never tell my brother anything. I'd be too scared of leading him astray.'

'Yes, well, I'm not like that. My brother and I have a very healthy relationship.'

'So it would seem.'

'What does that mean?'

'Nothing. Look, let's get some sleep.'

'How can I? Knowing that in the next room my brother's sleeping with some disease-ridden slut.'

'I'm sure she's not disease-ridden. Let's talk about this in the morning. Please? I'm really tired.'

'OK. I'm sorry. Goodnight.'

'Goodnight.'

time for bed

Alison had never been a big fan of dope, mainly because while it made her feel horny, it seemed to always have the opposite effect on her boyfriend. If she hadn't been going out with Adrian, she knew she would've given it up completely by now, and she rarely smoked properly, taking small puffs but handing it back well before she started to feel any real effect.

Tonight, however, she'd managed to get a pleasant buzz from smoking, and Adrian didn't seem too mashed to have sex. So when Suzanne left, Alison tested his mood by leaning across for a kiss. He responded with unusual enthusiasm, so she stood up and straddled his lap. He smiled and she pushed her weight down against his jeans. He looked back at her, as lasciviously as possible given his bloodshot, bleary eyes. She was pleased to see he had shaved recently, and kissed him again. When she broke away, he gently lifted her off of him so he could get up. She stood up and they went upstairs to their bedroom, Adrian reaching up under her skirt the moment they got through the door.

insomnia

Martin lay awake. He couldn't stop thinking about Tilly. It wasn't that he wanted to do anything untoward with her; he just felt eager to continue the conversation they'd been having at dinner without an audience. No doubt there would be other opportunities for this over the weekend, but now that he'd made the tactical error of telling Claudia about

Tilly's sexual history, he knew she'd be watching him intently even if he managed to steer her out of earshot.

No, he decided, he couldn't wait until morning. Claudia was a heavy sleeper, out the moment she closed her eyes and unlikely to wake during the night. He didn't know for certain, but it seemed possible that this tendency might run in the family, and if so, maybe Tilly was also awake alone and craving his company.

He climbed out of bed and tried to decide what to wear. He was planning to get Tilly to come out to the gazebo in the back garden, so it made sense to get dressed, but he was worried she might freak out and think it was a fire. Oh well, he thought, as far as he could recall she wasn't the type to panic.

Dressed, he left his shoes on the upstairs landing and slowly crept along the carpet until he reached the door to Julian's bedroom. The doors in the house had been fitted by an extremely inept carpenter and were hard to close satisfactorily. So, with a few soft taps Martin managed to get the door open. From the light of the landing he could see the faces of both Julian and Tilly. They appeared to be sleeping, although his operation was made potentially easier by the fact that Tilly was on the side of the bed nearest the door.

Martin dropped down onto the rug and slowly crawled towards Tilly. As he looked at her sleeping face he remembered his days in the Thélèmites and the time when she'd helped act out his own fantasy. It was a relatively safe fantasy, especially given Tilly's predilection. What he wanted to do was watch two women shaving each other's vaginas. Tilly had been kind enough to make a real show of it, somehow getting hold of a proper shaving-brush and a cut-throat razor. She also did it in one of the older college's dining hall, with both girls sitting in turn on a high-backed chair while the other went to work on her, which made the whole thing seem much less sleazy than it would've done in a college bathroom.

Tilly had always had an innocent face, and she looked even more untroubled asleep. Her hairstyle was exactly the same as it had been at university, a boyishly short set of loose brown curls that complemented her wide, mask-like, feline features. He remembered Claudia's comment to her mother about how she thought her brother was gay, and wondered whether homosexual or bisexual men were more or less interested in masculine women.

He reached out and gently pressed her lower lip, trying to make the touch feel like a kiss. She smiled, but did not wake, so he worked the tip of his finger slightly further into her mouth, not intruding too far in case she bit him. After a brief moment, it had the desired effect and she murmured awake. Starting slightly, she pulled back, clearly shocked to see his face by her bedside. But once she was properly awake her sense of fun seemed to take over (as he'd known it would) and she looked at him expectantly. He touched her lips again, warning her not to whisper, then took her arm by the wrist and straightened out her hand.

Using the index finger of his left hand, he shadow-wrote the word COME onto the palm of her hand. She nodded to indicate that she had understood, and he spelt out the second word in his secret message: OUTSIDE. She got confused halfway through and shook her head. He tried again and this time she got it. The next word was easy, two letters, TO, and she understood straight away. Same with the one after: THE. Knowing the last word would be difficult for her to work out, he did it so slowly that she almost started giggling, although maybe, he thought, that was because of the silliness of the word, GAZEBO.

She took his hand in return and spelt out her reply. *NOW?*
Not wanting to go through another long message, he held up
three fingers.

'Minutes?' she mouthed.

He nodded, and crawled back the way he had come.

Martin sat in the gazebo, finishing up a cigarette. Tilly
appeared in the darkness, clad in a long blue coat. He looked
at her bare feet and raised an eyebrow.

'You naked under there?'

'Maybe.' She smiled. 'Want to take a look?'

She walked towards him. Feeling mischievous, he opened
only one button, exposing her crotch. He gently stroked her
pubic hair.

'Remember what you once did for me?'

'Of course.'

He did the button back up. 'I need to ask your advice about
something.'

'My advice?' she asked, sounding surprised.

'Actually, it's not really advice. Well, it is, I suppose. What I
want to know is, do you think what we did at university was
dangerous?'

'AIDS, you mean?'

'No, not that.' He stared into the darkness. 'Do you believe
in demons?'

Tilly sat down. He looked round at her. She seemed
fascinated. He worried she expected him to spin some terrible
story of dark possession, and quickly continued, 'I don't
mean, literally, I mean, do you think if you do certain stuff it
changes you?'

She took his hand. 'Have you found religion?'

'I didn't lose it.'

'What d'you mean?'

'Well, y'know, I've always been a quiet Christian.'

'Do you go to Church?'

'No,' he admitted, 'but I read the Bible.'

She chuckled. 'I used to think I'd be struggling against my upbringing forever . . . then I managed to get over it in my first term.'

'I remember,' Martin said, 'people used to talk about you.'

Tilly didn't reply, looking away from him and trying to pull her bare feet up under her coat. He hadn't known Tilly that well at university (outside of the Thélèmites), but they had occasionally fallen in with everyone else by pretending they were characters in whatever novel they were studying that week and going round to each other's rooms for afternoon tea. He remembered their conversations as extremely erotic occasions, given an extra charge by their observation of the Thélèmites' rule that no one was allowed to talk about what had happened in their evenings, even people who'd taken part in joint activities together.

'Do you think the college knew what we were up to?'

'My God,' Tilly exclaimed, 'what we were doing was nothing. You wouldn't believe the stories I've heard since I left. But what's this about, Martin? Surely you're not worried about things that happened fourteen years ago?'

'No,' he admitted, 'there's something else. You know I told you I edit *Force* magazine?'

She nodded.

'Well, I got sacked today.'

'I'm sorry to hear that,' she said, sounding sincere.

'It's OK, I've been offered another job.'

'Great.'

'But I'm worried. I'm worried about what'll happen to me if I accept the offer.'

116

'Why? What is it? Contract-killing?'

'No, nothing like that. I've been offered the chance to create the world's first mainstream porn mag.'

Tilly chuckled. 'And why does that worry you? Do you think you're going to be tempted by all the models?'

'No, it's not that.'

'Are you faithful to your wife?'

'Sometimes.'

This response delighted her, and she fell into Martin's arms. 'Oh, fuck me, Martin, fuck me right here. I've never understood why we didn't fuck.'

It was a tempting offer, but he shook his head, in search of a different comfort tonight. 'I can't fuck you, Tilly, you're seeing my brother-in-law. Besides, I want to confide in you.'

'OK,' she said, clearly disappointed, 'tell me your worries.'

'I'm worried because I've had an unshakeable feeling recently that I've let something dangerous into my life. I don't know, maybe it's just some kind of puritan hangover, but . . . I've never been so into pornography that it's become a problem for me, but it feels like such a dark force, maybe because it's so bound up with guilt . . .'

'What happened to you, Martin?'

He looked at her, hearing a change in her voice and feeling unsure whether she was cross with him because he'd refused to have sex with her or because he was taking himself so seriously.

'What d'you mean?'

'You seem so lost. You never used to be like this.'

'I feel lost. I've felt like this for the last five years. Ever since I turned thirty.'

'OK, Martin, you came to me, so I'm going to give you some pointers. First of all, whether you take this job or not, nothing bad is going to happen to you. What you're suffering from is

117

good, old-fashioned fear of success. A mainstream porn mag is a pretty hot idea, and if it takes off you could become a world-famous figure. Of course that's scary, but it's stupid to get so superstitious. All this worry about dark stuff out there? That's bullshit. The only thing that's out there is opportunity.'

Martin sighed. He had chosen the wrong person again. Tilly didn't seem to have changed at all since university, and it was hardly surprising that she didn't understand. She was part of the problem, one of the earliest people to start shaping his current destiny. He needed someone with a moral centre, someone who at least had a conception of why he was feeling scared.

'You're right,' he told her, 'I'm sorry. I just had an attack of night-jitters.'

She kissed him. 'I know. It's fine. Let's talk again tomorrow.'

noises in the night

Alison often awoke during the night. This was understandable. They lived in a dangerous neighbourhood, their house was noisy, and there were often fights in the street outside. She wasn't as worried as she might be, knowing that Suzanne's irregular hours were a good deterrent to any criminals watching the house (she imagined them dressed in stripy jumpers and driving around in a big van), but she still occasionally did feel scared when she started in her sleep.

A few times recently she had awoken and known with absolute certainty that there was someone else in the room. She sensed an unknown presence and saw shadowy figures that took a few seconds to disperse when she set eyes on them. Tonight, however, there wasn't anything supernatural about the disturbance. The noises coming from the lounge were so loud that Alison decided she had to get up and go investigate. It was probably only a drunken Suzanne, but there was always the possibility that an aggressive customer had followed her home. Suzanne was cavalier about chucking people out of the club where she worked, and twice the police had interviewed her as a witness to violent incidents.

She grabbed her dressing-gown, tied it around herself, and slowly went downstairs. Creeping along the hallway, she headed towards the noise. When she reached the lounge, she hesitated, then, trying to keep hidden in the darkness, looked slowly round the door.

The man making love to her sister had his back to Alison. Suzanne was pushed against the back of the armchair, identifiable only by her hands and legs, tightly clutching the stranger. Alison knew she should leave, but couldn't take her eyes off the stranger's frizzy hair, which made her worry her sister was being fucked by Art Garfunkel.

After a few seconds, she heard her sister exhale loudly and realised she didn't want to watch this any more. She turned round and, taking great care to be quiet, returned to her bed.

Saturday

telling Claudia

'Would you like to make love?'

Martin rolled over, surprised by the question and waking from a dream where Tilly had tried to get him to help her raise the dead. 'What?'

Claudia smiled and stroked his hip. 'We overslept. Everyone else has gone out on a walk.'

'Oh . . .'

'Don't worry, it's OK, I spoke to mum. So, how about it?'

'Aren't you still angry with me?'

'No, of course not. Why do you say that?'

'We spent all last night arguing. You were furious with me because I wouldn't tell your brother about his girlfriend's sexual history.'

'I'm sorry, I was just overtired. I hate doing that drive.'

'So do you still want me to talk to him?'

'No, you're right. I've realised it's none of my business. I'll just get Abigail talking about her clinic and get her to spout loads of horrifying statistics at him. That'll get him to be careful.'

'Good idea.'

Claudia lay out on the bed, looking up at the ceiling. Martin turned on his side.

'Are you sure you're OK?'

'Yes. Why?'

'I don't know. You sound a little fragile.'

He leaned in closer and saw that she was crying.

'I'm sorry, Martin,' she said, 'I've been under a lot of stress recently.'

Martin held her arm, surprised. Although Claudia was frequently angry, she didn't often get upset and he couldn't remember the last time he'd seen her cry.

'Do you want to talk about it?'

'I don't know.'

'OK,' he said, knowing she would continue.

'It's just that if I do talk about it, it's going to make you angry,' she said, giving Martin a tentative glance.

'Why?' he asked.

'Because I'm different to you.'

Martin looked at her. 'What's this about?'

'It's Clive.'

'Right,' he sighed.

'He told me to leave you.'

'I see.'

'He thinks you're a scumbag.'

'Does he?'

'An exploitative, manipulative scumbag.'

'Funny, he's never said that to me.'

'He says that you're never going to change, and that I'm just a trophy wife . . . and if you loved me you'd divorce me so I could marry him instead.'

'Do you want to marry him?'

'Good God, no. I can hardly bear to be in the same room.'

Martin laughed. 'So where's the problem?'

'The problem is that men are different to girls.'

'So this is about biology?'

She slapped him. 'I'm trying to be serious.'

'OK, OK, tell me what's upsetting you.'

'It's easy for you. You can fuck a different girl every night and not get into trouble. They're all independent and perfectly happy to let you come and go as you please.'

'Hang on, Claud, I hardly fuck a different girl every night.'

'But you admit you fuck other girls?'

He looked at her warily. 'Are you saying you fuck other men?'

'I've tried, but every time I fuck someone they want to marry me.'

Martin knew better than to protest or get angry. He had yet to admit to any infidelities himself, and thought it might make strategic sense to concentrate on her adultery until she forgot about his.

'Maybe you're just fucking the wrong kind of men.'

'Right, I should fuck fruitcakes instead. Like you.'

'I didn't mean that.'

'Maybe I could fuck Naomi's boyfriend. He could pretend I'm Mel G and try to strangle me.'

'I just meant that you always go for such wimps. If you wanted, I could . . .'

'What? Pimp for me?'

Martin looked away.

'Why do we do it?' she asked. 'I know you don't enjoy it any more than I do.'

Martin didn't say anything.

'Do you enjoy it?'

'Sometimes.'

'Who did you fuck this week?'

'Come on . . .'

'What?'

'You don't really want me to tell you, do you?'

'Yes, Martin, tell me. Tell me who you fucked. You always said you would tell me if I asked.' She swung her legs back over onto her side of the bed and said coyly, 'I already know anyway. Naomi . . .'

'I've never fucked Naomi.'

'No?' she asked, sounding genuinely surprised. 'Who then?'

Martin rolled back and looked at the ceiling. Although he usually did anything possible to avoid a confrontation, and had never imagined a time when he would willingly admit his misdemeanours, for some perverse reason, today he felt like telling the truth. He could see Claudia was eager to get passionate about something, and even wondered whether she was provoking this conversation because she wanted their relationship to progress to a new level of honesty, so he said,

'Well, on Monday I went to a hotel with Gina.'

'Gina who?'

'Gina Mostyn, the journalist.'

'Who else?'

'There's no one else.'

Claudia seemed satisfied with this. Surprised he'd got off so lightly, he decided to press his luck. Taking her hand, he told her, 'I'm leaving *Force*.'

'What? Why?'

'I've been sacked.'

'What did you do?'

'Nothing. That's why it hasn't been in the papers. It's an amicable settlement and I'm going to do quite nicely out of it.'

'But what are you going to do?'

'Get rich,' he boasted, even though he had yet to discuss salary with his new employers, 'I've already got a new job.'

She kissed him. 'Oh, Martin, when were you planning to tell me all this? What is it? TV?'

'Not exactly.'

'What then?'

'Porn.'

'What?' she shrieked.

'Relax, Claud, it's not what you think. I'm going to be starting a new magazine. It's going to be a little risqué, but nothing too much. It'll be more arty than anything.'

'Oh, Martin, I'm so ashamed. Of all the things you could do. Whatever made you think this is a good idea. It's Naomi, isn't it, she put you up to this.'

'No one put me up to it. I know it sounds a bit shocking, but it's nothing to be worried about, really. You wait and see. It'll really help us consolidate our position.'

'How is you being a porn baron going to help us consolidate our position?'

'Look at Hugh Hefner, look at Bob Guccione. This sort of thing is really *in* now.'

'Oh, Martin, sometimes you can be so . . .'

'So what?'

'So fucking ridiculous. I'm going to take a shower. I suggest you stay here and come up with a different choice of career. Something more appropriate for a man of your age and position.'

Claudia slid out of bed and wrapped herself in a dressing-gown. So much for their Saturday morning sex. Martin closed his eyes and thought about Tilly, putting his hand around his helmet as he came, in a futile effort to stop his sperm spilling onto the sheets.

the man from last night

Alison awoke at eleven. She was in her usual morning position, stretched as far away from Adrian as was possible given the small dimensions of their duvet and mattress.

127

Managing to get out of bed without waking him, she went downstairs to make herself breakfast.

As she was boiling the kettle and toasting two pieces of thin white bread, the man from last night came into the kitchen. He was dressed only in a pair of blue jeans and his skin looked extremely pale. Now she could see his face, Alison realised he didn't look much like Art Garfunkel at all. He had an unpleasant, battered-looking face that made him resemble a boxer, although she doubted he'd ever felt the force of another person's fists. Alison looked at him, wondering whether she could bear being polite to another of Suzanne's anonymous conquests. Sometimes she felt sorry for them, but this one had a certain swagger to his morning-after walk, thrusting out his hand and announcing,

'Hi, I'm Joe.'

'Hi, Joe. Alison. Would you like some coffee?'

'Mmm, that'd be lovely.' He paused, then with a catch in his voice like he knew he was pressing his luck, he asked, 'And do you think it'd be possible for me to pinch one of those pieces of toast?'

time to go

Martin got out of bed and went through to the bathroom. Claudia had just finished in the shower and the room was thick with condensation. He went to the toilet, then washed his hands. He dried them on a still-damp towel and went down to the lounge.

Claudia was sitting on a leather chair in the corner of the room, a picture of mute defiance. Her hair was still wet, making it a darker shade than usual, almost more brown than blonde, and slicked back behind her ears. Her feet were bare and she was dressed in light beige trousers and a grey top. Claudia only initiated sex when she was really desperate for an orgasm, and he knew she must be irritated by the way the morning had worked out.

There was a scratching at the front door. Spencer, the family dog, was the first into the house, followed by the rest of the family, sweeping into the hallway in a bluster of mud and argument. Tilly perched on the edge of a chair and tried to get out of the pair of oversized wellington boots the family kept for ill-equipped visitors. Martin caught her eye and she smiled at him.

'How was your morning, Martin?'

'Pleasant.'

Claudia's mother finished changing her clothes and shoes and went out into the kitchen. She returned with a large green bowl of salad and placed it on a blue place-mat. Claudia was the first to the dining table. The others followed. Abigail picked up a wooden fork and started rooting through the salad bowl. Claudia slapped her hand.

'Ow,' she squealed.

'Stop that.'

'What's happened to the paper?' asked Julian.

Stephen looked at him. 'Oh, I'm sorry, it's still in my study. Would you like me to fetch it?'

'I wouldn't mind,' he said, 'but if you tell me where it is, I can get it.'

'No, no,' said Stephen, 'I'll go.'

He stood up. Martin didn't like Claudia's parents that much, but found her father, a brain surgeon, especially difficult. Claudia didn't get on with her father either, and he only really seemed to have time for Abigail, especially when she was talking about the most extreme cases at her clinic.

Martin was sitting opposite Claudia, and didn't like the way she was looking at Tilly. He could tell she wanted to belittle the intruder, especially after she had so clearly caught the interest of her brother and her boyfriend. His worst fears were realised when she opened her mouth to say, 'Martin's been telling me all kinds of tales about your college days.'

'Really?' she asked, unembarrassed. 'What stories has he been telling?'

Claudia looked round the room, making sure everyone was listening.

'He said you used to let men ejaculate on you.'

'Claudia,' her mother gasped, 'what on earth are you talking about?'

And after that, the room erupted.

another saturday afternoon

Surprisingly, Joe seemed to want to stick around. Usually Suzanne was so horrible to her men the morning after that they high-tailed it home as soon as possible. But maybe she was feeling lonely, even suggesting that the four of them went to a nearby park for an afternoon picnic.

'Yeah,' said Adrian, 'why not? Come on, Al, it'll be fun.'

'I didn't say I wasn't up for it. I'm just not sure if we've got any picnicky-style food.'

'We could get some Kentucky Fried Chicken,' Suzanne suggested, 'or burgers, maybe.'

'And some beers,' added Joe. 'Make an afternoon of it.'

'Are you allowed to drink in the park?'

'Of course,' said Suzanne. 'Go upstairs and get some blankets.'

on the way home

The argument started the moment they were back on the motorway. Martin couldn't believe Claudia had immediately betrayed his confidence and got them thrown out of her parents' house. From the way she was responding to his anger, it seemed Claudia couldn't care less about his undergraduate oath and was far more concerned about his change of career. Within seconds they were shouting at each other so violently that Claudia lost control of the car and crashed into the barriers.

It wasn't a serious smash, although Martin was shaken by the impact. Claudia was clearly much more upset, and the two of them sat in silence until horns blaring at them from behind forced Claudia to back up from the barriers and get back on the road.

'Is it safe to drive like this?'

'There's a service station a couple of miles up the road. Let's get there, then check the damage.'

the seven hour itch

Alison felt happy as they walked towards the park. There had been four noisy teenagers on the bus, and they had driven the driver into a frenzy by drumming their feet against the floor of the upper deck. Usually such yobbish high spirits made her anxious, but today she'd been able to share her sister's amusement at such exuberance.

'I'll get the chicken,' Joe offered, nodding towards the Kentucky place opposite the park.

'OK,' said Adrian, 'we'll get the beer and see you back by the gates.'

Joe nodded, turned his back, and ran across the road. Alison smiled at Suzanne.

'You're being surprisingly generous.'

'What d'you mean?'

'Joe. Usually they're out on their ear by now.'

'Alison,' said Adrian softly.

'What?'

'No,' Suzanne protested, 'I don't mind. What do you think of him?'

'He's nice,' Alison replied. 'A bit pale.'

She giggled. 'It was his idea, you know.'

'What?'

'The picnic. He suggested it last night.'

Alison looked at her sister, finding as usual that it was impossible to read her thoughts. Their mother had often said that eventually Suzanne would surprise everyone by settling down with some unlikely suspect. But she couldn't quite believe that this sallow ginger specimen would be the one.

assessing the damage

Martin remained in the passenger seat, waiting to see what Claudia would do next. Her fingers were trembling, and although she'd managed to get them to the service station and into a parking space, it was obvious that she'd been seriously shaken by their smash. Martin couldn't help feeling partially responsible for their accident, especially as Claudia was usually an excellent driver. After almost two minutes of sitting in silence, he said, 'There's no rush.'

She looked at him. 'What?'

'We can sit here as long as you like.'

Claudia appeared to interpret his comment as sarcasm and immediately opened her door. Martin unbuckled his seat-belt and got out. Claudia was already around the front of the car, assessing the damage. Martin's eye was hardly expert, but he could see the fender was smashed in and one of the headlights was broken.

'Aren't you meant to call the police in cases like this?'

'Shut up Martin,' she told him, 'please just shut up.'

Claudia brought her fist down heavily against the bonnet. He could tell she was more irritated by her accident than him, but he still kept quiet. She looked back at Martin, then started walking towards the entrance of the service station. He waited a moment, before following behind.

Claudia seemed to lose her purpose once inside the service station. Her slowing steps allowed Martin to catch up, and he swept his arm around her waist just as it looked like her legs might give way.

'Come on,' he said quietly, 'let's get a coffee.'

She didn't reply. He led her to the nearest restaurant that looked like it might serve anything other than cartoon food and sat her down at an empty table. She immediately took a packet of cigarettes from her handbag and lit up. He rubbed her arm.

'Food?' he asked.

She shook her head. 'Just a coffee.'

Martin nodded and walked away from the table. He picked up a tray and joined the queue snaking round to the cash registers. He looked at the food sitting in the plastic tubs behind the slanted glass and wondered whether he was up to eating a full meal. His stomach still felt queasy from the arguing and the accident, but it was now well after lunchtime and he hadn't even had chance to finish his breakfast. But the mounded carrots and curled sausages looked so unappealing that he decided to make do with a doughnut. He bought an extra one for Claudia in case she changed her mind about wanting to eat and waited for his two coffees. He paid for everything and carried the tray across to their table.

'I got you a doughnut.'

Claudia didn't say anything. Martin placed her coffee in front of her and handed across sugar and milk. She continued smoking, looking somewhere over his shoulder.

'I could call your family.'

'I don't want you to call my family.'

'I don't mean about the car. I could call them on Monday, tell them that stuff about Tilly was something I made up for a joke. Your parents have a sense of humour.'

Claudia looked away. 'I think we should get a divorce.'

'What?'

'I think that's the best idea.'

'Why?'

She puffed out her cheeks. 'Well, let's see. Maybe because you've been unfaithful to me. Or perhaps because I'm fed up of being humiliated. Or, who knows, maybe because I don't want to go out with the next Larry Flynt.'

Martin picked up his cup and threw it at the wall. A startled family at the next table shouted at him as pieces of china flew towards their table. He looked at them for a second, then snapped out of it and stood up. He started walking out of the restaurant.

'Where are you going?' Claudia shouted after him.

'What do you care? We just broke up.'

picnic II

Alison finished her final chicken-wing and dumped the gnawed bone back in the box.

'Do you reckon there's anywhere we can buy a Frisbee?'

Suzanne laughed.

'Or a ball. Even a ball would do.'

'Why don't you ask them if you can join in?' Suzanne suggested, pointing to a group of sporty men playing a makeshift game of cricket. 'I'm sure they'd let you.'

'No,' said Alison, 'I feel like playing catch.'

Adrian took another swig from his can and asked Suzanne, 'Do you reckon I can get away with skinning up?'

'Yeah, go on,' she told him, 'the worst that's gonna happen is some crusty coming across for a puff.'

'Or,' said Alison, 'we could get arrested.'

'Why are you so obsessed with us getting arrested? I reckon you like the idea of us all being in the cells together.'

'Have you ever been arrested?' asked Joe.

Alison quickly looked over at Suzanne and they both burst into giggles.

'We both were. Once.'

Joe sat up. 'What happened?'

'It was the first time I ever did drugs,' Alison explained. 'Proper ones, I mean.'

'Alison's eighteenth birthday. Our parents, who are pretty liberal . . .'

'Not that liberal,' Alison interrupted. 'Suzanne only thinks they're liberal cause she never takes any notice when they tell her off.'

'No, it's true, they do act all straight and serious. But underneath they're not as bothered by what I do as they make out. Although Alison's right, they're pretty normal parents really.'

'Your Dad's pretty strict,' Adrian added.

'Yeah. Anyway, our parents had gone away for the weekend so we could have a proper party in the house for Al without them worrying. So I did the sisterly thing and bought drugs for everyone.'

'Hang on,' said Alison, 'you *sold* drugs to everyone.'

'Bought, sold, who cares? I supplied the drugs, and hey, I was only sixteen.'

'So, anyway, Suzanne and I, for reasons I've long since forgotten, ended up breaking into our neighbour's house.'

'We'd run out of marge.'

'What? Is that why we did it?'

'Yeah.'

'You're kidding. Why didn't we go to the Spar?'

'The Spar was closed. It was four in the morning.'

'What about the all-night garage?'

'It was too far to walk. What d'you care, this was years ago. Anyway, it all got sorted out. But not before we'd spent some time in the cells.'

Joe laughed, and looked away. Alison wondered whether he'd raised this subject as a lead in to his own prison story, but it didn't seem so, not unless he'd been so shocked by the innocence of their anecdote that he couldn't bring himself to tell them how he'd once been done for multiple-murder.

Alison looked at her watch and decided she was going to buy a Frisbee after all. Gently lifting Adrian's head, she stood up and brushed the grass from her skirt.

'Anyone else want anything?'

'What are you buying?'

'Like I said. A Frisbee.'

Joe smiled. 'Pull me up and I'll come with you.'

a temporary reconciliation

Martin stood by the car. He'd been wandering around outside for twenty minutes and he fully expected Claudia to have driven home by now. But she was nowhere to be seen. Now that he'd calmed down he realised he didn't fancy being abandoned in the service station, and worried if he went back into the restaurant to look for her, she'd return from somewhere else and drive off. So he decided to risk being mistaken for a car-thief and remain where he was.

He only had to wait another ten minutes before Claudia appeared. Walking up slowly behind him, she said, 'You didn't get far.'

'No.'

'Are we still broken up?'

'It was your idea.'

'OK . . . in that case, I declare us back together. Shall I drive us home?'

'Feel up to it?'

'Come on, get in the car.'

Claudia walked round to the driver's side and unlocked the door. Martin climbed in. She reversed out of the space and drove out of the service station.

Joe

'How well do you know my sister?'

Joe turned back and looked at her. Alison could tell from his response that he was measuring the implications behind her question, and regretted asking it.

'I work with her.'

'Oh.'

'And have done for some time. So if what you're really asking is do I know about her reputation, then the answer is yes.'

Alison looked down, embarrassed. 'I didn't mean that.'

Joe laughed. 'Yes you did, don't make it worse by back-tracking. Now, where shall we try first?'

'There's a toy shop in the next street. We turn at the corner by the pub.' She walked behind him. 'Don't tell my sister what I said.'

'Alison, do you think Suzanne would think much of me if I gossiped like that? But I do think it's wrong of you to judge your sister.'

'I don't judge her. I'm just . . .'

'What?'

'Aware that others do.'

Joe stopped. 'How's your sister ever going to change if people close to her keep reinforcing her negative self-image?'

'Does she have a negative self-image?' Alison asked, taken aback.

He didn't reply. Alison felt too guilty to argue with him. They walked to the toy shop and bought a Frisbee. As they returned to the park, Alison said, 'I don't mean to go on about this, but you and Suzanne, this is more than a one-night thing?'

'That's up to Suzanne.'

'Right.'

'Why?' he asked as they crossed the road. 'Don't you like me?'

'No, no,' she said, 'you seem very nice. I was just wonder-ing.'

He looked at her as if she'd said something ridiculous. She

wasn't surprised. *You seem very nice.* Jesus. She sounded like her mother. Worrying about her sister always brought out the worst in her.

They got back through the park gates. Alison ran across to Adrian and Suzanne, holding the Frisbee aloft triumphantly. Then she noticed that the two of them were eating ice-creams.

'You bastards. Didn't you get me one?'

Suzanne grinned. 'We didn't know how long you'd be gone.'

'Where did you get them from?'

'The van came into the park. But it's driven off now.'

'Fuck,' said Alison, sitting down, 'I'd love an ice-cream.' She looked at Adrian. 'Can I have a bit of yours?'

He shielded it with his hand. 'No way.'

'Suzanne?'

'Sorry,' she replied, lying backwards and pushing what was left of the cone into her mouth.

'Bitch.'

'Steady on,' said Adrian, 'it's only an ice-cream. Besides, we were only mucking about. The van's over there.'

He pointed behind him. Alison felt embarrassed. She stood up and turned to Joe,

'Can I get you something?' she asked.

He shook his head. 'No thanks.'

Alison made her way across the grass to the ice-cream van, feeling guilty. Her strop when Suzanne had teased her had just been a moment of sibling brattishness, but Adrian's reaction had stung her, especially coming straight after Joe had criticised her attitude towards Suzanne. She supposed it was good that someone was sticking up for her sister, and she didn't want to dislike Joe just because he'd made her feel guilty, but there was definitely something upsetting about him. She wasn't too worried at the moment, knowing that no matter what he was planning it'd be unlikely he'd be around for long, but if Suzanne was still going out with him in a couple of weeks, she'd allow herself to think more seriously about whether he made a suitable partner for her sister.

Alison brought herself a '99' with raspberry sauce. She was surprised that she still felt so beleaguered. Looking back at the others, she imagined herself as a fat kid in a playground, given a treat by the teacher to stop her from crying. She walked back over and sat on the blanket. No one said anything as she quietly finished her ice cream. Wanting to break the tension, she picked up the Frisbee and asked, 'Who wants to play then?'

living space

Martin climbed out of the car and went back inside the house. Claudia had calmed down considerably during the drive home, and he'd done his best not to aggravate her again, keeping quiet and putting on one of her favourite classical CDs for the rest of the trip. Nevertheless, he still felt unsettled, and wanted to do something that would help him get back into a good mood. Calling Naomi was out of the question, but maybe Claudia wouldn't mind if he went upstairs and sent e-mails for a while.

He opened the front door. When they'd bought this place together, he'd been very resistant to the idea of having an office. He had enough trouble forcing himself to do anything at home as it was, and the idea of replicating his day-time workspace in his house depressed him considerably. Ever since he was a teenager, he'd always done any paperwork in the largest room available, preferably on a dining-room table. This had always annoyed his parents, but having coped with their complaints for six years, he thought from then on things would get easier. And because Martin had always lived at home before he got involved with Claudia, this had never previously been a problem. But Claudia had quickly let him know that he wasn't going to be continuing this tradition while he was living with her. So he accepted the compromise of having a room to himself, but designing it so it looked as little like an office as possible. It had a computer, of course, but he'd put in a table instead of a desk, and the bookcase was filled with magazines and videos instead of edifying tomes.

Claudia came up behind him.

'I'm just going to work for a while. If that's OK.'

'Of course. Do whatever you want.'

'What are you going to do?'

'Lie down for a while. This has been a very traumatic day.'

'Do you have any idea what you want to do tonight?'

'Oh God, you're not going out, are you?'

'No. I mean, I'm definitely not going anywhere without you.'

'I don't know, Martin, I really don't feel like doing anything at the moment.'

'Well, then shall we just get a video?' He looked at her. 'Unless you fancy going to the cinema.'

'Can we talk about this later? Just let me have a rest and calm down and I might feel up to doing something.'

Martin nodded and went up to his room. He picked up the black briefcase he used for hiding any good freebees that came into the office, looking through this week's batch of CDs to see if there was anything worth listening to. Choosing the one with the least effusive write-up on the back, he put it in his computer's CD drive and pulled out the stack of flyers and invites he'd swept off his desk into his bag before coming home from work on Friday, looking to see if there was anything he might be able to go to with Claudia.

going home

They played Frisbee until six, when Alison told everyone that she and Adrian needed to get back to prepare for the Elephant & Castle party. Joe and Suzanne made fun of her for going somewhere she couldn't take them, and Adrian took the opportunity to try and get out of the night ahead, but she still managed to shepherd them out of the park and onto the bus.

'Thanks for this afternoon, sis,' Suzanne said. 'It was fun.'

'For me too,' she said, squeezing her arm. 'Maybe we can do it again next weekend.'

Alison smiled and made her way down to the back seat.

They got back to the house just before seven. Alison took the phone and called Emma to confirm the plans for the evening. The group had decided to assemble outside Southwark station, then go looking for somewhere to drink. Alison told Emma that sounded fine.

persuasion

'And exactly how many of your weirdos will be there?'

Martin knew when he was being thrown a bone. He still had to be careful, but Claudia's open body-language suggested that she was prepared to be persuaded into going to the party. And he was great at these sort of situations, understanding he was being called upon to offer reassurance.

'None. I mean, I'm sure I'll know a few people, but there'll be no one you don't like, I promise. It'll be a much younger crowd.'

Claudia considered this. 'I do feel like going out. But the Elephant & Castle is miles away. How are we going to get back?'

'It says on the invite that there'll be a cab service running all night.'

'Yeah, that's fine if we don't mind being robbed and killed on the way back.'

'No, I know, well, I don't know them personally, but I've heard great things about the guys behind this magazine. They plan all their social events with the utmost precision.'

'Alright,' she said, 'but let's go late and not stay for long. I hate all that hanging around.'

Melissa's vibrator

Alison checked her reflection in the mirror. She rarely wore dresses to work, preferring to alternate between a jacket with smart trousers and a more casual look. She had a few designer items, but most of her stuff came from Karen Millen. She did, however, have a few favourite outfits that she'd mainly picked up on trips to visit friends in France or America, or been given as presents by her mother. Tonight she was wearing a silver dress her mother had bought her last Christmas. She thought she'd look a bit overdressed to begin with, but hopefully they wouldn't stay in a bar too long and she wouldn't feel out of place when they reached the party.

Besides, having a scruffy boyfriend was like matching an expensive outfit with trainers, immediately normalising her.

She spent another ten minutes touching up her make-up and then went to fetch Adrian from the lounge. It was a mild, warmish evening, and Alison decided to risk going out in the same light jacket she'd worn to the park.

When they got out of the tube at Southwark, Adrian seemed unduly impressed by the space-age design of the station, muttering to himself as they looked for an exit.

A man was standing alone across the road.

'Do you reckon he's with us?' Adrian asked Alison.

'I don't know. I don't recognise him. Let's go across and ask.'

The man turned out to be much taller than he'd seemed from a distance, not far shy of seven foot and almost albino in his colouring. His hair was shaggy. He seemed nervous as they approached him, only relaxing when Alison asked, 'Are you waiting for Emma?'

He nodded. 'Yeah.' He offered them his hand and said in a voice that immediately revealed he hailed from the West Country, 'I'm Steve.'

'Hi, Steve, I'm Alison and this is Adrian.'

He took off his walkman and looked back at the entrance to the station. A skinny man in a blue jacket stood with a slightly broader brown-haired man. The skinny man had spiky black hair and silver glasses. His friend looked more sure of himself, shouting hello to Steve as he crossed the road. Steve introduced the skinny man as Mike and his friend as Tony.

Mike seemed quite shy, beginning a conversation with Steve and Adrian, and leaving Alison to Tony. Alison felt nervous as Tony, who was quite a theatrical sort, started chatting her up, worried that her boyfriend would think she was encouraging this stranger's advances. But Adrian seemed absorbed in conversation with Mike and Steve, and Alison was surprised to hear him laughing every so often. She heard Steve telling Adrian that he was a comedian.

After a short while, the men fell silent. Alison followed Tony's gaze and saw the reason why they'd gone quiet. A beautiful blonde woman wearing a low-cut burgundy top was coming out of the tube station and walking towards them. Alison realised this woman was also part of their party.

The blonde woman seemed to be a friend of Mike and Tony's, but Alison couldn't tell whether she also knew Steve or not. She felt a churlish resentment of this new woman, who made her feel overdressed and under-attractive. The woman looked so good that Alison could tell she had to dress down just to get through the day unmolested. The minute she joined their cluster, Tony left Alison alone, and she had the upsetting sense that he'd been merely practising his lines on her.

When Emma arrived with four of her friends in tow, they decided to head for a bar, and inform the others where they'd gone on their mobiles. Of the nine people yet to show up, two weren't coming until ten, and the rest were due to join them at the party, so it wasn't too hard to organise. Alison was just relieved to be going to a bar, surprised by how strongly she was craving her first drink of the evening.

They found a hotel with a private bar and filed inside. Taking over the back room, they pulled two tables together and spread themselves out. Alison and Adrian were tucked in the corner with Tony, Mike, Steve and the attractive blonde woman. Tony offered to buy the blonde woman a drink and everyone on their side of the table chipped in with their orders. His friend laughed.

'Fuck you, Mike, you can get the next round.'

Alison leaned in closer to the blonde woman. 'I'm sorry, I missed your name.'

'Melissa.'

'I'm Alison. And this is my boyfriend, Adrian.'

Melissa leaned across and shook hands with Adrian. Her top was so low-cut that Alison not only noticed that she was wearing a red bra, but also that the material beneath her left breast had worn away enough to reveal the metal underwire. This made her feel fonder of the woman, even before she'd said anything. As she sat back, Melissa seemed to notice Alison staring at her bra. Embarrassed, Alison asked, 'So how do you know these guys?'

'She's been living with us,' Mike explained. 'In Steve's room.'

Steve wanted to explain. 'They kicked me out and gave my room to that slut.'

'Oi,' said Melissa, kicking Steve under the table, 'I hardly know you. So you don't get to call me that.'

'But Mike calls you slut all the time.'

'I'm allowed to. I've seen her vibrator.'

She turned to him. 'Thanks, Mike.' She looked at the others. 'It was a present, OK?'

'From Tony,' Mike explained, giggling and rubbing his hands. Alison was struck by how much he looked like a mechanical monkey.

'Yes. From Tony,' she repeated wearily, clearly used to this topic coming up.

'She's worn the batteries out.'

146

'OK, Mike, that's now officially enough. No one wants to hear any more about it.'

getting there

Martin arranged for the taxi to come at eleven. He and Claudia had kept away from each other during the earlier part of the evening and were now feeling companionable again. Martin made sure not to moan about the length of time it took Claudia to get ready, and she even gave him a long kiss before they walked out to the cab.

The taxi journey was long, but thankfully the driver didn't attempt to engage them in conversation. Martin contented himself with gently stroking Claudia's thigh as she looked out of the window. It was times like this that Martin felt pleased he was married, and, as he'd suspected that morning, it did seem that their argument had brought them closer together.

There was a line of cars leading up to the film studio, and the driver had to drop them off a short distance from the main gate. Martin paid him, got a receipt, then took Claudia's hand and led her towards the queue. He always enjoyed being outside at night, and was pleased that Claudia seemed excited by the size of the party. Seeing her like this made him wonder why he didn't bring her out more often.

'Is that Ronnie Herman?'

'Who's Ronnie Herman?'

'You remember,' Claudia told him. 'You introduced me to him. He's that rich guy who buys lots of art.'

'Dealer?'

'No, a private collector. Come on, let's go say hi.'

Martin let Claudia drag him across to the well-dressed art

collector. He really was a smooth piece of work, having achieved at the age of thirty an air of sophistication it would take most people a lifetime to achieve.

'Martin, hi,' he said, gripping his hand, 'so sorry to hear your sad news.'

Surprised, and not knowing how to respond, Martin ushered forward his eager wife.

'You remember Claudia.'

'Of course,' he said, giving her the briefest of smiles, 'but Martin, have you any idea what you're going to do next?'

'He's becoming a pornographer.'

Ronnie laughed. 'No, but seriously, Martin, what are you going to do?'

'A mainstream porn mag.'

'Oh, right, you are serious. But you don't mean actual porn do you? You're going to do something like Bob did with *Gear*.'

'No, it's real porn. Only in a mainstream context.'

Ronnie considered this. 'Well, Martin, I have to confess, I've got no idea what you're talking about. It sounds like madness to me. But that doesn't mean it's not genius. Tell me, are you looking for investors?'

gasheads

By the time of last orders, everyone had arrived and they decided to get taxis to the party. Alison shared her cab with Adrian and Melissa. She sat in the front, leaving the other two together in the back. The cab took them to the film studio where the party was taking place and they looked for the others in the queue.

As they were depositing their jackets in the cloakroom, the

rest of the group showed up. Going into the first room, Alison was immediately impressed by the scale of the party. There was already what looked like around five hundred people in the main room, standing around a kidney-shaped red neon bar. Hardcore pornography was being projected on one wall, a video of chimps playing with urine samples on another. The crowd was better dressed than she'd expected and Alison felt glad she'd decided on the silver dress. The music was white-boy's hip-hop, lyrics removed so everyone could feel comfortable getting off on the beats. So far she couldn't see anyone she knew, and she decided to stay with her group for the time being.

'Shall we check out the other rooms?' Emma asked everyone.

'Yeah,' said Steve, 'maybe we'll find a bar that's less crowded.'

They let him lead and followed behind. Alison smiled at Adrian and squeezed his hand, hoping he was happy to be at the party. The next room had more hardcore music, and almost everyone in the crowd was dancing. She looked at the scary specimens up on the podium and then realised it was probably her round. Mike had continued into the next room, and just as Alison was being served, he ran back in saying excitably, 'They're giving away free nitrous oxide outside.'

Alison laughed, despite herself. Free nitrous oxide seemed exactly the thing that would excite this strange, small, simian man. She distributed the drinks and everyone made their way through the next room and out into the forecourt. A small group was gathered around a man filling coloured balloons with the gas and handing them out. They walked across and joined the back of the queue.

Claudia and Ronnie

Once into the party, Claudia suggested trying to find some-where quiet to continue their conversation. Ronnie remained stubbornly beside them, and Martin concluded that Ronnie had no friends and had only come to the party to pick someone up. Martin wondered if Ronnie would attempt to chat up Claudia in front of him. It would take skill to be flirtatious enough with Claudia to ensure she'd go on a secret date with him while not being so obvious that he aroused Martin's anger.

Ronnie started by offering to buy them both drinks. Smooth, but obvious. Martin resisted the temptation to say something about Ronnie's behaviour to Claudia, finding it refreshing to be in the right for once. Martin hadn't always been as relaxed about infidelity as he was now, but preferred to think this was because he'd grown more mature rather than it being an indication of the state of their marriage.

Martin could tell Claudia was trying not to seem too anxious about Ronnie's return, and in spite of everything, he found himself feeling fond of his wife. Part of him just wanted to give her his blessing and leave the two of them to get it on, but he knew that would make her feel guilty. When he'd been younger, he'd hated this sort of scene, and part of the reason he'd ended up as he had was because he'd always been so terrified of becoming the jealous cuckold. It seemed far safer to get in with the first strike, and then, once he'd done it once . . .

'What are you thinking?' Claudia asked.

'Nothing much. Glad you came?'

'Yes,' she said, smiling, 'actually I am. I will give you one thing, Martin Powell, you know how to salvage a ruined day.'

He smiled, but didn't respond, not wanting her to qualify the compliment. But it was one of the qualities he admired in himself, and while so far it had only proved valuable in helping him sustain relationships with depressive girlfriends, he hoped that it would one day also help him to be a good father.

Ronnie returned with the drinks. 'What's with the balloons?'

'Some sort of gas. Why, want to try it?'

'Not for the minute.' Ronnie smiled. 'So, Claudia, tell me what you've been up to.'

McDonald's

Alison and Adrian left the party around three, accompanied by Steve and Melissa. Over the course of the evening (and much to the obvious irritation of Mike and Tony) Melissa seemed to have decided that she would be going home with the tall comedian instead of the two jokers, and now the four of them were looking for a taxi.

'Is anyone hungry?' Melissa asked as they reached the main road.

'I am,' said Steve, 'but I don't fancy walking far.'

'How about the drive-thru McDonald's? That's about a minute from here,' Adrian suggested.

'How do you know that?'

'It's on the invitation.'

'Can we get served there?'

'I think so. They usually have a walk-up window as well, don't they?'

Alison shrugged and the four of them walked to the

restaurant. After they'd been served, they walked across to the small picnic area outside and sat down.

'Good party,' said Steve, looking round at the others.

'Yeah,' Alison agreed, 'although I got a bit bored with the music.'

Adrian grinned at Melissa. 'Did he pull you at the party?'

'Adrian,' Alison admonished, shocked.

'No,' she said, 'it's OK. He didn't really pull me, as such. I've always had a soft spot for tall, funny men.'

'She twisted my arm,' Steve told them, 'although admittedly not very hard.'

'Lucky fucker.'

Melissa laughed.

McDonald's II

'I'll only be a minute.'

'And what am I supposed to do? Wait here for someone to rape me?'

'No one's going to rape you. Come on, Claudia, I'm starving.'

'Can't you wait till we get home? I'll make you a sandwich.'

'Seriously, Claud, I'll be back before you've noticed I've gone.'

She thrust her hands into her pockets and turned away. Martin left her to her mood and walked down to the McDonald's. There was no one queuing by the window so he went straight up and ordered a Big Mac meal. Taking his brown paper bag, he started walking back towards the main road when he noticed a group of four people sitting around one of the outside picnic tables. Although the two men looked like gimps, the women they were with were extraordinarily attractive. He didn't usually go for blondes, but even from this distance the woman looked incredible. Her friend was more his type, a thin, sexy woman in a stylish silver dress. She had hennaed hair, but he'd grown more used to finding that attractive since Alison had started working for him. He realised the women had noticed him staring, and got ready to move on, not wanting them to dispatch their boyfriends over to beat him up.

'Martin,' the woman shouted.

He looked again, surprised, and saw the woman *was* his assistant, beckoning him over with a friendly wave. Martin headed over. Alison stood up and came across, kissing him on both cheeks. Her lips were greasy from her fast food, but Martin didn't say anything, letting her give him a hug.

'Were you at the party?' She checked herself. 'Of course you were at the party. I didn't know you'd be there. I thought you went down to your wife's parents at the weekend.'

'Yeah,' he said, then not knowing what to say next, smiled and shrugged. She looked at him a second longer, before gesturing to the other people at the table and saying to Martin, 'You've met my boyfriend before, right? And this is Melissa and Steve.'

Martin smiled at them, but moved back slightly, finding the tall man strange and not wanting to shake his hand.

'Nice to meet you. Listen, Alison, I'm sorry, I'd better get back. My wife's waiting.'

'No problem. I'll see you Monday.'

'Yeah. See you.'

Martin ran back across the tarmac to where Claudia was waiting. He had already decided that he wouldn't tell her about running into Alison, even though he'd seen her pass Ronnie Herman her business card at the party. After all, he'd seen his assistant every day at work for months and months and never felt this way before. And there was no reason why he should feel this way again, as long as she didn't wear that dress into work.

Cause that's all it was, he told himself.

Just the dress.

Sunday

breakfast

'Pear and bananas?'

Martin looked up from his newspaper. 'OK,' he told her, 'but don't chop them up. Just give me the whole fruit.'

He watched her break off a banana from a bunch and put it in a bowl with a large green pear. The reason Claudia was offering him this particular combination of fruit was that they received a box from the organic distributors every Monday evening and by Sunday they were left to finish up the fruit that neither of them especially liked. He knew this was a waste of money, but as it was his only concession to healthy living, he felt reluctant to give it up.

'Orange juice?'

'Why not?'

She poured him a glass and placed it in front of him on the table.

'I called my mum.'

'Really? Are things . . . OK?'

'My brother's dumped Tilly.'

'Really? Oh God. She must hate me.'

'I doubt it. She seemed to think you were fairly fantastic. And it didn't look like she was that interested in my brother.'

'God.'

'What?'

Martin started peeling his banana. 'I was just thinking. What if she's told the other Thélèmites?'

157

'Your secret society? Oh, don't be ridiculous. No one carries on caring about that sort of thing after they've finished university.'

'The Thélèmites do.'

'Oh, stop being stupid. It's not like you see those people any more.'

'Are you kidding? I run into someone from Cambridge every single day. And besides, I still go to their reunions.'

Claudia turned on him. 'When? When do you go to their reunions?'

'Well, I haven't for a while,' he lied, not wanting to get in trouble, 'but I might want to in the future. And you don't understand, it's not even that which worries me. There were lots of *important* people in the Thélèmites. Reputations are at stake here.'

She stood looking at him for a moment. Martin tried to indicate how serious he was about this by keeping an entirely straight face.

'OK,' she said finally, 'if you're that worried, why don't you call my parents' house?'

the morning after

Alison had fucked Adrian with such ferocity when they'd got back last night that she awoke feeling unable to move from her bed. The energetic sex had been intended to stop her thinking about Martin, but she still dreamt about him doing all kinds of terrible things to her from the moment she passed into sleep until the final second before she woke up. She didn't really understand what had changed between them, but she knew that *something* had happened last night, and at the very least, Monday morning was going to be extremely difficult.

Julian

Martin crossed his office, sat down at his desk and dialled the number Claudia had written out for him.

'Hello?'

'Hi, it's Martin. Can I speak to Julian?'

The voice on the other end was stern and clipped. 'This is Julian.'

'Oh, OK,' Martin replied, wobbling slightly, 'the reason I'm calling is that I wanted to talk about yesterday.'

His stomach felt on edge as he waited for a reply. He'd never really liked Claudia's brother and he knew Julian wouldn't make it easy for him. If he wasn't genuinely afraid about the potential consequences, he'd curtail the conversation right now. But the danger was just real enough to make him press on.

'What about it?' he replied.

Martin sat down behind his desk. 'Claudia told me you broke up with Tilly.'

'That's right.'

'Well, I just wanted to check that it wasn't because of what Claud had said I said.'

'Why?' he asked. 'Wasn't it true?'

Martin put his feet up against the desk and pushed himself backwards. 'No, yes, it was true, but it was the way Claud put it. The thing is, you know how people are at university . . .'

Julian laughed. 'Not really, Martin, at least I know I never got lots of men to masturbate over me. Or women, for that matter.'

Martin sighed, sensing he wasn't going to get anywhere. It wasn't that he couldn't understand why Julian was getting upset. Nobody liked hearing about their partner's past sex-life, especially when it was as colourful as Tilly's had been. And he had felt bad that Claudia had talked about Tilly in front of Julian's family. But he knew he had to put such considerations aside if he was going to be able to protect himself.

'I understand why you're reacting like this, but I just wanted to put what I'd said into context.'

'I seriously doubt there's any context where being the target for a circle-jerk can be seen as respectable.'

'Well, no, but . . .'

'Look, Martin, I'm grateful for your concern, but to be perfectly honest, I didn't just break up with Tilly because of your sordid stories. Things weren't right between us.'

'But I thought you'd only been going out for a few months?'

'So? That was more than long enough to discover we weren't compatible.'

Martin picked up a pen from his desk. 'OK, I'm not trying to tell you how to run your personal life, I've said what I wanted to say . . . but Julian, I do have to ask you two favours.'

He didn't reply.

'The first is . . . and if it's genuinely true that you didn't break up with Tilly because of my story then this shouldn't be a problem for you . . . please can you not tell anyone that I told you about the Thélèmites?'

'And the second favour?'

'Could you give me Tilly's phone number?'

'Why?'

'Because I'd like to talk to her. Catch up on old times.'

Julian snorted, then gave Martin the number.

After Julian had hung up, Martin wished he'd asked for Tilly's e-mail instead, feeling scared that she wouldn't have believed Julian's excuses and might hold him responsible for the end of her relationship. But although he was trying to remain light-hearted about the whole thing, he was genuinely afraid that if his betrayal of her confidence did get back to some of the stranger members of his old secret circle, he could find himself in trouble. A career in magazines had taught him that most people took offence at the slightest opportunity, especially in London, where new friendships came cheap, and where it was always worth making a few extra phone-calls to check you hadn't upset anyone. So he steeled himself and dialled her number.

He wasn't sure whether Julian had given him the wrong number deliberately, but there was no response from the other end. No ansaphone either, and, peculiarly, the line cut off completely after three or four rings. He tried once more, then replaced the receiver and went back downstairs.

Martin looked across at Claudia, who was sprawled across the sofa, shuffling through the Sunday papers.

'Sorted?' she asked.

'Not really. I spoke to Julian but couldn't get through to Tilly.'

'I really wouldn't worry, Martin. It hardly seems the sort of thing one would want to talk about.'

He nodded, distracted. 'Do you feel like going out for a walk?'

'Now?'

'Why not? That's what we'd be doing if we were still at your parents.'

'But there's nowhere to walk round here.'

'Well then let's drive somewhere. I don't know, I just feel like getting some fresh air.'

'We could do that, I suppose. Maybe have a pub lunch.'

'If you like.'

'OK,' she smiled, 'I'll go and get ready.'

sunday lunch

Alison stopped outside Suzanne's room, wondering if it was worth trying to wake her up for Sunday lunch. Suzanne had to work until six a.m. on Saturdays, but she would often get angry if Alison ate without waking her. It amused Alison that in spite of all her wayward tendencies, Suzanne seemed much more influenced by their family's old habits than she was. Both their parents had been strong believers in maintaining the tradition of Sunday lunch. For years, it'd been the one time each week when the family got together and talked. Suzanne had got into huge fights with them over how hard it was to find someone chilled enough to drive her home from raves on Sunday mornings, but now she seemed just as committed an advocate of this meal-time as they had been. So Alison knocked.

A groan emerged from inside.

'It's only me,' Alison said quickly, 'Adrian and I are thinking of going to *The Falcon* for lunch in half an hour or so. Would you like to come with us?'

No response. Alison walked back towards the lounge. Then she heard her sister shout, 'Yes. Hang on. Don't go without us.'

Alison looked at Suzanne. She was wearing a blue T-shirt that had once belonged to her. Although Alison and Suzanne tended not to have the usual sibling fights about stealing each other's clothes, often Alison knew from the moment she bought something it would end up in her sister's wardrobe.

'No, like I said, you've still got half an hour.' She paused. 'Is Joe still with you?'

'Yeah,' she replied defensively, 'is that a problem?'

'Not at all. I was just curious.'

Alison went into the lounge and sat down in the chair next to where Adrian was sprawled on a settee, trying to get his elbows onto the coffee table so he could finish rolling his spliff.

'That bloke still with her?'

'Seems so. Why? Don't you like him?'

'Nah, he's alright. Just a bit scruffy.'

Alison laughed.

'What?' he asked.

'And you don't think you're scruffy?'

He scrambled up. 'I make an effort.'

Alison looked at her boyfriend's bedraggled blond hair and decided against prolonging the argument. But she did wonder whether his criticism of Suzanne's boyfriend meant there had been some romantic interaction between him and her sister after all, and she realised that even though this would be the perfect excuse for her to have an affair with Martin, she wouldn't be able to forgive such a serious betrayal.

Although she didn't consider herself an innocent person, Alison was always surprised when she heard that someone she knew was having an affair. Maybe she'd just always had super-secretive partners, but as far as she knew, no one she'd

163

ever been out with, apart from Adrian, that once, had cheated on her, and except for her one minor lapse, she had always remained faithful herself. Now and again there had been tiny overlaps, but she'd always hated those periods and had never been able to love more than one person at a time. Oh, she'd certainly thought she loved Martin before, but that had only ever been a silly crush. Which was why she now felt terrified about the possibility of it turning into something serious. She didn't want to go out with Martin: he was sleazy, untrustworthy, and maybe even a misogynist. He treated his wife like shit, and if she was to make her feelings known, she knew he'd expect her to have an affair with him. No, it was definitely best to keep quiet.

But what if she couldn't? What if last night was only the beginning? She knew there was something strange in her psychology that stopped her enjoying any kind of duplicity, and if she really started thinking seriously about Martin, it would only be a matter of time before something inside her made the connection a reality. She'd read enough magazine articles to know that it was healthy to occasionally fantasise about people other than your partner when making love or masturbating, but although she often needed to do that to reach orgasm, she was always careful to keep these imaginings abstract. Her private erotic life was full of anonymous individuals, or objects and fetishes, and last night's sex-dream seemed a dangerous omen. Martin was in her thoughts now, and it would be hard to get him out.

a marriage worth salvaging

Martin put his hand on Claudia's leg as she drove him to the park. She looked at him out of the corner of her eye and smiled. He now found he wanted to have sex with her, and wished he hadn't suggested going for a walk. Back in the house he'd thought that getting outside would give him the mental space to think about Alison, but now he realised that this made little difference. Often when he was with his wife the only way Martin could escape the pressure of her presence was to make love to her. He knew that if his body was servicing her, his thoughts would be his own, but as long as they were spending time together finding such peace was impossible.

'What are you thinking about?' she asked.

'Us,' he said. 'It seems odd, but very nice, to be spending a weekend together. I mean, I know we always spend our weekends together, but this feels different. Away from your parents, I guess.'

'I know what you mean,' she smiled, 'Martin . . .'

'Yeah?'

'I'm going to stop seeing Clive. At all. I don't think it's helping us. And although I don't want to spend another second talking about it, I've come to an understanding with myself about your affairs. Of course, I'd be happiest if you could stop fucking other people, but I'm not going to demean myself by asking you to do that. We've been through a lot, you and me, and I think it's worth us making an effort to save our marriage.'

'What about my new job?'

She rubbed her forehead. 'Oh God, Martin, what do you want me to say? Of course I'm going to be unhappy about being married to a pornographer, but I can see how it could be an exciting concept. Ronnie certainly seemed . . .'

'Ronnie.'

'Yeah.' She glanced at him. 'Well, he was desperate to give you money last night.'

'Are you going to have an affair with him?'

'What?'

'You gave him your card.'

'For business purposes. Jesus, Martin, the whole point of having this conversation is to convince you I'm going to concentrate on making us work.'

'You didn't answer my question.'

'Martin . . . what exactly do you want?'

'Huh?'

'It's a straightforward question. I'm here telling you that I'm prepared to put up with your affairs, can cope with you devoting your life to exploiting women and am willing to do just about anything to keep us together and you're interpreting that as me saying I'm going to have an affair?'

'It's a separate issue,' he said calmly, 'and I'm not worried, I just want to know.'

'No, Martin, I'm not going to have an affair with Ronnie.'

'Why not?'

'What?' she asked, her tone incredulous.

'Indulge me for a moment. Tell me why you're not going to fuck him.'

Claudia glanced across again. He smiled back. She leaned forward. 'You are so perverse,' she told him, sounding less angry than she had before.

'I don't mean to be. But we used to enjoy talking about this stuff, remember? Some man'd be hitting on you at a party and then we'd go home and you'd tell me why you hadn't been interested.'

'You really want me to talk about Ronnie?'

'I really do.'

'Well,' she smiled, 'he reminds me of Michael Douglas.'

'And that isn't sexy?' Martin asked, surprised.

'I suppose it could be. But I mean Michael Douglas in

that film where he plays an art dealer and tries to kill his wife.'

'*A Perfect Murder*?'

'Yeah.'

Martin smiled. 'He definitely wants you.'

'For an afternoon, maybe. But it wouldn't be worth it.'

'I feel like that sometimes,' he told her, 'when someone comes on to me and I know they only want me for a little while.'

Claudia didn't reply. Martin stopped talking, scared about what he might say next. His last remark had been intended as a compliment, but after he'd said it he realised it hadn't come out that way. He was glad Claudia didn't seem to have picked up on it, but just because she hadn't said anything didn't mean she wasn't turning it over in her mind. He knew if he carried on talking it wouldn't be long before he mentioned Alison, and in spite of the directions their relationship seemed to have taken over the weekend, he knew this could only be a mistake.

the Falcon

They had chosen a terrible time to show up at the pub. Families and small groups of elderly people staked out all the tables, most looking like they'd settled in for the afternoon. Alison was ready to leave, but just as they were about to do so a couple vacated a small square table by the door, and, grabbing two bar-stools, the four of them quickly sat down.

'Drinks?' Alison asked.

'Good idea,' Joe smiled, 'I'll have a pint of Pride.'

The other two told Alison what they wanted and she walked up to the bar. She was beginning to find it easier to get

167

her mind off Martin, mainly because she'd gone back to considering how their lives might change if Suzanne's relationship with Joe did become permanent. She still felt upset about the conversation she'd had with him yesterday, and had tried since then to get her current feelings about her sister straight. For all she knew, Joe might already have broken his promise not to tell Suzanne that she'd asked him about her reputation, and Alison thought she should prepare herself in case they ended up arguing about what she'd said. She knew it was terrible, but it was an undeniable truth that she'd definitely felt closer to Suzanne when they were both kids, and the promiscuity had been the only real factor in weakening their relationship. Joe could criticise her for that, but it didn't matter. It was, after all, only because she cared. She got far more upset about her sister's habits than her parents did, and no matter how hard she tried to see Suzanne's sex-life as some fantastic act of female emancipation, she just couldn't square this with the horny, fidgety, dead-eyed men her sister had spent several years bringing home.

Joe wasn't much of an improvement, but that didn't matter. What Alison found so exciting was the prospect of her sister dropping her silly, cynical act and actually admitting she cared about someone. So far she'd been tight-lipped about her feelings, but it wasn't as if Alison expected things to change overnight. This would be a slow process, but Alison truly believed that by the end of it she'd have her sister back.

Monday

monday morning

Alison lay in bed, listening to the chorus of *Lize* on her stereo-alarm and wondering why she'd yet to get up and switch it off. The lyrics were even more unsettling than usual today, and she knew Adrian would wake up if she let the tape play much longer. She scrambled down to the bottom of the bed and stretched across to where the alarm was perched on top of a pile of Adrian's dirty clothes. Switching it off, she sat up and got out of bed.

She walked across the upstairs landing to the shower. She had decided last night that no matter what happened today she definitely wasn't going to fuck Martin. For a while yesterday she had thought that in spite of everything, if he asked her in the right sort of way, she might find it impossible to resist. But now she had a handle on her feelings. It wasn't her relationship with Adrian that stopped her; it was the fact that it didn't fit in with the way she saw herself. True, she had cheated on her boyfriend once before, but that had happened at a time when they hadn't been getting on well and it'd even seemed conceivable that they might split up. And while she still didn't know how long she'd stay with Adrian, she wasn't sure she wanted this indiscretion in her past.

She took off her dressing-gown, hung it on the back of the bathroom door, and stepped into the shower.

reflection

Martin spat a mouthful of toothpaste and water into the sink and checked his reflection. He had been worried recently that he was beginning to develop a double-chin. Although most of his male friend's faces had started filling out by their mid-twenties, he had cut back on the boozing and managed to maintain his enviably square jaw for the next ten years. Now, though, after six months of increased indulgence, he was beginning to develop a small fleshy frog's belly beneath his chin. It was only slight, and not that noticeable apart from when it was shaded with stubble, but he couldn't help wishing it wasn't there.

He sat on the toilet, knowing that it was only his sudden infatuation with Alison that was making him vain. It seemed ridiculous that he was already worrying about ageing, especially as he still had a healthy mop of hair and a slim waistline, but he sensed that Alison would be harder to seduce than most women, and didn't want to start off feeling insecure.

He got dressed and walked out into the street to hail a cab. So far his last two months of employment were turning out to be less irritating than he imagined they would be, and he was already planning to waste as much of the company's time and money as was possible without getting caught.

gossip

Alison boarded the lift at the ground floor. This time when Gareth came in behind her she wasn't even surprised.

'I hear you went to a party with Martin at the weekend.'

'Where do you get this stuff, Gareth?'

He grinned, clearly pleased with himself.

'No,' she continued, 'tell me. Do you pay people? How do you do it? No, I didn't go to a party with Martin. I went to a party with some friends.'

'But Martin was at the party?'

'Yes, Gareth, Martin was at the party.'

'And you talked to him?'

'Purely in the interests of helping you get your facts straight I'll tell you the truth, Gareth. Steady yourself, G, cause this is pretty explosive stuff. I went to the party with some friends, Martin went with his wife. Then we ended up meeting at McDonald's and talked for about two minutes. Satisfied?'

The lift stopped and they both got out.

giving the game away

Martin sat in his office, waiting for Alison to show up. It was the first time he'd ever got in before her, and he worried that she'd take his early arrival as an indication of his new interest in her. *And what's so wrong with that*, he asked himself, *that's exactly what you want, isn't it?*

He'd spent a lot of time thinking about that moment outside McDonald's, replaying it over and over in a way he'd only previously done with the most erotic moments of his past existence. And although Martin wasn't an incredibly perceptive person, the more he thought about it, the more convinced he'd become that whatever happened had been a two-way thing.

Martin looked up from his computer. He couldn't concentrate. Maybe Alison didn't know he was in yet. Perhaps she was already setting up in her space outside his office. He got up and walked towards his door.

Just as he got there, Alison appeared.

the other side

Alison looked away, embarrassed. Although Martin always dressed well, he definitely seemed to have taken as much time over his appearance today as she had. Feeling light-headed, she asked, 'So where do we go from here?'

He quickly looked up. So she was right. And in spite of all her earlier promises to herself not to get involved, it already seemed too late.

Tuesday

tits

'Do we have to see her tits?' Lenny asked his sister.

'Are you kidding?' she exclaimed. 'Of course we have to see her tits. That's the whole point of the programme.'

'OK,' he said wearily, 'don't get heavy handed with the girl. Let me talk to the manager.'

Naomi dragged on her cigarette, cross. 'Christ. I can't believe we've ended up with a shy lap-dancer.'

'She's not shy, she's French. She doesn't understand what's going on.'

'Whatever.'

'And she's not used to dancing for so many people.'

'Alright, Lenny, alright. Go talk to the manager.'

Lenny looked from Naomi to Martin. 'Martin, come with me.'

'OK.'

They left Naomi with the cameraman and went to find the manager. He seemed an odd type to be in charge of a strip-club, looking more like a supply-teacher than Peter Stringfellow. As he started talking, however, Martin realised his authority came from his voice rather than his appearance.

'How's it going?' he asked in a carefully measured tone.

'Great,' Lenny replied, 'but listen, there's a problem with the girl.'

'Nikita? What's wrong with her? She's the best dancer in the club.'

'I know. She's great. But she doesn't want to show her tits

to the cameraman.'

He peered at them.

'Is he a weirdo?'

'The cameraman? No, of course not. He's one of our best.'

'Only the girls are very sensitive to that sort of thing. If she's not showing her tits, it's probably because he's giving off bad vibes.'

'It's nothing to do with his vibes. I think the problem is that there's a group of us.'

He nodded. 'Could be. Nikita only does lap-dances, y'know. She doesn't go up on stage.'

'Well, we really need a group in the programme, and we need tits. Do you have another girl we can use?'

'Nikita's our best girl. She's the one we want in the pictures. She's the face that'll bring people into the club.'

'Can you talk to her then? Reassure her that everything's alright.'

'I could do. But I don't know if it'll do any good. My French isn't up to much.'

'OK. Look. There's a guy in our party who's French. I'll get him to talk to her. But in the meantime, can you buy her a drink?'

'I can't do that.'

'Why not?'

'Not in front of the other girls.'

'Right,' said Lenny, exasperated. He started to walk away when the manager tapped him on the shoulder and gave him a few pieces of coloured paper.

'What's this?' he asked.

'That's the lap-dancing money we use in the club. Get one of your guys to buy her a drink and pay for a solo dance. That'll calm her down.'

Martin and Lenny walked back to the others. Naomi sipped

her drink and asked, 'What did he say?'

'Where's Benoît?'

'At the bar.'

She pointed to where Benoît was sitting with Laetitia, the two of them already engrossed in conversation with an auburn-haired lap-dancer and clearly on the verge of paying for a private show.

'Go and talk to him, Martin. Explain what's going on.'

'Why do I have to do it?'

'Huh?'

'It's your fucking programme. Why do I have to sort everything out?'

'Listen, Martin, I'm asking you as a friend. I don't want to talk to that freaky exchange-student. He gives me the creeps.'

'He gives me the creeps too.'

'But you know him. It's different.'

'I don't know him.'

'Enough,' said Naomi, 'Lenny, sit down. Martin, go talk to Benoît.'

Martin walked across to Benoît, Laetitia and the lap-dancer. Laetitia was the only one who turned to acknowledge him, the girl and Benoît continuing to flirt.

'Benoît . . .'

'Yes?'

'I need you to get a lap-dance.'

'Yes, Martin, I am about to get one.'

'Not with this girl. With Nikita.'

'Who's Nikita?'

'She's over there.'

He looked across. 'Is this for the programme?'

'Sort of.'

'Then I'm sorry, I cannot do it. My father . . .'

'We're not going to film you. The thing is, we need to calm

179

the girl down. She's not used to dancing for so many people and she doesn't want to show her tits. Basically, you have to let her dance for you and while she's at it, explain what's going on. Do you think you can handle that?'

'OK,' said Benoît. 'She is the girl over there?'

'Yes.' He handed him the coloured paper. 'And this is what you use to pay her.'

Benoît took the fake money and walked across. Martin took his empty seat.

'So, are you two actually dating now?'

She nodded. 'He's really nice. Once you get to know him.'

Naomi appeared at the table. 'What's going on? Is Pete supposed to be filming?'

'No, not yet.'

'Well, someone better tell him. He's going across.'

Martin watched as Pete walked over to the camera and started filming. As soon as Benoît noticed the camera, he immediately stood up and held his hand palm outwards, protesting. Then Nikita realised what was going on and shrieked and grabbed her dress from the floor, using it to cover her breasts.

'Oh Christ,' said Martin wearily.

Laetitia gave him an earnest look. 'Martin, distract Benoît and I'll do it.'

'Do what?'

'Get my tits out. It's not that big a deal. Besides, I've got a much better body than she has.'

'What's wrong with her body?' Martin asked, surprised.

'Oh, come on, her arse is huge. And her underwear is tacky. Look, come on, or I'll withdraw my offer.'

Martin looked at his watch. 'OK, you go tell Lenny and I'll check with the manager. He seemed pretty keen that we filmed Nikita.'

He stepped up from the floor area and went back to the manager.

'Tell that cameraman not to fuck with my girls.'

'Look, I know, but he didn't mean it. I should have told him, sorry.'

'Is Nikita OK?'

'I think so, but she still doesn't want to do the picture. What do you think about Laetitia?'

'Who's Laetitia? We don't have any girls called Laetitia.'

'No, Laetitia's the girl down there. The one who came with us. How would you feel if she was in the picture instead.'

'But she doesn't work here.'

'I know, but that doesn't really matter does it? If you've got a problem we can go to another club, but I really wanted to do the pictures here.'

'Which one's Laetitia?'

'The one in the pink.'

'And can she dance?'

'Well, she's not a professional, but I'm sure she can manage to make it look convincing.'

The manager looked away. 'Maybe, but I'd better come over to supervise. I don't want the people watching this programme to think we have amateur dancers.'

'OK, see that guy in black? He's Lenny, the producer. He's the one you have to talk to.'

Martin left them to it and walked over to Benoît. Putting his arm around his shoulder, he leaned in as Benoît said, 'That was very unfair of you, Martin. You gave me your word that you wouldn't film me.'

'And I promise they won't use it, Benoît. I'm sorry, he wasn't supposed to be filming. Lenny will make sure he erases the footage.'

'Good. Because it's wrong for friends to blackmail each

other.'

'No one's going to blackmail you, Benoît. Why don't you come outside with me for a minute?'

'Why?'

Stumped, Martin looked across to the booth where Aubrey was sitting with Helena.

'Hang on, Ben, I'll answer that question in just one minute.'

He took his arm from around Benoît's back and strode across to Aubrey and Helena.

'Hi, guys.'

'Hello, Martin, would you like something to eat? We've just ordered calamares.'

'No thanks, Aubrey. Helena, do you have any coke on you?'

'Of course.'

'Can I have it?'

'What?'

'Just for a minute. It's really important.'

She looked at Aubrey, who said helpfully, 'Go on, dear, I'm sure he needs it for a good reason.'

Reluctantly, Helena reached into her bag and handed over her wrap.

'Thanks,' said Martin.

Martin bounded back across to Benoît. He smiled at him and tapped the side of his nose.

'Ah,' said Benoît, smiling, 'now I see what you mean.'

little fingers

Alison took another sip of her cut-price cocktail. She looked back at the restaurant's entrance, sighing heavily as Suzanne flounced in. Her sister looked stressed, and her scruffy appearance indicated how reluctant she must've been to leave the house. She'd known Suzanne would think this was unnecessary, but also that it was the only way to do this.

Alison waved, and her sister came across. She pulled out her chair, slipped off her jacket, and sat down. Alison swirled the cubes in her glass and tried to make her expression as open as possible.

'So what's this about?' Suzanne asked. 'How come I couldn't bring Ade with me?'

'You didn't say anything to him.'

'No. You told me not to.'

'So where did you say you were going?'

'The video shop.'

'What?' she squawked.

'What's wrong with that?'

'We'd better not have anything to eat,' Alison said quickly, panicking.

'Why not?'

''Cause he's hardly going to believe we've been at the video shop for an hour, is he?'

'Does it matter? I'll tell him I ran into you by accident and we decided to go for a drink.'

'OK,' said Alison, calming down, 'let's order first.'

Suzanne opened the menu. 'I think I'll just have a starter.'

They called the waiter across and gave him their orders. Alison had another cocktail while Suzanne uncharacteristically ordered a Diet Coke. She wondered if Joe was responsible for her sister not drinking. As the waiter walked away, Alison said, 'I have something important that I want to share with you. But first you have to promise not to say anything to Adrian.'

'You're pregnant.'

'No. I know that if I ask you to keep a secret you probably

will, but probably's not good enough for this one, so although it pains me to do this, I'm going to have to ask you to do a little fingers.'

'No way.'

'Sorry, Suzanne, you know the rules. Mum said either of us could use little fingers whenever we needed it. So come on.'

Alison held up her left hand, little finger outstretched and the rest curled up. Suzanne glared at the finger, as if it were a wishbone she wanted to snap, then curled her own smallest digit around it.

'OK,' she said, 'we both know what this means. What I want to tell you is, I'm having an affair.'

Suzanne looked horrified. 'That is so fucking sick.'

'What?'

'Using little fingers for something like that. Mum would be ashamed of you.'

'No she wouldn't. She often used little fingers for stuff she didn't want us to tell dad.'

'But not about other men. Alison, how could you?'

'It's not a big deal, Suzanne. I know you like Adrian and you don't have to worry, I'm not going to leave him.'

'That's even worse. Maybe you shouldn't tell me anything more, Al, I don't want to have a low opinion of my sister.'

'What are you talking about? Why would this change your opinion of me? Please listen, Suzanne, let me tell you the whole story.'

'It's your boss, isn't it?'

Alison blinked. 'Yes.'

'You're so fucking stupid, Alison. You've got the perfect boyfriend, he totally loves you, and you're about to throw all that away to go after someone who's married. I can't believe you'd do something so pointless.'

'It's not pointless, Suzanne. You don't understand, it's different for you.'

'What does that mean?'

'Huh?'

'How is it different for me?'

'You've been with lots of men. I've never had anything like this.'

'Like what?'

'You know, an affair. A proper, grown-up adult one where everything's cool and we both know what we're doing and there's no chance of it becoming permanent, but that's because we don't want it to become permanent.'

Suzanne snorted. 'This is so lame I don't even want to carry on talking about it. I know you think your job makes you all smart and sophisticated, but the truth is, Al, you're acting like a total bimbo and I wouldn't be surprised if by the end of this you'll have had your stupid heart broken, lost your job, and your boyfriend.'

an open secret

Martin looked round the table and considered how their small group seemed to be becoming more stable. There were still odd energies surrounding the two new couples, Benoît and Laetitia and Aubrey and Helena, but the fact that these relationships had lasted over a week suggested they might go on to bring a new cohesion to their nights out. He was still worried about Naomi and her violent boyfriend, but she always seemed more together when she was out with her brother and working on a TV item.

Martin wondered how the group might respond if he started bringing Alison out with him. He'd always viewed these nights as his secret life, and although he wouldn't dream of bringing Claudia out with him, it'd be different with Alison. Wouldn't it? Probably not. He didn't know much about her background, but sensed she would be troubled by the nature of these evenings.

This wasn't the only secret he was keeping from his friends. He had yet to tell them about losing his job, which made him feel awkward, as he suspected Jennings had probably blabbed, but as yet no one had raised the subject with him. Neither did they know about the career-change he was currently considering. After tonight's visit to the strip-club, however, it seemed like a good time to confide in Naomi.

'Can I talk to you privately?' he asked her.

'Of course. Let's pretend we're doing coke and go to the bathroom.'

'We can't do that.'

'Why not?'

'Because Helena will think we really do have coke and get paranoid that we're hiding it from her.'

'Do you have any coke?'

'No.'

'Does she?'

Martin rolled his eyes. 'Of course.'

'Well, go get it off her.'

'I can't. I borrowed it once already.'

'When?'

'In the club. I needed it to distract Benoît.'

Naomi stared at him. 'So you've had some already?'

'I had to. Otherwise he would've got suspicious and found out that Laetitia was flashing her tits. Besides, why are you worried?'

'Well I don't want to go to the toilet with you if you're just

186

going to babble on at me. I thought you wanted to talk about something serious.'

'I do.'

'OK, Martin, hang on, in that case I'll ask Helena.'

Naomi got up and walked down to the other end of the table. Martin took a long gulp from his glass of wine, wondering how Naomi would respond to his news. She could be surprisingly sensitive sometimes, and when she gave him life advice it was usually sound. He supposed it should be more natural for him to confide in Lenny, especially as he'd be guaranteed an enthusiastic reaction. But Naomi was the one who counted, and who could be relied upon to disseminate the information to the rest of their mutual friends.

He pushed back his chair and followed Naomi to the women's toilets. She shoved the door open with too much force and it slammed noisily into the wall. Two women kissing by the sinks turned round with matching horrified faces, terrified their boyfriends had discovered them.

'Sorry,' said Naomi lamely.

The woman nearest them shrugged and went back to kissing her friend. Naomi moved towards the nearest open cubicle. She sat down on the toilet, waited for Martin to close the door and then asked, 'Do you actually want any of the coke?'

'Maybe. You go first. Get even with me.'

She nodded, stood up, and cut a couple of lines on the toilet seat. Doing them both, she turned back and asked Martin, 'So what's wrong?'

'Nothing's wrong. Just . . . some things have happened.'

'OK, what's happened?'

'I got sacked from *Force*.'

'What?' she said, shocked. 'Are you serious?'

'Absolutely.'

'Why? What did you do?'

'That's what Claudia asked me. Why does everyone think I did something? It was always obvious I wasn't going to last long in that job. You said yourself that you were amazed they gave it to me in the first place.'

Martin stopped, aware that his voice was becoming shrill and that everyone in the toilet could hear him. He leaned back against the cubicle wall, trying to make eye contact with Naomi easier.

'Well, yeah,' she replied, 'but I'm still surprised they got rid of you.'

'Why? It's a fairly standard tactic. Circulation is down, advertisers are pulling out, the magazine still doesn't have a coherent identity . . .'

'Who are they replacing you with?'

'Someone at *Nova* is the rumour. But I wouldn't be surprised if that turned out to be a smokescreen. I have an inkling they're going to promote somebody.'

'What makes you think that?'

'It just seems like their style. Anyway, that isn't the point. I already got a new job. Well, an offer, anyway, and if the money turns out to be OK I'm going to accept it.'

'And?'

'And what?'

'What's your new job?'

'Something you'll want to cover, I expect. I've been asked to come up with a concept for the first ever mainstream porn mag.'

Naomi stared at him. 'Oh, Martin, that's fantastic.'

'Is it?'

'Of course. And it's the perfect job for you. In fact, it'll be perfect for all of us.'

'Why?'

'It's obvious. We can promote you, you can promote us. And everyone loves pornography.'

'Are you sure? I was worried it might be over.'

'Are you kidding? It's just beginning. This is incredible. Have you told Lenny?'

'Not yet. I wanted to talk to you first.'

She hugged him. 'Let's go share this with the others.'

'There's something else,' he said slowly.

'OK,' she replied, her face open.

'I've sort of become involved with someone.'

Naomi looked nervous. 'In our gang?'

'Oh, no, nothing like that. It's my assistant, Alison. You've talked to her on the phone.'

'Right. So why are you telling me? Is it a big deal? Are you going to leave Claudia?'

'No, I just thought . . . maybe some time I could bring her out with us.'

Naomi smiled. 'You're so sweet, Martin. I know you see me as some kind of domineering queen bee, but you should know you don't have to ask my permission. After all, the others don't seem too concerned. And besides, I'm glad you've found someone who makes you happy.'

He looked seriously at her. 'Are things still difficult with Greg?'

'I don't want to talk about it, OK? Let's just do another line and go tell the others your good news.'

Wednesday

what do women want?

After his conversation with Naomi, Martin woke up feeling enthusiastic about his second meeting with Brad Russell. Brad had called him yesterday afternoon, worried there were a few things he hadn't explained properly and asking if Martin would be able to come into the office again. Hoping this second conversation would include discussion of his salary, he called Alison and asked her to make the necessary excuses.

He took a taxi over to Essex and went to the same building he'd visited on his previous trip. Brad was waiting for him and took him through to the same meeting room. Even Howard and Jerry were seated in the same positions behind him. Indeed, the only change this time round was the presence of a large colour monitor which had been set up in the corner. Martin peered at the screen, wondering whether it was showing a studio photo-shoot. But if it was, the pictures seemed to be for an extremely strange specialist magazine, as all he could see was a small group of elderly men.

'Focus-group,' Brad explained, 'but don't worry, that's not for your magazine.'

Martin nodded, reassured.

'Thanks for coming in again, Martin, and I hope this isn't a waste of your time, but the boys . . .' he nodded at Howard and Jerry '. . . thought that I might have left some things unclear last time you came in. The first thing, Martin, is that this isn't going to be just a men's magazine, OK? We're very keen that it's unisex.'

'OK.'

'Good.' He sat down, ready to listen. 'So what about women and porn, Martin? What do you think they like to look at?'

Martin considered this, trying to remember the few times he'd talked to women about pornography. Most of these occasions had been when he was out with Naomi's friends, and he worried their opinions might not be representative. Still, it was worth a try.

'Well, one thing's for certain,' he began, 'I don't think they get much joy out of women's porn mags. I think women actually get off on the idea of pornography. They may not want to look at the magazine, but I think they like the idea that it exists. All that innocence and exploitation.'

'You can't sell people an idea, Martin.'

'Why not? Look, take reader's wives, for example. On one level it's embarrassing and smutty, on another, it's one of pornography's greatest tricks. That's why I don't have any truck with the people who say that porn's demeaning to women. If all that was in the magazines was silicon tits and emaciated bodies, I'd agree, but porn is about the celebration of the female form in a way that's much, much more democratic than conventional modelling. I know there are some porn magazines that only ever feature the beautiful ones, but most British porn is all-inclusive. As long as you're prepared to open up for the camera, you can be a star.'

'Nice speech, Martin, but I think I got lost along the way. How are we going to get women to buy our magazine?'

'By making them feel that expressing their sexuality is empowering. It's the same con-trick we pulled on them in the men's magazines. Most people want to be pictured in their underwear, it's flattering. And while for lots of women there is a clear difference between pornography and glamour pictures, men's magazines have been slowly trying to eradicate that line.'

'I still don't follow.'

'OK. All I'm saying is that I think we ought to be careful about going all out for the erotica market. It makes far more sense not to try and hide the fact that this is going to be a porn mag. We should be completely upfront about what we're offering. But at the same time we should remember that women don't like to be patronised. The point I'm trying to make is that there should be nothing coy about what we're offering. As long as we steer clear of sexual hypocrisy, we're home free.'

Brad was staring at Martin. Worried he'd talked himself out of a job, Martin stared at his fingernails.

'Sorry,' he said quietly.

'What for?' Brad asked. 'We're looking for a man with a vision and it's clear you fit the bill. Now, is there anything you want to ask me?'

'Well . . .'

'Yes?'

'It's not really something I feel comfortable discussing in front of Howard and Jerry.'

'Guys, get out of here.'

They picked up their stuff and left the room. Brad stood up and walked over to Martin.

'OK, Martin, what's up?'

'My salary. We didn't talk about how much I'm going to get paid.'

'Oh, I see. You didn't have to get rid of the guys for that.'

'I don't like talking about money in public.'

Brad nodded. 'I understand. Well, what I had in mind was, if you write down what you're earning at the moment, put down the minimum you'd accept and the maximum you think you deserve, and we'll see what we can come up with for you.'

'OK.'

'Now, Martin, the boys were a little worried about your attitude to magazine pornography. I'm not so concerned myself, you said you watch videos and look up stuff on the net, and after all, we do want something different from conventional magazine porn, but I think it would probably be a good idea if you took away some of these magazines and got an idea of what we're talking about.'

'OK.'

'That's OK? Good. Give me your briefcase and I'll fill it up.'

Martin took a taxi back to the *Force* offices. He spent the journey thinking over this new development, wondering if he had it in him to produce the magazine Hendon Publications wanted. He had never imagined himself as a pornographer, but maybe Naomi was right, maybe he was scared of success. What would it be like to be a Hugh Hefner or a Larry Flynt, a man remembered for his contribution to masturbation? He'd been kidding himself that this new job would be no different from working at *Force*, but there was no question that getting involved with this would change his life forever.

If he succeeded in his mission, if he managed to break down the final barriers between pop culture and pornography, what exactly would he be responsible for? The main reason why it would be different from *Force* was that this magazine – his creation, although paid for and inspired by Hendon Publications – would be something new. And that made it dangerous. No matter what anyone said, pornography did have a huge effect on the world. It was up for debate whether that effect was good or bad, but there was no argument that it did impinge on almost everyone's life. And this influence was increasing – you didn't need statistics, it was evident even in people's sexual vocabulary. But to be the guy who took things one step further: was that a responsibility he wanted to bear?

The taxi stopped outside the *Force* offices. He took a lift to the seventh floor, checking his reflection and untying and reknotting his tie twice on the way up. He walked through the floor to his office. Alison had her back to him as he passed, and he didn't disturb her, not wanting to draw any further office attention to their affair.

Sitting down at his computer, he lit a cigarette and ran a hand through his hair.

The phone rang.

'Martin . . .'

He listened closely, and realised she was crying.

'Alison, why don't you come in here?'

She didn't answer, instead immediately appearing at the entrance to his office. Martin swallowed and rolled his chair back, wanting his desk to seem like less of a barrier between them. He remembered talking to Claudia about Alison and realised he should've anticipated something like this. In spite of all the screwing around, Martin had never quite been able to cultivate a proper persona to deal with this sort of stuff. Socially, Martin didn't seem to have a problem with letting people know that he wasn't that big on intimacy. But when it came to sexual relations, there was evidently something he did to encourage women to subsequently open up to him. Every time he slept with someone new he was amazed at the painlessness of the process, always forgetting that the problems arrived afterwards.

197

Alison moved closer to the desk, trying to stem her tears with the heel of her hand.

'I'm sorry,' she said, 'it's not you.'

'That's a relief.'

She laughed, the tears coming in a gulp. 'It's my sister. She was just, well, she was really horrible to me.'

'What did she do?'

'Nothing, really, it's just that I was talking about you, not in a big romantic way or anything. I was telling her, well, sort of about what happened, and how it was great because you and I were both totally cool about it, and she was just, I don't know, really cynical, and I didn't really care . . .'

'Alison . . .'

'I'm sorry,' she said again, 'it's not to do with the sex, I'm fine about that, but . . . oh, Martin, please let me carry on working for you.'

He stood up and walked across to the blinds, not wanting any of this to be witnessed by the rest of the office.

'Alison, I'm going to work for a porn magazine. You don't want to give up your position here for that.'

'Yes I do. And I was thinking, maybe I should get into writing. I'm sure I could manage to come up with the right sort of stuff. I mean, I'm more than happy to carry on working as your secretary, and if you think what I write is shit then you don't have to publish it, but let me come with you, please . . .'

Martin considered this, trying hard to disguise how flattered he felt.

'And this has nothing to do with the sex?'

'Nothing. I don't care if you never want to do it again or have me every day for a fortnight. I'm just so happy working for you.'

'But I'm a hopeless boss.'

'No you're not.'

'You don't have to lie. I'm proud of being hopeless. And this new job isn't going to be some sort of *succés de scandale*. All I'm interested in is pissing away my career as quickly as I possibly can.'

'Then let me piss with you.'

They both smiled at her unfortunate phrase.

'You're serious about this?'

'Yes.'

Martin looked at the beautiful woman smiling at him, and wondered how this had happened. When he'd been a twenty-something man and all his most fanciable female friends had been in the midst of affairs with worthless thirty-something men, the thought had depressed him, but now, for the first time, he understood how there could be love on both sides. This sort of love didn't have to be desperate, narcissistic and despairing; it could genuinely mean something. He fought the urge to kiss her, rubbing her shoulder instead.

strategy

Alison walked out of Martin's office, wondering whether letting her boss know how strongly she felt towards him had been a good idea. She also wondered whether giving up her job here and going to work on a porn mag was a sensible career move. It would be hard to tell her parents, no matter how liberal they were. Suzanne would find it funny. Well, she would've done, before last night. Now she'd probably just lay into her again, saying how stupid she was to throw every-thing away for a man who didn't give a shit about her.

And in a way, she was right. Alison knew she should feel pleased her sister was showing such concern, and accept that what she was doing now upset Suzanne as much as former promiscuity had upset her. She had been serious about attempting writing for this new magazine, but only because a few months earlier she'd met a glamorous girl who seemed perfectly happy writing for *Penthouse* and thought maybe she could use this opportunity to get into print. It was also likely that, in spite of Martin's low profile, there would be sufficient media attention focused on his new venture for her to be able to get at least some of the limelight. After all, editing a mainstream stroke-book was a lot more exciting than launching a film magazine or anything any other erstwhile editors had got up to.

She answered her phone.

'Hi,' said a familiar voice, 'can you put me through to Martin, please?'

New York

Martin felt nervous the moment he heard Gina's voice. This wasn't what he needed right now. He'd never had any willpower where she was concerned, and knew that even talking to her was a mistake.

'Hi, Martin, how are you?'

'Great.'

'Good for you.'

She went silent.

'And you?' he asked.

'Bad.'

'I'm sorry to hear that.'

'Way bad.'

'Are you sick?'

'My Mom wants to send me away.'

'Where?'

'Two words: *Girl, Interrupted*.'

'Aren't you a bit old for that?'

'Not in her eyes. Martin, have you got anything important that's keeping you in England?'

'Oh, Gina, no, I can't.'

'Why not?'

'It's complicated.'

'It's always complicated. Martin, I need you.'

'Gina.'

'OK, I don't need you, but I have to have you here. Just for a little while. If this is a fidelity thing you don't have to worry, I'm not going to jump you. I'm asking you as a friend. Please, Martin, I wouldn't ask if it wasn't a matter of life and death.'

strategy II

Alison avoided Martin's eye as he peered out of his office, looking for her.

'Al . . .'

'Yeah?'

'I need you to book me a ticket to New York.'

'When for?'

'This afternoon. There should be a flight around three or four out of Gatwick.'

She felt him take her hand. Turning round, she saw he was kneeling in front of her. 'Alison, did you hear who that was on the phone?'

'Gina.'

'Yeah. She's in a really bad way. I have to go on a rescue mission. But you don't have to worry, I'm not interested in her.'

Alison laughed. 'It's hardly my place to feel jealous.'

'Well, nevertheless, I don't want you to feel I'm taking advantage of you. Look, I know this seems like a mess, but we'll sort everything out when I get back.'

'When will that be?'

'Friday. I'm going home to pack an overnight bag. Can you fix it so I can pick up my ticket at the airport?'

surprise

Martin hailed a cab. He told the driver his address and looked out the window all the way home. Then he paid him, walked up to his front door, unlocked it and went upstairs to his bedroom.

The door was open. The couple inside on his bed were having such vigorous sex that neither of them noticed him standing there. And for a moment it was difficult for Martin to grasp that what he was seeing was real and not two actors on the set of a particularly lurid sex-movie. Then he said, in a quiet voice, 'Claudie?'

She opened her eyes, then started slapping the thighs of the man who was inside her. He had his back to Martin, but instantly realised what was going on and stopped moving, although he didn't turn round.

'I thought you said you weren't going to fuck him. I thought you said he reminded you of Michael Douglas.'

'And that isn't a good thing?' Ronnie asked, his voice surprisingly even.

Martin couldn't help laughing. Even with his wife sprawled out on their marital bed, clearly so fulfilled by Ronnie's sleek administrations that even in a situation as embarrassing as this she couldn't hide her delight. And who could blame her?

202

Ronnie looked a lot better naked than he did clothed, and his toned body suggested that he no doubt had much greater sexual stamina than Martin.

'OK,' he said, 'I'm actually in a bit of a hurry. As much as I'd like to give you two chance to finish off, I have to pack, so if you wouldn't mind, could you find another room to fuck in? But not my office, OK?'

a good secretary

Alison picked up the phone to call Martin. As she dialled, she wondered whether he would've got home yet.

He answered immediately. 'Hello?'

'Hi, Martin, it's Alison . . .'

'Yes?'

'I just wanted to check something with you.'

'OK.'

She hesitated, then said, 'You do know that the flight I've booked you on goes to Newark, not JFK?'

'Yes, Alison.'

'Oh good, I'm sorry, I'll see you when you come back.'

She listened while he ended the conversation and hung up. Part of her hated herself for returning to good secretary mode rather than letting him know how angry she felt, but after he'd gone she realised she was actually glad this was happening now so she could see what an unreliable person Martin was before she got too infatuated.

Still holding the phone, she cut the line and called home.

Joe answered.

'Hello?'

'Hi Joe, is Adrian there?'

'No.'

'What about Suzanne?'

'She's in bed. Can I help?'

'No. Not really. Can you get either of them to give me a call when they get in?'

on the way to the airport

On the way to the airport, Martin wondered again about what he was doing. It was clearly a good idea to be getting away from Claudia, but it didn't make sense to alienate Alison, especially as he now had the perfect excuse for continuing his affair with her.

What made things worse was that he couldn't even feel virtuous about going to New York. Gina always created these sort of dramas for herself, and wasn't grateful to the people she turned to for help. And he knew already that he would end up sleeping with her, and that the experience would hardly be a healthy one.

a peculiar situation

Alison's phone rang. She answered it. An initial throat-clearing revealed the caller as Adrian.

'What's up?'

'Are you going to be home tonight?'

'Nah. I'm going to a concert with Suzanne. But Joe will be home.'

'What concert? And how come you're going instead of Joe?'

'It's nothing special. I knew it wouldn't be your sort of thing so I didn't ask. And Suzanne isn't really into it . . . I had to blackmail her into coming by promising to take her to see some shitty boy-band next month.'

'Oh.'

'Nothing's up, is it?'

'No, not really. I just wanted a chat.'

'Well, Joe'll be here, you can always talk to him.'

'Why do you keep mentioning Joe?'

'What?'

'I don't want to talk to Joe, I want to talk to you. And to tell you the truth, I find it a bit creepy being left alone in the house with him.'

'Why? What are you talking about? Did he say something to you?'

'No . . . but it's a peculiar situation, isn't it?'

'What?'

'You being out with Suzanne, me alone with him.'

'Oh, come on, Al, you're being silly now. Look, if you really want to talk to me tonight I can try to get another ticket, although I'm fairly sure they'll have already sold out.'

'No, forget it, I'll be fine. You two go and have a good time.'

departure lounge

Martin had been certain there was an Internet Exchange at Gatwick airport. He could remember himself sitting there last Christmas, firing off a last few work-related e-mails as he waited for a delayed plane. But today, for some reason, he couldn't find it. There was, however, a long-haired man sitting with a laptop plugged into a large white pillar, and Martin was so desperate to apologise to Alison for his rapid departure that he swallowed his embarrassment and approached him.

'Hi.'

The man ignored Martin for a moment, finishing typing something before he looked up.

'Yes?'

'I was wondering whether I could borrow your lap-top.'

'What for?'

'I need to send an e-mail. It'll only take a second and I'll give you twenty quid.'

The man shook his head. 'I can't send e-mails. There's nowhere to plug in my phone-jack.'

Martin nodded and walked away. A woman came up behind him. 'I can send e-mails on my mobile.'

He smiled at her and took the proffered phone, listening as she gave him instructions on how to use it. He sent an e-mail to Alison, then tried to come up with something witty he could send to Claudia's mobile, realising that no matter how wounded his ego, he wasn't yet ready to start thinking about a divorce. Far better to use her deceit and infidelity as a way to punish her for her earlier sanctimoniousness, and get things back on an even keel. But after three attempts at a smart one-liner, he realised he was too hurt to reduce this to a joke. Instead, he gave the phone back to the woman and looked for his gate.

XXXXXXXXXXXX

Alison checked her in-box. She had two messages. One was from someone she'd never heard of; the other from someone anonymous who had blanked out their name with small crosses. *Force* had strict rules about e-mail abuse, although they still managed to contract every computer-virus going.

And today Alison didn't care how seriously she got in trouble.
She opened the mail:

The Dangers of Going Out With Thirty-something Men.
A Guide For Twenty-something Women.
By `One Who Knows.'

1) Thirty-something men are always much more self-
destructive than twenty-somethings. If they work in the
media, they are likely to be heavy drug-users, or alcoholics.
This will continue until their late thirties/early forties, at
which point they will either clean up and become very
boring, or be overwhelmed by self-loathing.
2) Thirty-something men may seem to be just as into the
latest developments in film, music, TV, drugs and clubbing
as you are. If you go out with one for any length of time,
however, you will soon discover that all their references are
slightly wrong. As strange as this might sound, you might
find you're better off going out with someone who has little
interest in modern media. A smart, well-dressed man into
classical music, for example, may be a better bet than you
first imagine.
3) Sexually, thirty-something men are a complete mess. No
matter how fed up you are with the inexperience of people
your own age, this is infinitely preferable to the hang-ups
you'll experience the second you get in bed with anyone
over twenty-nine.
4) Babies! No matter whether they have one, two, seven
or ten children already, as soon as the relationship
becomes serious, they'll want to prove themselves by
making you squeeze one out. And if they don't have one
already, you should really beware.
5) Money. By the time a man reaches his thirties, you will

be able to get an immediate sense of their attitude to money. And this is where a bit of inside knowledge really comes in useful: don't think that just because your man seems relaxed around money means he has a lot of it. Forget the kind of debt you're in now, even the most parsimonious of men can end up owing the bank several hundred thousand pounds once you factor in mortgages, company debts, school fees, etc. While some might argue that the best kind of man to go out with is one who isn't intimidated by debt, don't forget that most thirty-something men are now well on their way to their mid-life crisis, and if you're not very careful, they may well expect you to bail them out.

6) Finally, if your man is married, beware that this is a mixed blessing. On one hand, they will have to spend a lot of time at home and will leave you to get up to all the things you need to do to keep sane (or even have other affairs, etc, if the urge strikes you). On the other, most men are nowhere near as good at compartmentalization as they're supposed to be. This usually means that they'll either be incredibly wracked with guilt (it is always a danger sign if they start seriously pursuing therapy) or will try to legitimatise the affair in some way. In spite of everything else you've ever been told, beware of gifts, and never, ever do anything which will allow them to demonise you.

Hope this comes in handy.
Best wishes, A Friend.

Alison quickly looked round the office, wondering who had sent this to her. The tone seemed very female, which ruled out the usual office jokers like Gareth, but it seemed unclear whether the e-mail had come from a woman who had been out with Martin or someone who'd been burnt by another thirty-something man. Of course, there was no reason to believe it had definitely come from someone in the office.

She sighed and decided not to let it bother her. Clicking on the other message, she discovered it was from Martin. Alison read his few brief lines, and not seeing anything to change her mood with him, got up from her computer and walked across to join the art director and his two friends gossiping in cardboard cut-out celebrity corner.

flying

Martin lifted his black briefcase up onto the plastic fold-down tray and clicked the lock open. He knew it was stupid to attempt to write anything on an aeroplane (unless you were one of those sneaky types who brought along a lap-top to wangle an upgrade), but he had a few ideas for a final feature he might pen for his last issue and wanted to jot them down. He didn't remember the porn mags Brad had given him at their last meeting until the mother next to him tutted and turned her daughter's head away.

He quickly closed the case, and, deciding it was better to address his embarrassment head on, said to the woman, 'I'm sorry, I forgot they were in there. I mean, they aren't mine.'

The woman laughed. Her daughter looked up at her, surprised. Martin smiled and turned slightly towards them.

'I'm serious, they're not. My name's Martin Powell. I edit *Force* magazine.'

She didn't say anything.

'Have you heard of it?'

'No.'

'It's a men's magazine. And, well, recently, I lost my job. And there are these other guys who, well, they want me to edit a porn magazine for them.'

The woman had now turned almost completely from him. He didn't know why he was continuing to talk, or why he felt it was important to explain himself to this stranger. Sighing, he closed his case, stood up and placed it in the overhead locker.

He sat back down and took the entertainment magazine from the pouch in the back of the seat in front of him. None of the films looked that interesting, and if he wasn't so concerned with the woman next to him he would have brought the briefcase back down, found the magazines again and used them to help him get through the flight. Like, he believed, most people, he often found himself thinking about sex when he was in an aeroplane. He didn't really understand the connection, especially as air-travel was one of the most unerotic things imaginable. The ugly stewardesses, the proximity of too many other people, the loss of even the most basic sense of control. And yet, every time he stepped onto a plane, he immediately felt a nagging erection spring up in his trousers. So far he'd never done anything about it – mainly because the only woman he'd ever travelled in a plane with was Claudia, who had no interest in sex in public places – but he knew if he was ever seated next to someone even halfway attractive, he'd be doing his damnedest to join the mile-high club.

at home with Joe

Alison got through the front door and let herself collapse on the settee, too depressed to do anything except slump. As she did so, she noticed the table.

Her first thought was that Adrian had been teasing earlier and hadn't really gone with Suzanne to a concert. She had waited so long for someone to do something nice for her and now, at last, Adrian had finally taken the hint. She stood up and walked across, taking a glass of champagne from beside a place-setting and sipping from it.

Then Joe emerged from the kitchen.

'Hi, Alison.'

'Joe. I'm sorry, is this meant for Suzanne? I just couldn't resist a quick sip of champagne.'

'Relax. It's meant for you.'

She looked at him, suspicious. 'You've gone to a lot of trouble.'

He laughed. 'Why not? Those two are out enjoying themselves. I thought we might as well make the most of being at home.'

She looked across at him. He hadn't dressed up and was sporting a white T-shirt with blue jeans and a pair of trainers. His ginger stubble was approaching beard-length and his face looked pinker than usual. Since she'd met him, Alison had felt nervous around Joe, but this was mainly because he seemed secretive and more experienced than her sister – if not sexually, then definitely in life. But looking at him now, she decided that if Adrian and Suzanne were happy being childlike together, there was no reason why she and Joe couldn't act like adults for an evening.

'Alright, Joe, that's very kind of you. Just let me get changed.'

'Sure. Dinner should be ready in about five minutes.'

She nodded, pulled herself up off the settee and went to her bedroom. Sitting on the edge of the bed, she unbuckled the straps of her shoes and slid them off. Both sets of toes received a hard squeeze, and then she lay back again. Worried she was going to fall asleep, Alison sat up and took off her tights. Standing up and going across to the wardrobe, she fished inside for a spare hanger before stripping out of her top. Hanging it up, she unzipped her skirt and took that off too. Then she walked back across to the door and shouted,

'Joe?'

'Yes?' he replied.

'I know I'm being a nuisance, but is there time for me to have a shower?'

'No problem,' he shouted back, 'take your time.'

Alison took off her bra and knickers, wrapped herself in a towel and went to the bathroom. She climbed into the shower, checked the setting, and turned it on. As the warm jets sprayed over her, she decided she would put Martin out of her mind for the evening. Joe wasn't her ideal choice of dining-companion, but he had done something nice for her, which was more than could be said for either of the men she was romantically involved with. And she would reward him for his kindness by dressing up and acting as if she wasn't overburdened with emotional difficulties.

She washed her hair and then climbed out of the shower, wrapping herself in a towel. Alison returned to her bedroom and opened her wardrobe, trying to decide what to wear. She wanted to look elegant, but not too overtly sexy, as the last thing she needed was for Joe to start fancying her. She settled on a long black dress she'd bought in Paris the Summer after her graduation, although she didn't bother with expensive underwear, instead choosing a plain black bra and knickers. As soon as she was dressed, she went back to the lounge.

'I wasn't too long, was I?'

'No,' said Joe, 'take a seat.'

She sat down. 'What are we having?'

'Moules mariniere.'

'Lovely.'

'Followed by chicken.'

'Wow. So you're a proper cook? Does Suzanne know about this?'

He laughed. 'We both know she's hardly the fine dining type.'

'She hasn't taken you to Henry's then yet?'

Joe went back into the kitchen and returned with two large pots of mussels. He put Alison's down in front of her, then sat down with his own.

'What time do you think they'll be back?'

'Eleven or so, I expect.'

'This is fantastic, Joe. Where on earth did you find mussel-pots in our kitchen?'

'I didn't. They're mine. I brought them over.'

She nodded and started eating. 'Have you ever done this professionally? Cooking, I mean.'

'No, I'm not that great.'

She smiled. 'Sorry, I don't mean to be so effusive. It's just, you've no idea how nice it is to be cooked for. You know, the whole time I've been out with Adrian, he's only made me two meals, a bacon sandwich and some kind of weird red cabbage dish he and Suzanne saw on some daytime cooking show. I

213

keep dropping hints but he just ignores me. I think he's scared of seeming unmanly in front of my sister.'

'You think cooking is unmanly.'

Alison looked up. 'Oh no, of course not, I think it's very manly, I love it, but you know what Suzanne's like, she teases him.'

He dropped another empty mussel shell into the lid of the pot. 'Do you ever wonder about them?'

'Who?'

'Adrian and Suzanne.'

'What d'you mean?'

'They seem very close.'

'They are very close.' She swallowed. 'Like brother and sister.'

He chuckled. 'Oh, I think there's a little more to it than that.'

Alison's heart dropped. 'Do you have any proof?'

'Only her reputation.'

'I thought you said that wasn't important.'

'Reputation isn't. Character is.'

She laughed.

'What?' he asked.

'You sound so solemn.' She smiled as she discarded another shell and wiped her fingers on a piece of kitchen-towel. 'I really wouldn't worry, Joe. I know my sister and I know she'd never do anything with Adrian. Besides, what happened to all that stuff you said to me at the weekend? That made a lot of sense, and convinced me that you're the right person to be with Suzanne.

'I realise her relationship with Adrian seems unusual, but you've got to remember that the two of them have spent every single day together for the last few years.'

Joe didn't reply. Alison hoped he'd got the hint. She didn't want to continue with this unpleasant topic, but needed Joe to understand that she wasn't going to put up with any criticism of her sister, especially not after he'd made her feel judgemental last time they'd talked about Suzanne.

She finished her mussels and he came across to take out her plate. Alison was puzzled by Joe's behaviour, but chose to believe he was acting like this because Suzanne had started to stifle him, the same way Adrian sometimes constrained her. If that was the case, she didn't need to feel guilty about enjoying his food and attentions, as she was giving him something Suzanne was not only incapable of, but also uninterested in, providing.

He returned with the chicken. Alison suddenly remembered a question she had been wanting to ask Joe since the weekend. It was a dangerous question, especially in light of the remarks he had just made about her sister, but she hoped it would stop him becoming too sanctimonious.

'What were you in prison for, Joe?'

'Who said I was in prison?'

'So you weren't in prison?'

'It was nothing. A misunderstanding.'

'What kind of misunderstanding?'

'I defended myself.'

'Against whom?'

He smiled. 'Gravy?'

'Thanks.'

'It was an ex-girlfriend's mother. She tried to kill me.'

'Why?'

'She thought I did something to her daughter.'

Alison swallowed a large piece of chicken. It was delicious. She remembered something Martin had told her in the Tenderloin after they had slept together about a friend of his whose father had been a barrister and made his daughter go out with him and his client the night before they went to trial. She tried to imagine herself in that girl's position, with Joe as the client.

She finished her dinner and then said to Joe, 'I'm going to get changed. We don't want Adrian and Suzanne getting jealous.'

'Don't you want dessert? Or coffee?'

'In a moment. I'm going to get changed first.'

She pushed back her chair and returned to her room. She started undressing. A few seconds later, she felt eyes on her back.

'I think you're so much sexier than your sister.'

Alison didn't reply. There was still no reason why this had to turn nasty. If she didn't acknowledge the comment . . . if she looked disapproving enough . . . maybe then he'd get the hint. She glared at him.

He smiled. 'Why don't you get rid of that bra and come over here?'

'Why don't you fuck off?'

'Why don't you fuck me?'

'Get out, Joe.'

'Come on, Alison, don't pretend you're a good girl. I know all about you, and if you don't play nice, it won't be long before Adrian does too.'

'And what exactly are you going to tell him?'

'I haven't decided yet. But I thought I'd start by letting him know you've been fucking your boss.'

She turned on him. 'What do you expect to get out of this?'

'Huh?'

'Well, you must realise if you blackmail me into going to bed with you I'm not going to enjoy it. Does that matter to you? Or is that what turns you on?'

He looked away. 'Just take your fucking clothes off.'

216

'No.'

He got up off the bed and walked towards her. He was clearly intending to be intimidating now, and Alison readied herself to stand up to him. She didn't know what he was going to do, but doubted it would be physical. At least that's what she thought until he reached out and tried to rip off her bra.

immigration

For Martin, the worst part about travelling was the delay getting out of the airport. The experience of editing a magazine over the last sixteen months, plus the year before that when things were getting set up, had been so stressful that he'd developed a strange coping strategy of always thinking three or four hours ahead, anticipating problems and preparing solutions beforehand. Most of the time this strategy worked fine, but if he was presented with a problem beyond his control, he experienced a mental file-systems error, everything in his head crashing to a halt. Contemplation of the amount of airport dead-time he'd have to endure before getting to Gina had triggered this problem, and now he was waiting at the back of a queue that wound back on itself four or five times before reaching passport control he found it impossible to think beyond the immediate present.

Standing in front of him in the queue were two twentysomethings to whom he'd taken an immediate dislike. Although the woman was clearly extremely proud of being an experienced traveller, dressed in clothes that showed the required disdain for cleanliness and fashion, she clearly hadn't spent any time in America, and kept coming out with stuff that showed a staggering stupidity.

'I brought loads of gum, right, in case we couldn't get it here.'

'Great,' said her male friend, 'what type?'

'Juicy Fruit.'

Martin stuffed his fist into his mouth, not wanting to draw attention to himself. He kept expecting the girl's male friend to say something, but he seemed as dense as she was. The pair kept up their inane dialogue as the queue shuffled forward at three or four minute intervals, each new exchange tormenting Martin even further. For a while he found himself unable to do anything except listen, and as much as he didn't want to pay any attention to them, there was something about the way that everyone they knew seemed to have three names that drew him in to their monotonous conversation. In the space of a single anecdote one person was referred to as Stiv, Steve and Diggy. It felt like hearing a Russian novel reinterpreted by characters from *Home and Away*. When he finally managed to stop listening to them, he tried to kill time instead by looking at the queue and wondering whether there was anyone waiting whom he could conceivably fancy. The process reminded him of the sort of selection he made when looking at internet porn, and the way he'd always been unable to have sexual thoughts about someone if he didn't like what they were wearing. Most of the women didn't look that hot after the flight, but there was one who caught his eye. She had a nice Kristen Scott Thomas thing going on, and seemed to be travelling alone. He smiled at her for a while, but she didn't respond. Good job, too, he supposed, what with Gina waiting for him outside. If she could be bothered to show up, that was. He wouldn't put it past her not to have got it together enough to make it to Newark airport.

The queue lurched forward again, this time allowing Martin to make it round into the next twist. The attractive woman was now almost alongside him, and he had chance to admire her closer. He felt especially drawn to her eyebrows, which she'd clearly carefully plucked. He thought this kind of grooming only really worked on certain women. It was most attractive on women who looked like they only took such precise care on one or two bits of their anatomy, sexy in the same way as a girl who didn't care about her clothes but obsessed over her lipstick. She was just the sort of woman he'd like to see naked, and he wondered what would happen if he approached her about his forthcoming magazine. He had no idea how one solicited women to appear in pornography, but he thought it would be much more satisfying to go up to someone on the street than look through a modelling agency's books. He remembered reading about Don Simpson auditioning women for naked roles in non-existent movies and wondered whether he'd ever be able to become that shameless.

fight

Alison had responded immediately to Joe's attack, managing to get an instantly effective blow to the underside of his jaw. He staggered back and stood there with a smirk on his face as he stared at her breasts. This was just long enough for her to get a knee up hard into his groin. Although this winded him, he managed to fight back, grabbing her from the side and twisting her onto the bed. 'Joe . . .' she whispered, hoping to disarm him. 'Let's not do it like this.'

He leaned down on her. 'Do what?'

'What if I told you I fancy you too? What if I said I think you're sexier than Adrian.'

'Anyone's sexier than Adrian.'

'Let me get up.'

Joe released her arms and rolled over onto the mattress. Initially, she had planned to get out of the house the second she had the opportunity, but now she thought there might be a safer way of resolving this. After all, if she left him alone in the house there was no telling what he might do to the place or even her sister once she got back.

The exertion of fighting him had felt strange, especially since the only time she'd done anything like that before had been play-fighting in a sexual context with other men. She knew she wasn't responding in a sensible way . . . even now her brain was racing down inappropriate lines of thought instead of snapping into survivalist mode. But she had never been one for over-reacting, and saw nothing to be gained from turning this into *Cape Fear*. Their fighting had been too clumsy to terrify her, and the only moment that had genuinely chilled her was when he pulled her bra off, and even then, he seemed so shocked when he managed to do this that all she really thought at this point was that it should now definitely be possible to defeat him.

She realised he was crying. This made her furious for the first time, and she found it hard to resist laying into him. Maybe he'd realised this was the only way he'd get out of this; maybe he was genuinely upset about what he'd done. Either way, she was not about to take pity on him.

Nevertheless, it made strategic sense to feign gentle feelings. Suzanne needed to be the one who got rid of him, and she wouldn't do that until Alison had told her what he'd done. And she also needed to make sure that he knew what would happen to him if he attempted any form of revenge. It would be horrible that Suzanne would have to carry on working with him, but maybe Alison could persuade her to leave her job.

She couldn't bring herself to hold him. But she put her hand on his shoulder and said, 'This doesn't have to be a big deal.'

'Don't make me go.'

'What?'

'Please. Don't make me go. I don't have anyone.'

Alison considered this. It wasn't that she was taking his request seriously, just that she hadn't yet decided on the best way of getting rid of him. She sat up.

'Do you mind if I put some more clothes on?'

He shook his head. 'Of course. Alison . . .'

'Yes?'

'I'm sorry.'

She got off the bed and walked across to her wardrobe. As she found a different bra and top, she said, 'You say you don't have anyone. But you have your own place, right?'

'Yeah.'

'Well, why don't you go there? Just for tonight.'

'Why? So you can tell Suzanne I molested you?'

'No, Joe, I give you my word I won't do that. But if you stay here and Suzanne comes home and sees us both together, she's bound to sense that something's happened. Give me some time alone to forget about this.'

He sat up. 'OK,' he said, 'but don't betray me.'

Newark

Martin had never got through a flight without having his bags searched at one end or the other. He knew today would be no exception, and had already mentally prepared himself for the process. Several times he had tried to work out the point where the officials decided who they were going to pull over so he could try to look respectable for at least ten seconds, but so far had failed to manage it. He'd even once called up Channel Four and requested tapes of a documentary series they did on customs and immigration, but even that failed to give him the information he needed.

Every time he got stopped, the process was always the same. They would treat him with brusque disrespect until they went through his bags and found a copy of his magazine, and then, after he'd ostentatiously informed the person searching that he was the editor, they'd complete their task with less enthusiasm and more caution, seemingly afraid that they would show up in a feature.

It wasn't until they approached him and took him to one side that he remembered that not only did he not have a copy of *Force* with him today, but also that his briefcase was stuffed with a selection of Britain's finest top-shelf titles. For a brief moment he was terrified, worried that it was illegal to bring this sort of material into America. But he told himself to relax, knowing that things would only get worse if he looked scared. Besides, it wasn't as if he had any specialist stuff. These magazines were freely available in England, and anyway, weren't American laws about what was acceptable much more lax?

A large, uniformed Hispanic woman stood waiting in front of him. He handed her his briefcase and waited while she flipped up the two locks and looked inside. He knew that even discounting the pornography his belongings must look weird – most people don't stuff their underpants in with their work papers – but there was no law against being weird. And besides, he hadn't felt like bringing along an overnight bag as well as his briefcase. Sure, the sensible solution would've been to just bring the overnight bag and forget the briefcase, but he had been in a hurry and, as he kept reminding himself, just

222

suffered considerable emotional distress. She looked up at him and started taking stuff out of the case and putting it on the table between them. He felt as embarrassed now as if a dietician was sorting through the contents of his stomach, or a psychiatrist the contents of his mind. She didn't say anything, but he could tell from the look on her face that she sincerely regretted pulling him across. He hadn't seen such disdain from this sort of official since a cavity-search brought forth unexpected bounty several years before at Heathrow.

'What did you say the purpose of your visit was, sir?'

'I'm attending a conference on the dangers of pornography on the adolescent mind. That stuff in my briefcase . . . they're items for debate.'

'And where is this conference taking place, sir?'

Martin considered this. Every time he got on a plane and was faced with the boring prospect of filling out his green and white cards, after resisting the urge to lie and say he was a communist drug-addict with involvement in past Nazi atrocities, he realised that, once again, he didn't have the address he was staying at with him. The only American address he ever remembered was one for those friends in Chelsea, so that was what he scribbled down every time (apart from one occasion when he'd explained his predicament to a sexy fellow passenger and she'd dared him to put down Sesame Street), always secretly believing that one day the airport staff would send secret agents to this address and find out he'd been lying. Now, though, he faced a whole new challenge, and worried that this would finally be the occasion when he was caught out.

'Chelsea,' he said, 'the conference is taking place in Chelsea.'

'Where in Chelsea, sir?'

'Um . . . I'm not sure of the exact address . . . I'm staying with friends.'

'They're not providing you with accommodation?'

'Who?'

'The conference guys.'

'No.' Martin straightened his collar around his neck, 'well, you know, they offered, but . . .'

She picked up a copy of *Club* and flipped through it. 'You know what I really hate about these magazines?'

Martin shook his head.

'The pussies. They always look so dry. And where's the fucking dick?'

after the show

The front door opened. Alison immediately sat up, unsure whether it was Suzanne and Adrian, or Joe returning for another attack. Then she heard her sister giggle. The two of them burst into the living room.

'Good show?' she asked, her voice tremulous.

'It was alright,' Adrian replied.

'Alright? It was dead boring. Some strange little man with no stage presence.'

'He doesn't need stage presence. He's a musical genius.'

'Alison?' asked Suzanne. 'What's wrong?'

She sniffed. 'Now's probably not the best time to talk about it.'

'What d'you mean? What happened?'

'Joe attacked me.'

'What?' demanded Alison. 'How?'

She looked worriedly at Suzanne. 'He tried to sexually assault me.'

Suzanne stared at her blankly for a second, before turning on her heel and leaving the room.

Newark II

Although Alison sounded concerned on the phone when she'd informed him that he'd be flying into Newark instead of JFK, he actually preferred (whenever possible) to use this airport. While he had been forced to spend years cultivating suitably showy likes and dislikes for his magazine, his natural instinct was always to go for the low-key. And Newark was about as low-key as airports got. There was hardly ever anyone holding up cards like they did in the waiting areas of every major British airport, and the people milling around the front entrance always looked like they were desperately in search of a beer.

Martin scanned the crowd for Gina. She wasn't the sort of person to make things easy, so he checked every possible area apart from the women's restrooms. Then he went outside to see if she was waiting in her car. When that didn't work, he checked his watch and saw that it had taken him over an hour to get through passport control. He wasn't worried that she'd come on time and then gone home, but he did suspect she might not have shown up yet.

Irritated, he looked for a phone.

after the show II

For once, Adrian had shown some tact and left Alison alone with Suzanne. Alison couldn't really tell how either of them were taking it, but she was more worried about her sister than her boyfriend. She knew Suzanne would be angry with her, even if what had happened had hardly been her fault. She wanted to apologise to her, but found it impossible to summon up any sincerity.

'So what exactly happened?' Suzanne asked.

'I don't want to tell you.'

'That's ridiculous. You can't expect me to take your side if you won't tell me what happened.'

'He attacked me.'

'So you said. But talk me through it. Tell me exactly what happened.'

'Suzanne . . .' she said wearily.

'What?'

'A little sympathy wouldn't go amiss.'

Suzanne tucked her legs up on the sofa. 'Alison . . . I realise this has been hard for you, and I do believe that what you said happened happened, but this is a man I slept with. And you've got to understand that hearing that he almost raped you . . .'

'It wasn't rape. It was assault.'

'OK, see, I need to hear this. And if you're going to go to the police . . .'

'I'm not going to go to the police.'

'Why not?'

'Because it was horrible, but not serious. Just as long as you don't see him any more.'

'But what about work?'

'Yes, I did think of that. And I think I've come up with a solution.'

'Which is?'

'He's coming back tomorrow. I think the three of us . . . you, me and Adrian . . . we need to talk to him. We have to make it clear that if he doesn't leave us all alone and quit his job, we'll take this further. He's not going to like it, but I'm pretty sure he'll be too scared to protest.'

something came up

The first time he called there was no response. Ten minutes later, he tried again. He got the ansaphone, but just as he was about to hang up, there was a click and she said, 'Hello, Martin, it's Gina . . . listen, something's come up.'

'Right. So you can't get to the airport?'

'No, well, it's more serious than that. Can you keep yourself occupied for the next couple of days and come see me on Friday?'

He caught the next flight home.

Thursday

a shot of strychnine

Martin arrived home just after ten. It was the first time he'd ever taken two flights in quick succession, and he was surprised how well he was holding up. Unable to sleep on the return trip, he had so far just about managed to stave off complete exhaustion, and believed that if he could get into bed within the next ten minutes, he could sleep through till four and function for the evening.

First, though, there was the small matter of Claudia's letter.

He knew it was important because she'd sealed it in a white envelope and left it waiting with a glass of what looked like water. The drink was an odd touch, and he had an idle fantasy that she'd left a shot of strychnine and an invitation to join her in a suicide pact.

He opened the letter.

Dear Martin,

I know I don't have to say any of this, and that the simplest thing for both of us would be if I just left with no explanation. Well, not that an explanation is needed. I know you pretended not to care (which, as always, was very cool of you), but it must've been truly horrible to come home and find me and Ronnie having sex. I know it sounds silly after everything else, but I do genuinely feel guilty. Not about the sex, especially, but the way it must've seemed. I was going to write that I felt guilty about the lies, but there have been so many between us that to write about them now seems stupid. Anyway, I did want to say a few things. Firstly, when we had that conversation about Ronnie, when I said I was going to give up seeing Clive, well, I was telling the truth. I wasn't going to fuck Ronnie, but then he asked, and it just seemed stupid to say no, especially as I knew that if I said anything to you, you would've told me to go for it. Secondly, I just wanted to say that I know you always tried to protect me from anything you did, and although I know other people wouldn't understand this, I am grateful for the consideration you showed me in those matters. In fact, Martin, I'm grateful for everything, and I'm really sorry our marriage didn't work out.

Love,
Claudia.

rollercoaster

Alison was amazed to find a message on her voice-mail from Martin, telling her he'd be in later that afternoon. At first she thought he hadn't gone to America at all, although as he continued speaking she realised he'd gone and come back. He didn't explain why. She told herself not to get excited, remembering how miserable she'd been when he left yesterday afternoon, but she found it impossible. Her emotions felt completely out of control at the moment, and it was increasingly hard for her to respond to her life in a normal way. She knew she should be angry at Martin, and take this running around after other women as evidence that he was completely wrong for her, but instead it just seemed romantic and glamorous, as if he'd been chasing her instead of Gina.

She hadn't felt like dressing up this morning – especially after what had happened with Joe – but now she knew Martin was coming into work she considered going home to change. Maybe on her lunch-break she could buy something. She turned on her computer and checked through her e-mails. There was another one with crosses and a blanked-out name.

She opened it and read:

What did I tell you?

A Friend.

Alison couldn't help glancing up from her computer, even though she knew it was stupid to think she'd suddenly spot someone watching her and looking guilty. The last e-mail had seemed funny and relatively innocuous, and although she'd spent a few minutes trying to work out who'd sent it, she wasn't really that bothered, thinking it was probably some- one who'd been burnt by an affair with an older man. This time, though, it seemed more personal, and she worried it had come from someone who'd had (or was having) an affair with Martin. That didn't matter if it was Gina, but there was always the possibility that it was another girl in the office, and that would be much harder to cope with.

headache

Martin woke up at three-thirty. He didn't feel properly rested, but thought trying for more sleep was probably futile. He worried about seeing Alison in this state, suffering from a hellish headache and knowing he was likely to snap at her for no reason, but since reading Claudia's letter, he wasn't so sure a relationship with her wasn't doomed anyway. Without his wife he knew he'd be a much less attractive proposition to a single twenty-something girl, and didn't feel strong enough to convince Alison she wouldn't have a lot of serious emotional fall-out to contend with should she become his full-time lover.

He washed and shaved, trying to remove the bleary smudge from his features. Usually losing his stubble was enough to make him presentable, but that didn't seem the case today. Perhaps, he considered, it was best not to go into work at all. Then again, his present mental state was so fragile that a day without any human contact didn't seem a good idea.

Dressed, he walked out into the street and hailed a taxi.

breaking up

She had decided against going home, and couldn't be bothered to go clothes-shopping at lunchtime. When she saw Martin she felt glad she hadn't gone to any extra effort. He looked terrible, and more miserable than she'd ever seen him. She hoped it wasn't disappointment at failing to hook up with Gina that had left him in this state. He walked down the floor of the office and stopped by her desk.

'Can I talk to you for a minute?'

'Of course.'

She stood up and followed him into his area.

'What's up?' she asked.

'I want us to stop . . .'

'Stop what?'

'Doing what we've been doing.'

'OK.' She swallowed. 'Can I ask why?'

'My situation's changed.'

'Why does that mean we have to stop?'

'I'm not in any fit state to be with someone . . . in any capacity. I'm sorry, Alison, but I hope you realise how strongly I feel about you.'

Alison nodded, but didn't reply. She was surprised she hadn't considered this possibility. One of the reasons she'd taken so long to have a proper affair was that she found it hard to even kiss someone without imagining a future where she'd end up married to that person. But with Martin she really hadn't thought beyond the immediate present. This wouldn't be so difficult if her lover was more domineering. In fact, what she needed now was someone to bully her, to take away her freedom of choice and tell her exactly what to do.

She knew this wasn't Martin's style. He seemed as helpless as she was, and she didn't feel up to doing this alone. He also seemed less attractive without his usual quiet confidence, and more like her father than ever.

So she said, 'It's OK, Martin, I completely understand.'

the end of the working day

Martin stayed in work until six, waiting until Alison had safely left the building. The last two hours had been extremely awkward, and although he'd intended to attempt to get through the rest of the day without talking to her again, he found he couldn't complete even the simplest of tasks without consulting her. Depressed by his ineptitude, he decided not to do anything at all and sat staring at his computer screen until he was ready to go home.

He got the taxi to stop at a Japanese restaurant and bought enough food and beer to get him through the evening. Then he stopped at an off-licence to get a bottle of whisky to finish off the job. There, he told himself, that should get me through to tomorrow.

betrayal

Alison could tell from the silence when she entered her home that something was wrong. But she didn't realise how serious it was until she went into the lounge and found Joe sitting with his arm around Suzanne. She didn't say anything to either of them, instead leaving the lounge and going straight to her room. She put her bag down on the floor and sat on the bed. Seconds later, Suzanne came in.

'Do you want to hear my side?'

'Your side of what? I don't remember you being there when he attacked me.'

'He admitted it, Al. He admitted it and explained everything.'

'Oh, I see, that's OK then. Did he tell you that he told me

that I was much sexier than you? Or how he told me to get my fucking clothes off?'

She looked away. 'Yes. But he also told me that you said you found him more attractive than Adrian.'

'Jesus Christ, Suzanne, I only said that to stop him raping me.'

'I wasn't going to rape you.'

Alison looked up and saw Joe standing in the doorway.

'OK, Joe, whatever you say. Jesus, Suzanne, I can't understand what makes you so fucking stupid. This guy is a psychopath. He could really hurt you.'

'I'm not a psychopath.'

There was a moment of silence.

'Adrian thinks you should be the one to leave,' Suzanne said in a calm voice.

'What?'

'He knows everything. And he doesn't take your side. In fact, funnily enough, he doesn't want to see you ever again.'

Alison looked at her sister, astounded by the anger in her expression and incredulous that she could betray her in so many different ways in the space of a single afternoon.

bedtime

Martin could feel the Nytol kicking in, and after downing the remainder of his glass of whisky, he decided to swap the sofa and television for bed. He staggered to the bathroom and cleaned his teeth. He washed his face, then headed straight for his mattress. Collapsing down on it, he pulled the duvet around him and grabbed the two softest pillows.

Ten minutes later, the phone rang. Feeling incredibly groggy, he nevertheless managed to answer it.

'Claudia?'

'No,' he heard Naomi tearfully reply, 'it's me.'

'What's wrong?'

'He hit me.'

'Who? Greg?'

'Yeah. So I've left him. It's only a matter of time before he flips out completely. And I don't want to be there when that happens.' She paused. 'Where's Claudia?'

'What?'

'When you picked up the phone you thought I was Claudia. Has she gone too?'

'Yeah. Naomi, do you need a place to stay?'

'Thanks for the offer, Martin, but I managed to pull some strings and get a suite at The Tenderloin.'

'That's great.'

'I know. So, anyway, I'm going to have a moving-in party tomorrow. Are you free?'

'Sure.'

'So I'll see you at ten? And, Martin, I'm sorry about Claud. But don't worry, I'm sure you'll work things out.'

Friday

truth or dare

Martin took Friday off. He'd had more than enough humiliation for one week and didn't wake up until two o'clock anyway. He couldn't be bothered to get dressed until dinnertime, and even then only did so in order to go to the restaurant at the end of his street without feeling embarrassed.

He still had a couple of hours to kill before Naomi's moving-in party, so after dinner he went to a bar alone and drank three pints. No one there tried to talk to him and he enjoyed his isolation, feeling that he'd returned to the way he used to be before starting work in the magazine business. He watched the people around him getting drunk and wondered what would happen to him if he didn't take the porn-mag job. He always saw situations in such absolutes, unable to recognise a middle-ground between success and failure, doing well and desperation. But whenever he had a set-back and was forced to think seriously about his life, he usually came to the same conclusion. Like most of his peers, he had been swindled into believing that a life out of the limelight was no life at all. And if he had no discernible talent of his own, he might as well benefit from the glamour of association. Somewhere along the line, however, he had got bored with celebrities. Now the famous faces were eight years younger than him, and he couldn't work up the enthusiasm to care about them. Mandy and Giles were right to get rid of him. All the celebrities he really liked were yesterday's men, from his favourite film-stars (Alec Baldwin and Kevin Costner) to pop heroes (Prince and Michael Jackson.) But now he had a career: he was in magazines. And if he couldn't sell celebrity, he'd have to make do with naked women.

What he really needed to do was start all over again. He had to leave this life behind and find one of those jobs that nowadays people only had in films. It was too late to be a doctor or a dentist, but there must be some nice middle-class vocation that'd suit a man like him.

He finished his drink and went to the hotel.

Naomi let him into her room. She looked incredible, even by her normal high standards. Putting a finger to her immaculate lips, she shushed Martin and led him to the bathroom.

Helena was chopping out lines on one of the large marble tops. Naomi smiled and sat down on the toilet behind her. Laetitia waved at Martin from her space beside Benoît in the shower tray.

'I appreciate the club vibe, kids, but can't we do this in the other room?'

Naomi smiled. 'Room service is coming.'

'So? I'm sure those guys are used to this.'

'I know,' she said, 'but then I'll have to go through that whole stupid routine. He turns a blind eye, I have to give him a ridiculous tip. Then every afternoon some creepy hotel-sanctioned drug dealer will sidle up to me and ask if I want him to get me some stuff.'

'Besides,' said Helena, looking up at them through her fringe, 'I'm an addict. I don't like to share.'

There was a knock at the door. Naomi gave Martin a ten-pound note.

'Take care of him, will you?'

He went over to the door and opened it. Blake smiled back, dressed as always in a sharp dark suit.

'Where are the girls?' he asked. 'In the bedroom already?'

Martin tapped his nose. 'Bathroom.'

Blake came inside. Martin noticed the room-service guy coming up the corridor with a trolley and stood back as he pushed it into the living-room. He gave him the cash and closed the door.

'OK,' he said, 'he's gone. You can bring the drugs in here.'

No response. He banged on the bathroom door. The others came out and went across to the sofa and chairs in the other room. Naomi pulled out a selection of bottles from the drinks cabinet and put them on the coffee table. Helena sat on the floor and started racking out lines.

'Eat some food first,' Naomi told them, 'I don't want you lot losing your appetite and leaving this stuff to stink up my room.'

Blake took an oyster. 'I never lose my appetite.' He looked round. 'Where's Aubrey?'

'I don't know,' said Helena. 'He was supposed to meet me at seven.'

Blake sat down and took a bottle from the table. Martin moved in beside Helena and did two lines of coke.

'So how'd you like your new home?' Blake asked Naomi.

'I'm very happy here.'

'And Greg's getting your place?' asked Blake.

'I don't want to talk about it.'

'Let's play a game,' Helena suggested.

'Yeah,' agreed Naomi, 'come on, boys, two girls without their boyfriends. Be imaginative.'

'OK,' said Blake, downing his bottle in one. He put it on the coffee table and span it. Helena put her hand protectively around the space she was using for her coke. The bottle

243

stopped, pointing at Naomi.

'Helena,' said Blake, 'snog Naomi.'

Helena looked at her and licked her lips. 'Girl on girl, huh? OK, let me just do another one of these.'

She snorted another line. Naomi advanced on her. Helena backed off, grinned at the two men, then leapt towards Naomi. The two of them grappling together made Martin think of fighting lions. Their kiss was long and deep, with lots of pawing. After a moment, they broke apart, both women eyeing the other warily. Martin looked at Lenny, disturbed by the way he was taking in the scene in silence and wondering again about the relationship between the two siblings.

'Naomi,' said Helena, 'can you explain something to me about English women?'

'OK.'

'What we just did, that was like a joke, right? You wouldn't see it as a big deal?'

'Of course not.'

'Right. That's what I thought. But there was this English girl I was staying with when I first moved here, and she was straight, OK, she had a boyfriend. And we were friends. But one night we went to this party together and there was a boy who was coming on to both of us. So we went to the toilets to talk about it, and I said she could have him, but she said, "No, we'll share him." But when we went back out into the party he'd gone home and we were both, sort of, worked up, and we looked round for someone else to take home with us, but it was too late, the party was breaking up. So we went home, and then after I'd gone to bed, the girl came into my room, and got into my bed behind me and started rubbing my breasts and doing all these suggestive things. So we ended up sort of having sex. And I thought it was all, not a joke, but, you know, not very serious. But she got really upset and kicked me out the next morning.'

'Uptight bitch,' said Aubrey.

'So you wouldn't be upset if your girlfriend went with another woman?'

'Of course not,' he replied. 'It doesn't count with girls, does it, Martin?'

Martin ignored him. Lenny span the bottle. It pointed at Naomi.

'Hey,' she said, 'this isn't fair. How come the girls are getting all the dares?'

'Want me to spin again?' asked Lenny.

'No, no, it's OK. What do I have to do?'

Lenny kneeled down, putting his hands on his knees and, staring his sister straight in the eye, said, 'Take your knickers off.'

Naomi stood up. 'You're so twisted.'

She pulled down her knickers, tugged them over her shoes one foot at a time, and threw them at Lenny. He tucked them into his jacket pocket. Helena reached down and span the bottle. It stopped at Blake.

'Is it just dares,' asked Helena, 'or can we ask questions?'

'You can ask me a question,' he told her, 'if you want.'

'How long have you been fucking Naomi?'

Naomi laughed. 'How did you know?'

Blake moved round next to her. Naomi took his hand.

'Well,' he said, 'the first time was many years ago. But that was the only time. At least until last night.'

Naomi kissed him. Blake span the bottle. It pointed to Martin.

'Snog Naomi,' Blake told him.

'Oh, come on, Blake, I can't.'

'Why not?'

'Not in front of you. Not now you're . . .'

'Why not? Helena just did.'

'But that's different. You said it yourself. Girls don't count.'

'Neither do friends. Come on, Martin, it doesn't have to be graphic. Just have a nice friendly snog.'

Martin looked at Naomi. She smiled encouragingly, so he moved towards her and they started kissing. As usual, she tasted of mint chewing-gum. He broke away first, and leaned across to spin the bottle. It rotated twice and pointed at Lenny.

No one said anything. Then Blake, with a chuckle, suggested, 'Eat out your sister.'

Martin felt a horrible tension in his stomach. Things often got like this when he was out with Lenny and Naomi and their friends, but he couldn't remember a situation quite as horrible as this arising before. He knew Blake was just being a drunk, cokey fool, but the atmosphere in the room had already turned nasty, and he knew that Lenny and Naomi weren't the sort of people to back out of a situation like this. He looked up at Lenny, still waiting to see what he'd do.

treats

Alison lay across the hotel bed, cradling the phone.

'I know it's a funny name.' She paused to listen to her mother's reply. 'No, I'm going to move somewhere cheaper in a couple of days, I just wanted to treat myself.' She listened again. 'Because everyone in the office was talking about it. It's like that in London. There's one hip hotel, one hip restaurant, one hip club.' Another pause. 'It's hard to explain what it's like. It's kind of deliberately tacky. No, I don't think it'd be your sort of thing.'

She listened to her mother talk for a while, wondering whether it was worth returning to the subject of her sister. So far all she'd told her was that they'd had a terrible argument, it was to do with her new boyfriend, and she'd been forced to leave home and move into a hotel. Alison wasn't always entirely open with her parents – preferring them to think of her as a good daughter rather than an honest one – but she knew this was a situation where they'd want to hear the full story. The trouble was, the consequences of giving them the truth were likely to be overwhelmingly negative. She knew the moment her father found out about Joe he'd immediately take Alison's side, drive up to their place and demand Suzanne left with him. And of course Suzanne would refuse, and then Joe and her dad might end up having a fight, and even if that didn't happen, lines would be drawn, the family divided, and Suzanne might disappear from their lives forever.

'Are you OK, Al?' her mother asked, obviously sensing she was no longer listening.

'Yeah, fine. Sorry . . . I was just thinking . . . have you heard from Suzanne?'

'You already asked me that.'

'Did I? I'm sorry. What did you say?'

'No, we haven't heard from her in ages. You know she never calls us if she can help it. But why did you fall out? I still don't really understand.'

'You know what she's like, Mum.'

'Yes, but I also know what you're like. And I know you wouldn't leave home over something trivial.'

'It was just a difference of opinion, Mum. To do with her new boyfriend.'

'What's wrong with him?' her mother asked. 'And why doesn't she want us to meet him?'

'Oh, you know, she gets embarrassed,' Alison mumbled, aware she was becoming less convincing the longer the conversation continued.

'And where does Adrian figure in all this?'

'Huh?'

'You haven't mentioned Adrian. Has he left home with you?'

'No. He and I aren't getting on very well at the moment. And he's always been close to Suzanne.'

'But he's your boyfriend,' she exclaimed.

'Yeah, well . . .'

'Isn't he?'

'We're kind of separated at the moment.'

'What? Why? Because of Suzanne?'

'No, because of me.'

'I don't understand any of this, Alison. What aren't you telling me? It's not like you to be so secretive.'

'It's nothing, Mum, honestly. I'm only being vague because everything's so up in the air at the moment. But I'm sure in a couple of days everything'll be sorted.'

'But . . .'

'Listen, Mum, I've got to go. I'll call you on Sunday, OK? And don't worry . . . none of this is that serious.'

Alison hung up before her mother had chance to argue.

knocking on doors

'We'll do their dare,' said Laetitia, grabbing Martin by the hand.

'Yeah,' said Martin, 'and Lenny can do my next one.'

'No,' said Lenny, 'I'll . . .'

'Shut up, Lenny,' Laetitia told him, 'Benoît, clear a space on the coffee table so I can get up.'

Benoît looked furious. 'No, Laetitia, you are my girlfriend, I will not let you . . .'

'Relax, Ben,' said Martin, 'this is only a between friends thing. It's the English way.'

'I'm sorry, Martin,' said Benoît, 'I like you very much, but I will not allow you to perform cunnilingus on my girlfriend.'

'Well, look, I have to do it to someone. How about I do it to Naomi?'

He looked around. Hearing no protests, he disappeared under her skirt.

After that, the game seemed to lose its entertainment value and the group decided to leave Naomi and Blake to their hotel room and go on to another party. Martin and Helena walked down the corridor together, as she took instructions from a mobile phone.

'Hello? No, I've used up most of it. Oh God. Of course. Where? Hang on . . . Martin, do you have a pen?'

'Sorry, no.'

'Can you find one?'

'Where?'

'It's a hotel. Knock on some doors. Someone's bound to have one.'

'I can't just knock on people's doors.'

'Martin,' she said wearily, narrowing her eyes at him.

He knocked on a door. No response.

'Try another one.'

He knocked again. The door opened.

'Martin,' said Alison, her voice trailing upwards in delighted surprise, 'who told you I was here?'

'You know this person?' Helena asked, momentarily distracted from her phone. 'Oh well. Small world. Ask her if she has a pen.'

'Alison,' said Martin, 'I . . .'

Alison looked at Helena, and then back to Martin. 'You have cocaine all over your face,' she told him, before closing the door.

'Wow,' said Helena, 'who the fuck was that bitch?'

Martin ignored her, instead continuing to knock on Alison's door. She didn't respond. Helena came across and took him by the hand. 'Martin, if you can't find a pen, remember this address, OK? 42, Merchant's Drive.'

Martin didn't reply.

'You got that? Well, it's not too hard. One of us'll remember.'

She started walking down the corridor towards the lift. Martin gave up knocking and followed Helena. She pressed the down button and they waited for the lift to reach their level. The doors opened and they went inside. Martin examined his nostrils in the mirror. Not seeing anything, he turned to Helena.

'You can't see any coke on my face, can you?'

She studied him. 'There's kind of a white crust on your cheek. But I think it's mainly love-juice.'

He scratched at his cheek with a thumbnail. The lift reached the ground floor and they walked out into the lobby.

the end of a bad week

Alison sat on the bed, resting her face on her fists and trying not to cry. She'd known when she decided to stay in this hotel that she'd bump into someone, but had assumed it'd be some writers from the magazine utilising the late-night bar rather than a drugged-up Martin sneaking out of a hotel suite with a dodgy-looking woman. Of course, after the way the rest of this week had gone, it was hardly surprising that her Friday night would end with such a serious disappointment. Alison had always been the kind of person who could deal with other people's bad behaviour much more easily if she wasn't directly confronted with it. She didn't have an overactive imagination and wasn't keen on torturing herself, so if someone had told her that Martin had celebrated breaking up with his wife by going to a hotel and getting out of it she wouldn't have given it a second thought. In fact, hearing something like that would've made her more likely to wait a few weeks and start going out with him again, pleased he'd purged all the self-destructive anger out of his system. But seeing him like that upset her in a new, deeper way she couldn't really explain to herself, and after this, she held out little hope of them ever getting back together again.

the mirror man

Helena hailed a cab. Martin got in and waited for her to tell the driver where they were going. Instead she said, 'Do you have money?'

Martin took out his wallet and looked through it. 'A hundred pounds.'

'Great. You're up for buying some more blow before we go, aren't you?'

'OK,' he replied anxiously.

She took out her mobile and dialled.

The taxi stopped outside the Mirror Man's flat. Helena leaned forward and said to the driver, 'Keep the engine running, OK?'

Benoît and Laetitia stayed in the cab. Martin and Helena got out and walked up the front path of an anonymous looking semi. Helena rang the doorbell. A scrawny looking man in his underpants answered the door.

'Billy, this is my friend, Martin.'

Billy stared at Martin and said in a low monotone, 'You got gak on your face.'

Martin looked back at Helena. 'I thought you said it was gone.'

Helena laughed, and they went inside. The hallway was filled with abandoned weight-lifting equipment. They continued through to the lounge. In the corner of the room was a man wearing a dressing-gown and white gloves. He was doing magic tricks in the mirror, watching himself intently.

'Hi ya, Mirror Man,' said Helena, 'caught yourself out yet?'

He didn't answer, instead continuing to do tricks. Billy hovered in the corner of the room. Martin and Helena sat down.

'This is only a flying visit, I'm afraid.'

The Mirror Man nodded. 'Billy, get Helena her wrap.'

Billy went out into the kitchen and returned with a small wrap of cocaine. Martin noticed the wrap was a folded-up page from a porn mag. He got up to go.

'I'll leave you a line here, OK, Mirror Man?'

He nodded. Helena put out a thin line on the table. Billy came across again and waited for Martin to give her the money. Martin handed across the cash and the two of them stood up to leave. Billy showed them out.

hotel bars

Alison looked at her watch. Earlier in the evening, between her mother calling and seeing Martin, she had been enjoying the experience of being alone in a hotel room. Telling herself it counted as research for her new job as Martin's porn-mag assistant, Alison had flipped her television onto the adult channel and watched the first half of *Mirror Images II*, a sex-movie about two sisters. Although both sisters were played by the same actress, and the plot was soft-core nonsense, Alison found it uncomfortably close to home. The conceit of the sensible sister wanting to assume the role of the slutty one reminded her of how whenever she attempted to analyse her feelings about Suzanne's former promiscuity, she often found herself with the uncomfortable awareness that along with the disdain went a certain amount of envy. It wasn't that she wanted the same experiences, it just seemed peculiar that two people sprung from the same place should have such different destinies. She remembered what Joe had been saying about the importance of character, and although she felt uncomfortable considering the opinion of an obvious lunatic, it did somehow feed into what she was thinking.

Alison knew that if she left the hotel room she'd end up getting in trouble. It already seemed a foregone conclusion that before the night was over she'd end up sleeping with a stranger. But if she didn't go down to the bar, that couldn't happen. If she just stayed here, everything would be fine, and she could wake up tomorrow with no regrets.

She put her shoes back on and left the room.

skank

'How come you gave some of your stuff to the Mirror Man?'

'That's the rule. Always leave a line for the dealer. Don't you do that?'

Martin looked sheepish. 'I don't have a dealer.'

The taxi pulled up outside another anonymous semi. Everyone got out. Martin paid the driver and asked Helena, 'So who's party is this?'

'You ever here of a band called Skank?'

'No.'

'They were more famous when I first came here. But in the last two years they've very lost the plot.'

She pressed the buzzer. The door clicked and they went inside.

subbacultcha

Alison walked into The Tenderloin bar. It looked like Steven Tyler's bedroom. *Subbacultcha* was playing on the stereo-system and she used the song to help pace her walk to an empty table. The last time she'd heard *Trompe le Monde* was over seven years ago in an ex-boyfriend's mini, and it seemed a perfect song for this evening. She sat alone and checked out the other people in the bar. At the moment the tables were filled mainly with single men and women. All the men looked too old and the women too young. At least this wasn't the kind of place where the hotel staff would make her feel like a prostitute. A waiter appeared at her table and asked her what she wanted to drink.

'Just a vodka-tonic please.'

He nodded and turned away.

television and drugs

Helena led Martin, Laetitia and Benoît through to a lounge area where people were doing coke from a coffee table and watching a huge TV screen with the sound down. Martin sat next to a hippyish woman in her late thirties. Opposite him was a tall man wearing heavy jewellery and an old-skool tracksuit. Next to Laetitia, Benoît and Helena sat a goth woman with a striking ugly-beautiful face.

'Who's blow is this?' asked Helena.

'Diana's,' said the goth woman.

Helena looked anxiously at her. 'If you let us join in, we have some more stuff for when this runs out.'

'Whatever.'

Helena immediately concentrated on the drugs. Feeling tired and bored, Martin looked at his watch. Diana noticed this and turned her attention to him.

'So what's your name and what do you do?'

'I edit a magazine.'

'That sounds cool.'

'What about you?'

'Me? Nothing. I mean, I deal a little here and there. But I can't have a proper job because I'm a single mum.'

'How old is your kid?'

'Nine.'

'And she's not in school?'

Diana ignored this. After an awkward silence, Helena turned to Martin and handed him a straw. He tried to pass, but Helena pressed him. As he leaned down to snort, the tall, tracksuited man looked across at them with disturbingly spaced-out eyes.

'Diana, what's in this stuff?'

'Nothing,' she said quickly.

'No, I don't mean that, I mean, there's no like, smack . . .'

'Of course not. It's just blow.'

'Are you sure?'

'Yes I'm fucking sure.'

'Then I don't get it. I'm feeling really sick.'

He got up and staggered across the room. He clutched his forehead, then emptied the contents of his stomach onto the carpet. A few guests looked surprised, but the people sitting down quickly returned their attention to the television and drugs.

Greg

A man showed up halfway through her second drink. He just appeared opposite her, sitting down without invitation. Amused, Alison felt like she was in a rock video. The man had small, close-together eyes, long curly hair and a tight jaw that made it look like he had no teeth. As he started talking, she realised he was American.

'Hi, I'm Greg. Are you staying in the hotel?'

She nodded.

'I thought you were.' He looked around. 'Me too. But people come here who aren't staying in the hotel too, right? It's the kind of joint where people hang out?'

'Yes. It's one of the most fashionable bars at the moment.'

'See, that's what I heard too. Do you think this is an expensive hotel?'

'Definitely.'

He leaned in closer. 'So where are you from?'

'Oh no, I mean, I'm from here. London, I mean.'

'But you don't have a place?'

'It's a long story.'

'That's OK. I understand. You don't have to tell me.'

Alison sighed. 'Buy me a drink and I'll tell you everything.'

stuff

Martin lay on the sofa, too coked up to sleep, but too wasted to do anything other than watch television. His lips were going too, twisting involuntarily every fifteen seconds or so. Diana and the goth woman had gone in search of someone else more interesting to talk to, and he had room to stretch out. In the sofa opposite was the tall, sick man, clearly in a seriously bad way. Laetitia and Benoît had gone upstairs to bag one of the bedrooms. Helena suddenly appeared alongside him, tapping the crown of his head.

'Come with me.'

'Where?' he asked wearily.

'Just come with me.'

She led him out into the hallway and pushed him into the bathroom. She immediately crouched down by the toilet, putting the lid down and starting to chop up coke.

'Diana's about to run out of stuff,' she said speedily, 'and although she's not saying anything about it yet, I think pretty soon she'll start wanting our blow, so I thought . . .'

'Didn't you say you were going to share your stuff with them?'

'Well, yeah, I did say that, and if we get caught they may make us keep our word, but at the moment everyone is so fucked that if we're really clever about it . . .'

Someone started hammering on the door.

'Hang on,' said Helena sharply.

'Helena, it's me, let me in.'

Martin looked at Helena.

'Open the door.'

'Are you sure?'

'Yeah. But do it quick, before anyone else notices.'

Martin opened the door. The goth woman came into the bathroom.

'I know what you're up to, Helena,' she said, 'and if it was just me I wouldn't care, but you know, there's a protocol to be observed at this party. Diana gives out her coke to everyone, even though it's the only way she can support her kid, and you're in here being stingy.'

Helena cut her off by kissing her.

'Mmm,' said the woman as she broke away, 'that was nice. OK, this makes things different. Move over, let me get in here with you.'

They all shuffled round.

'What about him?' asked the woman, pointing at Martin. 'Can I kiss him too?'

'Martin?' asked Helena.

'Oh, what the hell,' he said, leaning over and taking the woman by the back of the head.

'Great,' she said, 'now let me do a couple more lines with you and you can go.'

greg II

Alison had known she was going to sleep with someone that night before she'd even left her hotel room. She didn't decide that Greg would be the lucky man until after she'd finished telling him about everything that had happened to her in the last couple of weeks. It wasn't just that he was a good listener, or the fact that throughout her story he offered no advice, no criticism, or any comparative experiences of his own. Any stranger in a bar could do that. What made her feel something towards him – enough, at least, to contemplate giving herself to him for the night – was the careful, silent way he weighed up the information afterwards, as if instead of telling him about her life she'd been explaining the faults in a car he was about to buy. She knew this wasn't a particularly sexy response, but it seemed right for tonight, and the kind of adult attitude they would both need to get through this.

He bought her another drink and started talking about himself. He was much more general and vague than Alison had been. His manner was funny enough to convince Alison that he'd done this sort of thing before, but not so slick that she thought he'd been doing it every night. After a while she started ignoring his words and building up a mental picture of his background from what he left unsaid.

She could tell he was married, even if there was nothing as crass or obvious as an untanned strip of flesh around his finger. She also thought he probably had kids, although she suspected they weren't that old. There was something slow and considerate about his behaviour that suggested his temperament had been affected by spending time around children, as well as a palpable sense of gratitude to be spending time with another adult.

He said he worked in the music business, but refused to give specifics. It did cross Alison's mind that he could actually be really successful and just acting bashful – maybe even a singer in some band big in America but unknown here – but she suspected he was more likely to be some session musician or a studio technician. She was tempted to play harder to get in order to make him boast, but realised she didn't have the mental energy for that kind of game-playing tonight.

They finished that round and he offered to buy another. Deciding it would be simpler if she made the first move, Alison placed her hands over his and suggested it was time they went upstairs.

Not wanting to make a flirty joke about who's room they should go to, she led the way out of the bar and across the lobby to the lifts. He followed her and they went up to her room. She smiled at him as her plastic door-card didn't work first time, and he leaned across to give her a quick peck as her second attempt was successful.

back at Helena's

Dawn. Martin, Benoît, Laetitia and Helena staggered out of the taxi and made their way up the garden path to the front door of her house. She unlocked the door and left it open. He watched her take her shoes off, then followed her into the main room.

'Where's your bedroom?'

'Upstairs.'

He stood up and went out into the hallway, hoping he had enough energy to get himself upstairs before he passed out. *Come on Martin*, he told himself, *it's only a few steps.* Suddenly Benoît and Laetitia came up behind him, Benoît pulling Martin's legs back as Laetitia raced to get ahead. The horseplay gave him the renewed energy he needed and he struggled past both of them to be the first to dive into the empty bed. Benoît groaned, then directed Laetitia into another room.

Martin closed his eyes, knowing this time he could definitely get to sleep. But before he had chance, Helena was beside him again.

'What are you doing?' she demanded.

'I really need to sleep.'

'No, come on, Martin, that's just because of the taxi ride. Do another line and you'll feel fine.'

'Really, Helena, please, I stayed out with you, now let me just get some sleep. Even if only for a little bit.'

'I'll get you a glass of water.'

'I don't want a glass of water. I want some sleep.'

Helena ignored him and walked out of the bedroom. Martin sat up, took off his shoes and loosened his shirt. Curling up on the bed, he tried to sleep. Seconds later, Helena returned and slapped his face hard.

'Fuck,' he uttered, immediately awake, 'ow . . .'

'I told you not to go to sleep.'

'What?'

'Take your water.'

'Thanks.'

'Now we'll do some more coke and you can decide what you want to watch on TV.'

'Seriously, Helena, I just want to sleep.'

'It's not just normal TV. We have satellite. And I have videos. Have you heard of *Enter-Animation?* I have my friend Gina send me tapes of it from America.'

'Your friend who?' asked Martin, waking slightly.

'Gina.'

'Gina Mostyn, the journalist?'

'Yeah. I used to stay in her place in Chelsea and watch the show all the time.'

'What show?'

'*Enter-Animation.* Send us fucking e-mail.' She repeated this three times, in a throaty, sing-song voice. 'There's like this pig and you have to like call in and the pig says stuff like "You're a fucking gaylord, you reek of shit."'

'I think I'm too wasted to get harassed by a talking pig. I'll watch it in the morning.'

'It is the morning.'

'Helena, I'm serious. If you keep on at me, I'll go home.'

'Alright. But please do a couple more lines with me. Then I'll give you a roofie.'

'But if I don't do the lines I won't need a roofie.'

'Do the lines with me.'

Martin picked up his coat, put his shoes back on, and headed for the door.

Saturday

the Thélèmites

Once outside, he immediately wondered whether he'd made a mistake. He knew from experience that it was extremely difficult to find a taxi at this time in suburban areas, especially on a Saturday. He had no idea where he was, but also doubted that there'd be a tube station nearby and saw no one around to ask.

But he couldn't bring himself to go back into Helena's, even if only to call for a taxi. She scared him, and he desperately needed to sleep. A double-dose of jet-lag added to his twitchy exhaustion, and if a taxi didn't come soon he'd collapse in the street. Suburban areas at this time in the morning always seemed so haunting. In the city it was fine to be up early, and amusing to be surrounded by night-owls and early risers, people either out of bed for exercise or staggering back from a punishing night out. Here, though, just to be awake at this time seemed an admission that there was something wrong with your life.

Three streets later, he came across a taxi parked outside someone's house. Not having any other options, he rang the front doorbell and waited to see if he'd get a reaction. A light went on inside and an old man came to the door.

'Yes?' he said, blinking at Martin.

'Hi, I'm sorry to wake you.'

'You didn't wake me.'

'Good. I'm glad. Is that your taxi outside?'

'Jesus, I knew I should've parked it out back. What is wrong with you people? Let me guess, you've been with that German girl, right?'

'Huh?'

'Did she tell you to come here?'

'No, I . . .'

'She's bad news, that one. I don't know why you can't all see it. Oh well, how much are you willing to pay me?'

They agreed on a price, and the old man went back inside to get his keys and coat. Martin walked across to the taxi, leaning on it to keep himself upright.

'Here,' said the driver, 'I brought you a piece of toast.'

'That's kind of you,' Martin replied, 'but I don't think I can eat anything.'

'Just as I thought,' he said, unlocking the doors. 'Do you have any idea of the damage you're doing to your body?'

Martin looked at the driver, wondering whether he could cope with being lectured all the way home. He decided he had no other choice and climbed into the back of the cab.

'What does she do, that woman?'

'Helena? I don't think she does anything.'

He shook his head. 'And you? Do you have a job?'

'Not any more. Listen, I'm sorry, but do you mind if I just close my eyes for a while? I could really do with some rest.'

Martin didn't awake until they reached his street. Then the driver asked for the number of his house and slowly continued down the left-hand side of the street until he found it.

'Someone's kicked your door in,' said the taxi driver.

Martin struggled up. It was five a.m., he was more wasted than he'd ever been in his life, he was looking at his house from a distance, but nevertheless, the evidence was unquestionable.

'Yeah,' he said slowly.

'Any idea who did it?'

'No.'

'You don't want to go in there alone, mate. I'll come with you.'

'It's OK.'

'Nah, mate, it's no trouble. Besides, I got a shooter in the boot.'

'We don't need a shooter.'

'Alright, mate, I'll tell you what. I'll stay out here, you go inside, check out everything's OK, then if you're alright, come back outside and give me a signal and I'll go. How does that sound?'

'OK,' said Martin, too weary to argue.

He paid the driver then pushed open the door of the taxi and put his feet down on the pavement. Standing up, he tried to prepare himself for what he might find in the house. Although there were lots of people who could've done this, Martin was fairly certain he knew who the culprits were. He'd had a niggling anxiety ever since he'd been unable to get through to Tilly, and in spite of all Claudia's protests that he was being paranoid, he knew what sort of people the Thélèmites were, and that they would want to punish him for being so loose-lipped. As he walked up the garden path, he remembered how one of the Thélèmites favourite punishments for people who threatened their circle was to break into their student bedrooms and turn all their furniture upside down. He hoped what awaited him inside the house was only something this innocent, as he wasn't sure if he was up to finding something truly horrible.

He reached his broken door and gingerly looked inside,

timidly assessing the damage as if he was doing nothing more worrying than clearing up after an especially raucous party. It was much worse than he thought it would be. It looked like someone had taken a chainsaw to his banisters and a pneumatic drill to the wall. He was amazed by the scale of the destruction, wondering who hated him enough to go to all this trouble.

He walked through to the lounge and found Gina sleeping on an almost destroyed settee. She was wearing a red T-shirt with the words *But he said he loved me . . .* written in small print across her breasts. She'd taken her red trainers off and left them beside the sofa.

'Gina,' he said.

Her eyes opened. 'Martin, hi.'

'Why did you smash up my house?'

'I didn't. It was like this when I arrived. It was fortunate in a way because otherwise I wouldn't have been able to get in.'

'Gina,' he said wearily, 'I'm really not in the mood for this.'

'Relax, you're insured, aren't you? Who do you think did it?'

'I'm not sure. Maybe a secret society.'

'What secret society? You don't know any secret societies.' She looked around. 'Where's your wife, by the way?'

'She left me.'

'You're kidding. Why?'

'All the fucking around. What are you doing here?'

'I felt guilty.'

He laughed.

'What?' she said defensively. 'You don't believe I could feel guilty? I didn't think you were going to turn round and go home. I thought you'd have stuff you could do in New York. To be honest, I thought you'd relish the time alone.'

'Did they get my drink?'

'What?'

'My alcohol. Is that all smashed up too?'

'I don't know. Shall I go out and look?'

'Nah, relax, I'll do it. Although, shit, yeah, fuck, forgot, I've got this taxi driver waiting. Can you go and tell him everything's OK?'

'Do I have to pay him?'

'No. He was just waiting in case there was someone in here waiting for me. I mean, other than you. Like a big guy with a gun.'

Gina looked perplexed for a moment, then nodded and went outside.

greg III

Alison awoke with a thick twist of Greg's hair in her mouth. Using her fingers to fish it out, she found it was still attached to his head. He was sprawled right across her bed, and showed no sign of being about to move. Wanting to get the taste of his hair out of her mouth, she walked through to the en suite and poured herself a glass of water. After she'd drunk two mouthfuls, she sat down on the toilet and stared at her bare feet as she urinated. She was still trying to get a handle on her mood, and to decide whether what had happened last night was a good or bad thing. The thing was, there was something in her psychology that connected this sort of sex with danger, and even though she'd made sure that Greg had used a condom and they hadn't done anything really risky, she still felt compromised in some way. It all went back to the way she felt about her sister, and her knowledge that Greg was exactly the sort of person Suzanne would've gone for. When she was thirteen and fourteen, Alison had spent a lot of time fantasising about one-night stands, but the way she'd pictured them had always been something naughty and innocent, a child-like pursuit of pleasure that ended up in sex. And if she had felt any jealousy about Suzanne's strike-rate, it was only because she hadn't enough experience of this sort of one-night stuff to realise that most of the time you didn't find this sort of childish conspiracy but instead an adult weariness that made sex seem more like some sort of arcane exercise than something people would do for fun.

She wiped herself, washed her hands and went back into the bedroom. Greg was beginning to stir, and she wondered what to do next. She didn't feel the repulsion towards him that she'd expected, and although she was slightly embarrassed that she'd slept with this man, she felt that she wanted to bring this experience to a proper conclusion.

'Hi,' she said softly, 'how are you?'

He grinned. 'Good.'

Alison noticed the lascivious way he was looking at her, and suddenly felt self-conscious. It hadn't occurred to her that he might want to have sex again. This did make her feel uncomfortable and she retreated back into the bathroom to pick up a complimentary bathrobe.

Aubrey and Jennings

They hadn't touched his alcohol. In fact, it looked as if whoever had done this had deliberately not smashed up his bottles, allowing him this small courtesy as if to show that although they'd had to smash up his house they weren't really bad people.

He took a bottle of scotch, grabbed two glasses and went back into the lounge. He was still looking for somewhere to sit when Gina walked back in with the cab driver and Aubrey, who was covered in blood, all of it stemming from a deep puncture-wound just below his left shoulder.

'Um,' said Gina, 'this guy . . .'

'Martin,' cut off Aubrey, 'I know who did this to your house.'

'Who?'

'The same guy who stabbed me. Jennings. I fought him off and he must've come straight round here.'

'Jennings smashed up my house?' asked Martin, incredulous.

'Yes. He stabbed me, and . . .'

'Why the fuck would Jennings want to smash up my house? I made him a contributing editor, I gave him more articles than anyone else . . .'

'Yes, well, the thing is, I don't know why he did this to you, but I think he stabbed me because of that argument we had in his house when he told me about my dad buggering him.'

'Look, hang on a second, Aubrey. How did this happen? Jennings came up to you with a knife?'

'Well, yes . . . but I mean, he was wearing a Balaclava.'

'So it might not have been Jennings at all?'

'Of course it was Jennings. I've fought him before, I know what his body feels like.'

'But this time you didn't fight him, he came up to you and stabbed you.'

He lifted up a bloody, cut hand. 'I fought him off.'

'Right, but still, Aubrey, you do acknowledge that you're not a hundred percent certain that the man who stabbed you was Jennings?'

Aubrey looked away, his face defiant. Martin looked at the others, realising he quickly needed to take control of this situation.

'Right,' he said, 'let's all calm down.' He looked at the taxi driver, who had a strange, smug expression on his face. 'Why are you still here?'

'Your friend here wants to sort this Jennings bloke out. I say we take my shooter and pay him a little visit.'

'Will you stop going on about your bloody shooter? Aubrey, I think we should get you to hospital.'

'No, Martin,' he protested, 'not just yet. Listen, I came round here because we need to do something. Jennings has stabbed me, smashed up your house, and God alone knows what he might be doing to the others.'

'If we all go round his house now, we'll be able to catch him asleep and sort him out.'

Martin sighed, uncapped his bottle and took a long swig from it.

'OK, this is what's going to happen. I'm happy to go round his house, but once we get there we call the police and don't do anything unless he tries to leave, and then all we do if that happens is restrain him, right. I don't want any crazy vigilante behaviour from any of you. Agreed?'

'Agreed,' said the others.

'Right then, let's go.'

morning

'What time is it?' Greg asked.

'Oh, really early, I just tend to wake up like this when I've been drinking.'

Greg didn't say anything, instead turning over on the bed and fluttering the sheets. Alison finished her glass of water and, deciding against getting back into bed, walked to the wardrobe to get dressed.

'Is it too early for breakfast?' Greg asked.

She turned back at him and smiled. 'You're forgetting this is supposed to be a rock and roll hotel. They don't start serving breakfast until lunchtime. But there's a twenty-four hour cafe.'

'How about we go down and get something then?'

'Yeah,' she said, 'OK, that'd be nice.'

pesky kids

The taxi driver stopped outside Jennings' house. Aubrey fell back heavily against the seat, groaning in pain. There were lots of things about their vigilante taxi driver that surprised Martin, but the main one was that he didn't seem at all worried about Aubrey bleeding all over his cab.

'Aubrey,' said Martin, 'do you promise that when we've sorted this out you'll let us take you to a hospital?'

'Yes,' said Aubrey, 'believe it or not, Martin, I would actually like to go to a fucking hospital. I just want to get hold of this jerk first.'

'Right, then,' said the taxi-driver. 'I think this is how we should do it. One of us should stay in the cab . . .'

'Aubrey,' Martin suggested, still worried about how he was slumped.

'Yes, OK, that makes sense. Now, as for the rest of you . . . somebody should stand by the front door and two of us should go round the back.'

'I'll stand by the door,' Gina offered.

'Good girl,' said the driver admiringly, 'but the thing is, that does put you in a vulnerable position. So you take this.' He handed her the gun. 'But you mustn't use it, no matter what happens. You're American, aren't you?'

Gina nodded. 'But I spent the first twelve years of my life in England.'

'Well, I'm afraid I don't think that makes any difference, as far as the law is concerned. But I shouldn't worry, luvvy, the threat of the gun should be more than enough to stop this psychopath.'

Gina took the gun. She seemed delighted to be holding it. Martin looked at her. It suited her, somehow, not just the gun, but this whole situation. It was exactly the sort of drama she was usually trying to construct for herself, only this time it was unarguably real.

'So that leaves you and me,' said the taxi driver. 'You ready?'

Martin nodded.

'Then let's go.'

eggs and bacon

Alison was impressed by the range of food available at six o'clock and the number of people already up and eating. She ordered a bowl of fruit, eggs and bacon, coffee, and a glass of orange juice. Greg stuck with cereal. She felt a bit wobbly with lack of sleep and immediately started on the coffee the second it was placed in front of her. Greg watched her drink, and she could tell he was trying to think of the most suitable thing to say.

'So what are your plans for today?' he asked, eventually.

She stared into her coffee cup, trying to decide whether he seemed as if he wanted to spend the rest of the day with her. Now they were having breakfast the absurdity of the previous evening seemed much clearer, and she felt keen to get away. But she didn't have any plans or anywhere to go, and worried that she'd be too heavy-handed if she tried to make something up. She considered turning the question back at him, but then realised that would sound as if she wanted to spend the day with him. So, a lie would have to suffice.

'I'm meeting my sister.'

'That's nice.'

'Yeah. We're going to the cinema.'

'Cool. What are you planning to see?'

'I'm not sure yet.'

The waitress reappeared with their breakfasts. Alison decided to start with the fruit. Greg eagerly tucked into his cereal, and for the moment both of them were silent.

the ladder

The taxi driver had instructed Martin to stand by the patio doors. While Martin kept watch there, the taxi driver was going down to the bottom of the garden to retrieve a rotten-looking wooden ladder in order to check out the upstairs window. Martin thought that if Aubrey was in the house asleep, this sort of activity would definitely wake him up, but the taxi driver claimed he'd done this sort of thing plenty of times before and knew how not to be too conspicuous.

Martin stared through the patio doors, unable to stop himself feeling impressed by the quality of Jenning's furnishings. He knew most of the money came from Jenning's wife, the notorious nymphomaniac who'd done almost as much good for her own career as her husband's by her endless and indiscriminate fucking, but he couldn't help feeling jealous, especially given the wanton destruction that had recently been visited on his own house. The events of this morning were coming so thick and fast that his thinking three or four hours ahead strategy was completely failing him, and he worried that by the end of today he'd only ever be able to live in the present. Indeed, right now, for the first time in years his brain was playing catch-up, still trying to process the implications of everything that had happened since last night in the hotel.

The biggest question was what was he going to do about the women in his life. Standing there at the window, he started thinking back through his current situation. Claudia. He had been married long enough to have a fairly definite sense of her character, and knew that in spite of everything she'd said in her letter, the main reason why she'd finally decided to bail out on him was embarrassment about being caught having sex with Ronnie. And there would be a certain pleasure in getting back together and making her feel guilty for a change. But, in truth, when it came right down to it, he realised he was glad to be rid of her. And in a way, in a strange, perverse way, he was also glad that his house had been destroyed. He would be really pissed off if it did turn out that Jennings was the man behind it, but only because he'd given him so much work and never really wanted him in his life in the first place, and he knew that was probably better than being the target of a secret sex-society, and at least that would make the divorce that much clearer. Split the insurance down the middle and make a fresh start.

Alison. Probably still alone and upset with him back at the Tenderloin Hotel. Now he'd had time to think about it, the fact that she'd been upset about seeing him with Helena was definitely a good sign, and he believed that if he just cut out all the crap and concentrated on making her his girlfriend it would work out. But he still wasn't sure if he was ready for that. He couldn't carry on like this, that much was definite, and if he did he'd probably end up dead. Going from his marriage with Claudia straight into a relationship with Alison seemed too intimidating a possibility to contemplate, especially given the fragility of his current mental state. They'd only slept together that one time, Monday afternoon in the same suite at the Tenderloin where he'd fucked Gina the week before, and although it had been incredible and amazingly natural and for once he'd managed to come before his partner started getting bored, there was still something unsettling about it. It wasn't that he had some stupid notion of her being especially innocent, but he was surprised at how different it had felt, like drinking water after a lifetime of whisky and coke.

Gina. Now, this was where things started getting complicated. He knew there was more to this relationship than he'd been pretending, and the fact that he'd been prepared to abandon Alison to head to New York to rescue her had to mean something. And he had felt seriously hurt when she didn't show up at the airport, and happy – although somewhat confused – when he'd found her in his house. Separating from Claudia had unpinned all the certainties in his life, and now he no longer had the excuse of a wife to stop him going beyond purely sexual relationships with other women, he had to look for new excuses for staying away from Gina. The most obvious one was that she was crazy, although he had a suspicion that everything she'd said about her parents wanting to have her committed wasn't true. The other excuse, and the one he'd always held to before, was that there was no prospect of any long-term future to a relationship with Gina. But maybe a brief, torrid affair was exactly what he needed.

'OK,' shouted the taxi driver from behind him, 'I think I'm going to need your help to get this up against the wall.'

Martin turned round, scared by the sight of the taxi driver

swaying towards him carrying the heavy ladder. He rushed across and helped the driver steady his steps and then bring the ladder against the house without breaking a window.

'Right,' he said, 'I'm going up.'

Martin held the ladder until the taxi driver was halfway up and looked safe. Then he returned to the patio doors. When the driver reached the top, he turned back and shouted, 'Looks like we've got the right guy.'

'What makes you say that?'

'There's someone in there. I can't see her face but she's all chained up. He's probably stabbed her and is about to do some sick sex-thing.'

As he said this, Martin saw Jennings come into the lounge. He was naked except for a black leather sex-mask and holding a knife.

'Shit,' shouted Martin, 'he's got a knife.'

'Right,' said the driver, 'you go and get my shooter from your lady friend, I'll get down and find something to smash the window.'

Martin ran round to the front of the house. He was amused to see Gina pointing the gun at Jennings' front door, one eye squeezed tight.

'Gina,' he said, 'give me the gun.'

'Why?'

He walked across and took her by the hand. 'Please, I need it now, come with me.'

Together, they went round the back of the house and found the taxi driver about to hurl a metal garden chair at the patio doors.

'Wait,' shouted Martin.

The driver froze mid-throw. 'What?'

'We can't smash his patio doors. What if he's innocent?'

'Martin,' said Gina, 'he trashed your house and you're worried about his patio doors?'

'Besides,' said the driver, 'the girl inside might still be alive.'

He brought the garden chair up over his shoulders and towards the patio doors. It bounced off without breaking them, but the glass shuddered so violently that Jennings immediately looked round. Taking off his sex-mask and using one hand to try to hide his springy, hard penis, he held out the other in a conciliatory gesture and came over to open the doors.

'Martin,' he said, looking at him, 'what's going on?'

'Did you smash up my house?'

'What?'

The taxi driver took the gun from Martin and trained it on Jennings.

'What are you doing with that knife?'

'Huh?' He looked embarrassed. 'Well, Martin, you know what Jemima's like.'

Martin laughed. 'Oh god, don't tell me.'

'It's just a bit of fun, that's all.'

'What's he talking about?' asked the driver. 'Who's Jemima?'

'His wife. Look, Nick, you're going to have to let us check out that it is really her.'

'Martin, she's ... well, you know, she's kind of in a compromising position right now. I can't let you all go up there.'

'OK,' Martin replied, 'I understand what you're saying. We'll all sit here, you go and untie her and bring her down.'

He nodded. 'Would you like a cup of tea?'

'Oh, yes please, mate,' said the taxi driver.

'The stuff's in the kitchen. You can do it yourselves, right?'

Jennings started walking up the stairs. The taxi driver waited until he was out of sight and then asked, 'So what do we think?'

'His wife is very kinky,' Martin admitted.

'How do you know?' Gina asked, crossly.

Martin looked away. 'Well, I always thought he was innocent.'

'What if he's lying and he's up there killing that woman?' asked Gina.

'He's left his knife on the table.'

'So? He could be strangling her.'

'And how would he get away? We're all sitting round here waiting for him to come down.'

'What about the ladder?'

'Lady's got a point. Martin, why don't you go outside and move the ladder? I'll do the refreshments. What do you want? Tea?

'Coffee, if they're is any. Black.'

The taxi driver nodded and went out into the kitchen. Martin walked back through the open patio doors. He was still feeling a bit dazed about being up this early, and the morning chill didn't help. Jennings didn't seem to have absconded, so he picked up the ladder and staggered across with it to the back of the garden. Having completed his task, he walked back through to Jenning's lounge.

'Oh, Gina, I forgot to tell you. Aubrey, that stabbed guy in the taxi, he's going out with Helena.'

'Who's Helena?'

'German girl. Bit of a fiend for the white powder. Said she stayed with you in Chelsea.'

'Oh, right, Helena. I know Helena. Is she in England now?'

'Yeah.'

The taxi driver came back through from the kitchen. 'Does somebody want to take this cup out to Aubrey?'

'I'll do it,' said Gina.

She took the cup and went out through the house to the front door. The taxi driver gave Martin his coffee. He wrapped his hand around it and relaxed back into the sofa.

'Wow,' said the taxi driver as he looked up the staircase.

Martin scrambled up, trying to get a look at Jenning's wife, Jemima. He could see why the taxi driver was so impressed, and worried what Gina would say when she came back in. It was no surprise that almost all of the most influential men in London had fallen for Jemima's charms, and the way she'd dressed this morning was exciting enough to get an instant reaction out of Martin's exhausted body.

'Martin,' she said cheerfully, 'what's all this about?'

He was barely able to reply, still taking in her incredible body. She was wearing a pair of black strappy leather shoes with a high square heel that were so perfectly placed between porn star and schoolgirl that Martin just knew she probably only wore them for sex, along with a white shirt that flapped open at the bottom to reveal the crotch of a pair of pink knickers with a tiny black polka dot pattern. Utter tat, the sort of thing that would completely horrify Claudia, but that Jemima could completely pull off. Her defiantly curly red hair had clearly been recently styled and her face was heavily made up. As she came across and leaned over Martin to give him a kiss, he noticed red ridges around her wrists.

'Aubrey's been stabbed,' said Martin. 'He thought Nick did it.'

Jemima looked sternly at her husband. 'Nick, did you stab Aubrey?'

'Of course not. I've no idea why he would think that.'

'Come on, Nick, you two did have a fight last time you went round to his house.'

'Yeah, but we finished that there and then.'

'He kicked you out. It's hardly surprising that he might think you'd want to retaliate.'

Jennings exhaled, exasperated. He sat down heavily on the sofa, and Martin noticed he'd managed to put on a pair of black pants. 'Martin, you know me better than that. I take all kinds of abuse from everyone and I never retaliate. OK, sure, I did have that one fight with Aubrey, but that was only because he wouldn't accept the sacrosanctity of my relationship with his father.'

Jennings looked across at the doorway. Martin followed his eyes and saw Gina standing there, looking considerably upset.

'Martin,' she said in a half-sob.

'Yes?'

'Aubrey's dead.'

next

Alison didn't have any trouble getting rid of Greg. He waited until they'd finished breakfast, then stood up, dabbed his lips with a serviette, and offered her his hand. She shook it, he smiled, and then he walked off and left her alone at the table.

Once he'd gone, she realised she now felt even worse. It wasn't the guilt of the one night stand, but instead a sense of total disconnection. She had nowhere left to go, no one she could turn to. Talking to her mother last night had been fine to begin with, but once they'd got into the problem of her sister and Joe, it just reminded her of the unpleasant nature of her current situation and made her feel much worse. Her father was usually the more sympathetic of her parents – or at least, the one with whom she had the better relationship – but there wasn't that much she could say without telling him the truth, and she knew that would be a bad idea.

It was only then that she realised Greg had left her to pay for breakfast. As post-sex crimes went, it wasn't very serious, hardly up there with Brad Pitt stealing Thelma's dollars or even the bad behaviour of some of Suzanne's previous conquests, but it did depress her, especially as she suspected that not only had it not been an accident, but that he'd probably also taken a certain masculine pleasure in stiffing her.

She signalled for a waitress. A woman came across, smoking ostentatiously. Alison could tell she was probably encouraged to do this to make the cafe seem more authentic, and wondered how they got round the health and safety regulations.

'Yes dear?'

'Can I pay?'

'It's already taken care of. Greg has a tab whenever he comes here.'

'Are you sure? He told me it was his first visit.'

She smiled. 'Did he? Nah, he's friends with the owners. He's here all the time.'

The waitress cleared the table and Alison stared into space, trying to work out whether this made things better or worse.

statement

Aubrey wasn't dead. He'd fainted from loss of blood, which made everyone more serious about getting him to the hospital. Unfortunately, once they got there, an officious nurse made them explain exactly how Aubrey had been injured, and before long, the group was escorted to the nearest police station.

'So why didn't you take him to the hospital straight away?' the police woman asked, her pen poised.

Martin sucked on his cigarette. 'Well, I did think that would be a good idea. And in fact, I did try to persuade him. But he was worried Jennings might stab someone else.'

The woman interrogating him looked back through to the earlier pages of his statement. Martin knew he was proving a terrible witness. There were two main problems with his testimony. One was that he was struggling to make his behaviour over the last few hours sound respectable, and consequently kept lapsing into lies and half-truths. The other was that he could see everything the woman was writing and as she continued to turn his speech into bland biro bubble letters, she kept missing the nuances of the situation and making it seem as if he was continually contradicting himself.

'But,' she said, 'I thought you said that Jennings didn't stab Aubrey?'

'Yes, that's right, I don't think he did.'

'But he did smash up your house?'

'No, I don't think he did that either. I mean, I don't know any of this for definite. But when we challenged him about it he seemed genuinely surprised.'

'So who do you think smashed up your house?'

Martin looked at his fingernails, wondering if they deliberately kept the temperature high in the interrogation room. He could feel his body pushing out the toxins of the previous night and desperately craved another cup of water. He knew he shouldn't talk about this sort of stuff, but was currently feeling so paranoid that he thought he might be safer if the police knew everything.

'Some people from university.'

'Which university? The one you went to?'

'Yes.'

'And that was?'

'Cambridge.'

'And who are these people?'

'I don't know. Look, I know this sounds weird . . . all of this must sound weird . . . but I used to belong to this secret society . . .'

The woman listened to his story. After he'd finished, she screwed his statement into a ball and said, 'I think we'd better start again, don't you, Mr Powell?'

phone call

Alison went back upstairs to her hotel room. She sat on the bed and flicked on the television, idly wondering if she could get through the whole day without going outside.

The phone rang. She answered it.

'Is this Alison Hendry?'

'Yes.'

'I have a man called Martin Powell on the line who wants to be put through to you.'

'That's fine.'

'OK.'

Alison looked down at her feet, waiting for Martin to come on the line. She lay back on the bed.

'Alison?'

'Yeah?'

'Um, I need to talk to you. This isn't just about last night, and I am really sorry about that and wish you hadn't seen me with Helena and I understand why you're angry.'

'I'm not so angry now.'

His voice sounded strained. 'That's really good, but the thing is, look, a friend of mine, I can't remember if you met him or not although I'm sure you heard me talking about him, Aubrey, well, he got stabbed.'

'What?'

'Yeah. And I think I might be in danger. I've been in the police station, I'm rambling, I'm sorry, they smashed up my house.'

'Martin? What are you talking about? Look, come here, OK? Room 407.'

'OK, thanks, Alison. I should be there in about an hour.'

only to photograph

Martin replaced the receiver in its cradle and walked out of the telephone box. He knew the others – especially Gina – would be cross with him for ditching them in the police station, but he really couldn't cope with them right now. Besides, none of them were in danger, and even if they were, the taxi driver could protect them with his blasted shooter. He needed to see Alison, she would help him out. It didn't matter about their relationship, he just needed someone who could make him calm down. After this morning, he didn't feel like taking another taxi, so he started walking towards the tube.

Two streets later, he was attacked from behind. Whoever did it whipped the mask over Martin's face so quickly that the only thing he could do was wonder whether he was being abducted or suffocated. He didn't move until he felt a gun pointing into his back, and then, bizarrely, could only think of the taxi driver.

Not knowing what to do, he instinctively started to walk in the direction he was being pushed. He kept going until he bashed his knees on something hard and fell slightly forward. Hands against his back guided him into what had to be some kind of van. He felt his arms being taken away from him and then the pinch of cuffs. A small thin gag that tasted faintly of petrol was pulled around his mouth, and then nothing for a second before the slam of the van doors.

problems

Alison felt pleased Martin was coming over. It made her happy that he was turning to her in a time of crisis, even though she knew this was vaguely pathetic. But it wasn't as if she didn't have her own serious problems and maybe it wouldn't be so bad if they helped each other work things out.

She caught her reflection in a mirror and decided to change. She hadn't felt relaxed enough to dress properly when Greg had been in the room, worried that if she made herself look too attractive he'd either want to sleep with her again, or would think she wanted him to hang around. There was also the whole discomfort factor of dressing in front of a stranger, which oddly felt more unnerving than undressing the night before.

The phone rang. Worried that it was Martin calling to say he'd changed his mind about coming over, she considered not answering. But she'd never been able to ignore a ringing phone.

'I have a Suzanne for you.'

She sat back down. 'OK.'

Her sister came on the line. 'He's gone.'

'What?'

'Joe. Adrian kicked him out.'

'Because of me?'

'Sort of. They had a fight.'

Alison didn't say anything, listening instead to her sister's breathing and wondering about the edge in her voice.

'What was the fight about, Suzanne?'

'Me and Adrian.'

'What about you and Adrian?'

'Nothing. That's the point. That's why we kicked him out. He thought there was something happening between me and Adrian.'

'I know. He said that to me too. But there isn't, right?'

'Of course, you know that.'

'So, who exactly kicked Joe out?'

'What?'

'First you said Adrian kicked him out, then you said you both did it. I wondered what was the true story.'

Suzanne sighed. 'Adrian did the actual kicking-out. I stood by and supported him and told Joe I never wanted to see him again. Any particular reason why you're being so pernickety?'

'I just want to get things straight.'

'OK,' she said, 'so when are you coming home?'

Alison started crying. Not wanting her sister to notice, she changed ears and, stretching the cord around her arm, said, 'I'm sorry, Suze, I don't think I am coming back. I mean, maybe for a couple of days while I sort out somewhere else to stay, but that's it . . .'

'Al . . .'

'It's just not a good idea, OK? I'm not going to get back with Adrian and I can't see any other way the three of us living together is going to work. Don't worry, though, I won't leave you short on money.'

'It's not about that.'

'I know. Listen, sis, I love you, OK, and I promise I'll see you soon.'

only to photograph II

Martin tried breathing. As he did so, he realised he had been waiting for this to happen. It wasn't just the usual drugs paranoia, but a fear that he'd never been able to confront and consequently banish. This fear struck him any time he heard anyone talking about any kind of violence, and consisted of a sense that somehow by listening he was involving himself in a chain of events that one day would lead to someone, for some unknown reason, coming to get him.

When he had imagined this happening, he'd always thought it would be over in an instant, like dying in a dream. He hadn't realised that between being caught and being killed, there would be the same prosaic period of waiting that accompanied everything else in his life.

It wasn't until the van started moving that Martin realised he wasn't the only one imprisoned in the back. He didn't know who the other person was, but they were flailing violently, landing several kicks against the side of the van and the rest into his leg. Somehow the other person managed to get rid of their gag and, after they'd been driving a short while, began shouting and screaming at the driver in German.

Martin could feel the van speeding up, and he began to be pulled backwards and forwards across the floor of the vehicle. Bumps on the road made his arms wrench agonisingly, as he tried to keep himself in place by pushing his own feet against the opposite wall of the van.

The German woman was getting increasingly emotional. So

their kidnapper was German. Of course. In that moment everything became clear to Martin. This wasn't his story. After all his paranoia. All his fears about everyone in his life. All the unhinged loonies, from Jennings to Naomi's boyfriend, from the Thélèmites to the mysterious porn magazine men. After all that, the real threat had turned out to come from one of the strangers, one of the women he barely knew, a German girl called Helena with a scary story about her father the barrister and a sex-criminal who had once kidnapped her.

He thought back to the night when Aubrey had first picked up Helena, remembering the taxi ride from the art gallery to the restaurant. What had she said about the man who kidnapped her? She said it wasn't so bad. That he didn't want to hurt her. Only to photograph. But he hadn't wanted to hurt *her*. This didn't mean he felt the same way about men he suspected of being involved with her. After all, he'd already stabbed Aubrey, and tried to destroy Martin's house. These were acts of frustration, a psychotic anger aimed at anyone he believed was involved with the object of his adoration. And what about Benoît and Laetitia? Were they imprisoned elsewhere? Or already dead?

The van continued to speed up. Martin remembered being on the motorway with Claudia, and the way their argument had caused her to crash. He joined in with Helena's noise-making, flailing as loudly as he could. He heard the driver shout something at them in German and then accelerate again.

Martin wondered where they were being taken, and whether when the driver tried to take them out of the van they might at least have one last chance to escape. But then his unhelpful imagination pictured the driver parking inside a lock-up garage before carrying them out. Or maybe his plan wouldn't even be that elaborate. Perhaps he'd just drive them to an abandoned area and dispatch them both with a bullet to the head. He considered shouting to the driver that he had nothing to do with Helena, that he barely knew her and there was no reason for him to feel jealous. If only he'd learnt to speak German. Then he might be able to come up with an explanation that would stop this psychopath from trying to kill him.

The van was now moving so fast that Martin allowed himself the optimistic hope that someone had witnessed the abduction and decided to give chase. Helena's kicking, screaming and shouting continued to increase in volume, getting louder and louder until she was momentarily silenced by a sudden bump and a horrendous scraping noise. Martin felt himself being thrown backwards, pulled forward, and then tried to keep very still as the van tipped up on one side. Terrified he was going to lose his hands, he pulled as hard as he could and with another heavy jolt he felt the cuffs ping free from whatever he'd been pinned to. Then he was thrown forward again, smacking his face so violently into the side of the van that as he fell back all he could taste was blood.

Nothing was happening. Helena was silent; there were no sounds from the driver. Worried he was stuck here with two dead people, Martin used his cuffed hands to get the gag out of his mouth. He breathed in and wondered whether it made more sense to keep the mask on. He could tell his face was a bloody mess, and worried that peeling off the material might do more damage. Then, swearing to himself, he pulled it off anyway, pleased it didn't cause him too much pain.

Helena was huddled in a ball in the far left hand side of the van. He moved across to her and slapped her face.

'Are you alive?'

Her eyes opened and she let out another scream, much louder than before. She didn't stop screaming or sobbing, but did manage to punch out the words,

'My fucking arms. I think they're broken.'

Martin didn't reply. He knew he had to get out of here. This wasn't anything to do with him. Getting into trouble for fleeing the crime scene later was fine by him; he just didn't want to be involved with these people any more. Ignoring Helena's cries, he moved down the van to the double doors at the back and, using his fingers and elbows, finally managed to get them open.

A crowd had already began amassing around the upturned van. No one tried to stop Martin as he walked away, feeling like The Fugitive with his bloody face and cuffs. He kept walking until he reached the nearest tube. Expecting someone to apprehend him, he was amazed when he had no trouble buying a ticket and two guards even held open the plastic barrier to allow him through.

He went down on the escalator and caught the first train. It was a long journey to the Tenderloin and he had to change twice. He went back up on another escalator, through the gates, then walked the few streets to the hotel.

Martin was more careful as he went through reception, trying to hide the cuffs as he shuffled towards the lift. He got in the lift alone and went up to the fourth floor. Walking down the corridor, he found Alison's room and raised his clipped hands to knock. He waited for a second, then heard her footsteps and the door swung open. He could see the questions bubbling up inside her. But before she could say anything he raised a bloody finger to his lips and, attempting a smile, told her, 'Don't ask, OK, just don't ask.'

Acknowledgements

Neil Taylor, Rose Billington, Nick Guyatt, Tibor Fischer, Richard Thomas, Katie White, John Gray, Jin Auh, Sarah Ballard, Alexandra Heminsley, Borivoj Radakovic, Drazen Kokanovic, James Linville, Laurence Bowen, Scarlett Thomas, Kate Le Vann, Nicholas Blincoe, Leila Sansour, Daren King, Ben Richards, Lillian Pizzichini, Rowan Pelling, Annie Blinkhorn, Dea Brovig, Lawrence Norfolk, Huda Abuzeid, Katy Guest, Bo Fowler, Sarah Waters, Sarah Harris, Candida Clark, Lucy Luck, Toby Litt, Jim, Jamie and Catherine Shaw, Jim Giraffe, Gabrevil, Rebbecca Ray, Ross Gillfillan, Lana Citron, Stefan Marling, Jo Rideout, Jim Flint, John Rush, Kaye, Dave and Louise Thorne.

All Orion/Phoenix titles are available at your local bookshop or from the following address:

Mail Order Department
Littlehampton Book Services
FREEPOST BR535
Worthing, West Sussex, BN13 3BR
telephone 01903 828503, *facsimile* 01903 828802
e-mail MailOrders@lbsltd.co.uk
(Please ensure that you include full postal address details)

Payment can be made either by credit/debit card (Visa, Mastercard, Access and Switch accepted) or by sending a £ Sterling cheque or postal order made payable to *Littlehampton Book Services*.
DO NOT SEND CASH OR CURRENCY.

Please add the following to cover postage and packing

UK and BFPO:
£1.50 for the first book, and 50p for each additional book to a maximum of £3.50

Overseas and Eire:
£2.50 for the first book plus £1.00 for the second book and 50p for each additional book ordered

---

BLOCK CAPITALS PLEASE

name of cardholder _____   *delivery address*
                     _____   *(if different from cardholder)*
address of cardholder _____   _____
_____   _____
_____   _____
_____   _____
        postcode _____   *postcode* _____

☐ I enclose my remittance for £_____

☐ please debit my Mastercard/Visa/Access/Switch (delete as appropriate)

card number ☐☐☐☐☐☐☐☐☐☐☐☐☐☐☐☐

expiry date ☐☐☐☐   Switch issue no. ☐☐

signature _____

prices and availability are subject to change without notice